Emily Sarah Holt

Earl Hubert's Daughter or the Polishing of the Pearl

A Tale of the Thirteenth Century

Emily Sarah Holt

Earl Hubert's Daughter or the Polishing of the Pearl
A Tale of the Thirteenth Century

ISBN/EAN: 9783743423848

Manufactured in Europe, USA, Canada, Australia, Japa

Cover: Foto ©Andreas Hilbeck / pixelio.de

Manufactured and distributed by brebook publishing software (www.brebook.com)

Emily Sarah Holt

Earl Hubert's Daughter or the Polishing of the Pearl

Earl Hubert's Daughter

Or

The Polishing of the Pearl

A Tale of the Thirteenth Century

BY

EMILY SARAH HOLT

AUTHOR OF "MISTRESS MARGERY," "SISTER ROSE," ETC.

" Lost is my realm ; yet I shall not repine,
If, after all, I win but that of Thine."
—KING EDWARD THE SECOND.

NEW EDITION

LONDON
JOHN F. SHAW AND CO.
48 PATERNOSTER ROW

PREFACE.

THE thirteenth century was one of rapid and terrible incidents, tumultuous politics, and in religious matters of low and degrading superstition. Transubstantiation had just been formally adopted as a dogma of the Church, accompanied as it always is by sacramental confession, and quickly followed by the elevation of the host and the invention of the pix. Various Orders of monks were flocking into England. The Pope was doing his best, aided by the Roman clergy, and to their shame be it said, by some of the English, to fix his iron yoke on the neck of the Church of England. The doctrine of human merit was at its highest pitch; the doctrine of justification by faith was absolutely *unknown*.

Amid this thick darkness, a very small number of true-hearted, Heaven-taught men bore aloft the torch of truth—that is, of so much truth as they knew. One of such men as these I have sketched in Father Bruno. And if, possibly, the portrait is slightly over-charged for the date,—if he be represented as a shade more enlightened than at that time he could well be—I trust that the anachronism will be pardoned for the sake of those eternal verities which would otherwise have been left wanting.

There is one fact in ecclesiastical history which should never be forgotten, and this is, that in all ages, within the visible corporate body which men call the Church, God has had a Church of His own, true, living, and faithful. He has ever reserved to Himself that typical seven thousand in Israel, of whom all the knees have not bowed unto Baal, and every mouth hath not kissed him.

Such men as these have been termed " Protestants before the Reformation." The only reason why they were not Protestants, was because there was as yet no Protestantism. The heavenly call to " come out of her " had not yet been heard. These men were to be found in all stations and callings; on the throne —as in Alfred the Great, St. Louis, and Henry VI.; in the hierarchy—as in Anselm, Bradwardine, and Grosteste; in the cloister—as in Bernard de Morlaix; but perhaps most frequently in that rank and file of whom the world never hears, and of some of whom, however low their place in it, the world is not worthy.

These men often made terrible blunders—as St. Louis did when he persecuted the Jews, under the delusion that he was thus doing honour to the Lord whom they had rejected: and Bernard de Morlaix, when he led a crusade against the Albigenses, of whom he had heard only slanderous reports. Do we make no blunders, that we should be in haste to judge them? How much more has been given to us than to them! How much more, then, will be required?

CONTENTS.

CHAP.		PAGE
I.	FATHER AND MOTHER	1
II.	"WHAT DO YOU LACK?"	26
III.	BELASEZ	53
IV.	THE TIME OF JACOB'S TROUBLE	81
V.	NOT WISELY	103
VI.	THE NEW CONFESSOR	127
VII.	THE SHADOW OF LONG AGO	152
VIII.	IN THE DARK	175
IX.	PAYING THE BILL	200
X.	TRUTH TOLD AT LAST	227
XI.	WHAT CAME OF IT	247
XII.	WHAT IS LOVE?	272
XIII.	FATHER BRUNO'S SERMON	294
XIV.	EVIL TIDINGS	316
XV.	AT LAST	337

"' Lay thy veil aside, my maid.' said the Countess with most unusual kindness,
considering it was a Jewess to whom she spoke."—p. 53

EARL HUBERT'S DAUGHTER.

CHAPTER I.

FATHER AND MOTHER.

"He was a true man, this—who lived for England,
And he knew how to die."

"Sweet? There are many sweet things. Clover's sweet,
And so is liquorice, though 'tis hard to chew;
And sweetbriar—till it scratches."

"LOOK, Margaret! Thine aunt, Dame Marjory,
is come to spend thy birthday with thee."

"And see my new bower?[1] O Aunt Marjory,
I am so glad!"

The new bower was a very pretty room—for the
thirteenth century—but its girl-owner was the
prettiest thing in it. Her age was thirteen that

[1] Boudoir.

day, but she was so tall that she might easily have been supposed two or three years older. She had a very fair complexion, violet-blue eyes, and hair exactly the colour of a cedar pencil. If physiognomy may be trusted, the face indicated a loving and amiable disposition.

The two ladies who had just entered from the ante-room—the mother and aunt of Margaret—were both tall, finely-developed women, with shining fair hair. They spoke French, evidently as the mother-tongue: but in 1234 that was the custom of all English nobles. These ladies had been brought up in England from early maidenhood, but they were Scottish Princesses—the eldest and youngest daughters of King William the Lion, by his Norman Queen, Ermengarde de Beaumont. Both sisters were very handsome, but the younger bore the palm of beauty in the artist's sense, though she was not endowed with the singular charm of manner which characterised her sister. Chroniclers tell us that the younger Princess, Marjory, was a woman of marvellous beauty. Yet something more attractive than mere beauty must have distinguished the Princess Margaret, for two men of the most opposite dispositions to have borne her image on their hearts till death, and for her husband—a man capable of abject superstition, and with his hot-headed youth far behind him—to have braved all the thunders of Rome, rather than put her away.

These royal sisters had a singular history. Their father, King William, had put them for education into the hands of King John of England and his Queen, Isabelle of Angoulême, when they were little more than infants; in other words, he had committed his tender doves to the charge of almost the worst man and woman whom he could have selected. There were just two vices of which His English Majesty was not guilty, and those were cowardice and hypocrisy. He was a plain, unvarnished villain, and he never hesitated for a moment to let people see it. Queen Isabelle had been termed "the Helen of the Middle Ages," alike from her great beauty, and from the fact that her husband abducted her when betrothed elsewhere. She can hardly be blamed for this, since she was a mere child at the time: but as she grew up, she developed a character quite worthy of the scoundrel to whom she was linked. To personal profligacy she added sordid avarice, and a positive

incapacity for telling the truth. To these delightful persons the poor little Scottish maidens, Margaret and Isabel, were consigned. At what age
Marjory joined them in England is doubtful: but
it does not appear that she was ever, as they were,
an official ward of the Crown.

The exact terms on which these royal children
were sent into England were for many years the
subject of sharp contention between their brother
Alexander and King Henry III. The memorandum drawn up between the Kings William and
John, does not appear to be extant: but that
by which, in 1220, they were afresh consigned
to the care of Henry III., is still in existence.
Alexander strenuously maintained that John had
undertaken to marry the sisters to his own two
sons. The agreement with Henry III. simply pro-
vides that "We will also marry[1] Margaret and
Isabel, sisters of the said Alexander, King of Scotland, during the space of one full year from the
feast of St. Denis,[2] 1220, as shall be to our
honour: and if we do not marry them within that
period, we will return them to the said Alexander,
King of Scotland, safe and free, in his own terri-

---

[1] This meant at the time, "cause to be married."   [2] Oct. 8.

tories, within two years from the time speci-
fied." [1]

This article of the convention was honestly
carried out according to the later memorandum,
so far as concerned Margaret, who was married
to Hubert de Burgh, Earl of Kent, at York,
on the twenty-fifth of June, 1221. Isabel, however, was not married (to Roger Bigod, Earl of
Norfolk) until May, 1225.[2] Still, after the latter
date, the convention having been carried out, it
might have been supposed that the Kings would
have given over quarrelling about it. The Princesses were honourably married in England, which
was all that Henry III. at least had undertaken
to do.

But neither party was satisfied. Alexander never
ceased to reproach Henry for not having himself
married Margaret, and united Isabel to his brother.
Henry, while he testily maintained to Alexander
that he had done all he promised, and no further
claim could be established against him, yet, as
history shows, never to the last hour pardoned

---

[1] Patent Roll, 4 H. III.; dated York, June 15 [1220].

[2] "In the octave of holy Trinity" [May 25—June 1], at Alnwick.
—Roberts' Extracts from Fines Rolls, 1225.

Hubert de Burgh for his marriage with the Scottish Princess, and most bitterly reproached him for depriving him of her whom he had intended to make his Queen.

The truth seems to be that Henry III., who at the time of Margaret's marriage was only a lad of thirteen years, had cherished for her a fervent boyish passion, and that she was the only woman whom he ever really loved. Hubert, at that time Regent, probably never imagined any thing of the kind: while to Margaret, a stately maiden of some twenty years, if not more, the sentimental courtship of a schoolboy of thirteen would probably be a source of amusement rather than sympathy. But at every turn in his after life, Henry showed that he had never forgiven this slight put on his affections. It is true that his affection was of a somewhat odd type, presenting no obstacle to his aspersing the character of his lady-love, when he found it convenient to point a moral by so doing. But of all men who ever lived, surely one of the most consistently inconsistent was Henry III. In most instances he was "constant to one thing—his inconstancy." Like his father, he possessed two virtues: but they were not the same. Henry was not a lover of cruelty for its own sake—which John was: and he was not personally a libertine. Of his father's virtues, bravery and honesty, there was not a trace in him. He covered his sins with an embroidered cloak of exquisite piety. The bad qualities of both parents were inherited by him. To his mother's covetous acquisitiveness and ingrained falsehood, he joined his father's unscrupulous exactions and wild extravagance.

I have said that Henry was not a lover of cruelty in itself: but he could be fearfully and recklessly cruel when he had a point to gain, as we shall see too well before the story is ended. It may be true that John murdered his nephew Arthur with his own hands; but it was reserved for Henry, out of the public sight and away from his own eyes, to perpetrate a more cruel murder upon Arthur's hapless sister, "the Pearl of Bretagne," by one of the slowest and most dreadful deaths possible to humanity, and without any offence on her part beyond her very existence. Stow tells us that poor Alianora was slowly starved to death; and that she died by royal order the Issue Roll gives evidence, since one hundred pounds were delivered to John

Fitz Geoffrey as his fee for the execution of Alianora the King's kinswoman.[1]

It is not easy to say whether John or Henry would have made the more clever vivisector. But assuredly, while John would have kept his laboratory door open, and have sneered at anæsthetics, Henry would have softly administered curare,[2] and afterwards made a charming speech on the platform concerning the sacrifices of their own feelings, which physiologists are sorrowfully compelled to make for the benefit of humanity and the exigencies of science.

Thirteen years after the marriage of Margaret of Scotland, when he was a young man of six-and-twenty, Henry III. made a second attempt to win a Scottish queen. The fair Princess Marjory had now joined her sisters in England; and in point of age she was more suitable than Margaret. The English nobles, however, were very indignant that their King should think of espousing a younger sister of the wife of so mere an upstart as Hubert de

---

[1] This terrible fact has been strangely ignored by many modern historians.—*Rot. Exit., Michs.*, 25–6 H. III.

[2] A drug which deadens the sensibilities—of the vivisector—by rendering the victim incapable of sound or motion, but not affecting the nerves of sensation in the least.

Burgh. They grumbled bitterly, and the Count of Bretagne, brother-in-law of the murdered Arthur and the disinherited Alianora, took upon himself to dissuade the King from his purpose.

This Count of Bretagne is known as Pierre Mauclerc, or Bad-Clerk: not a flattering epithet, but historians assure us that Pierre only too thoroughly deserved the adjective, whatever his writing may have done. He had, four years before, refused his own daughter to King Henry, preferring to marry her to a son of the King of France. The Count had undertaken no difficult task, for an easier could not be than to persuade or dissuade Henry III. in respect of any mortal thing. He passed his life in acting on the advice in turn of every person who had last spoken to him. So he gave up Marjory of Scotland.

Three years more had elapsed since that time, during which Marjory, very sore at her rejection, had withdrawn to the Court of King Alexander her brother. In the spring of 1234 she returned to her eldest sister, who generally resided either in her husband's Town-house at Whitehall,—it was probably near Scotland Yard—or at the Castle of Bury Saint Edmund's. She was just then at the latter. Earl Hubert himself was but rarely at home in either place, being constantly occupied elsewhere by official duties, and not unfrequently, through some adverse turn of King Henry's capricious favour, detained somewhere in prison.

"And how long hast thou nestled in this sweet new bower, my bird?" said Marjory caressingly to her niece.

"To-day, Aunt Marjory! It is a birthday present from my Lord and father. Is it not pretty? Only look at the walls, and the windows, and my beautiful velvet settle. Now, did you ever see any thing so charming?"

Marjory glanced at her sister, and they exchanged smiles.

"Well, I cannot quite say No to that question, Magot.[1] But lead me round this wonderful chamber, and show me all its beauties."

The wonderful chamber in question was not very spacious, being about sixteen feet in length by twelve in width. It had a wide fireplace at one end —there was no fire, for the spring was just passing into summer—and two arched windows on one of its longer sides. The fireplace was filled with a

---

[1] This was in 1234, when our story begins, the English diminutive of Margaret, and was doubtless derived from the French Margot.

grotto-like erection of fir-cones, moss, and rosemary : the windows, as Margaret triumphantly pointed out, were of that rare and precious material, glass. Three doors led into other rooms. One, opposite the fire-place, gave access to a small private oratory ; two others, opposite the windows, communicated respectively with the wardrobe and the ante-chamber. These four rooms together, with the narrow spiral staircase which led to them, occupied the whole floor of one of the square towers of the Castle. The walls of the bower were painted green, relieved by golden stars ; and on every wall-space between the doors and windows was a painted " history "— namely, a medallion of some Biblical, historical, or legendary subject. The subjects in this room had evidently been chosen with reference to the tastes of a girl. They were,—the Virgin and Child ; the legend of Saint Margaret ; the Wheel of Fortune ; Saint Agnes, with her lamb ; a fountain with doves perched upon the edge ; and Saint Martin dividing his cloak with the beggar. The window-shutters were of fir-wood, bound with iron. Meagre indeed we should think the furniture, but it was sumptuous for the date. A tent-bed, hung with green curtains, stood between the two doors. A green velvet settle stretched across the window side of the room. By the fireplace was a leaf-table; round the walls were wooden brackets, with iron sockets for the reception of torches; and at the foot of the bed, which stood with its side to the wall, was a fine chest of carved ebony. There were only three pieces of movable furniture, two footstools, and a curule chair, also of ebony, with a green velvet cushion. As nobody could sit in the last who had not had a king and queen for his or her parents, it may be supposed that more than one was not likely to be often wanted.

The Countess of Kent, as the elder sister, took the curule chair, while her sister Marjory, when the inspection was finished, sat down on the velvet settle. Margaret drew a footstool to her aunt's side, and took up her position there, resting her head caressingly on Marjory's knee.

"Three whole years, Aunt Marjory, that you have not been near us ! What could make you stay away so long ? "

"There were reasons, Magot."

The two Princesses exchanged smiles again, but there was some amusement in that of the Countess, while the expression of her sister was rather sad.

Margaret looked from one to the other, as if

she would have liked to understand what they meant.

"Don't trouble that little head," said her mother, with a laugh. "Thy time will come soon enough. Thou art too short to be told state secrets."

"I shall be as tall as you some day, Lady," responded Margaret archly.

"And then," said Marjory, stroking the girl's hair, 'thou wilt wish thyself back again, little Magot."

"Nay!—under your good leave, fair Aunt, never!"

"Ah, we know better, don't we, Madge?" asked the Countess, laughing. "Well, I will leave you two maidens together. There is the month's wash to be seen to, and if I am not there, that Alditha is as likely to put the linen in the chests without a sprig of rosemary, as she is to look in the mirror every time she passes it. We shall meet at supper. Adieu!"

And the Countess departed, on housekeeping thoughts intent. For a few minutes the two girls —for the aunt was only about twelve years the senior—sat silent, Margaret having drawn her aunt's hand down and rested her cheek upon it. They were very fond of one another: and being so near in age, they had been brought up so much like sisters, that except in one or two items they treated each other as such, and did not assume the respective authority and reverence usual between such relations at that time. Beyond the employment of the deferential *you* by Margaret, and the familiar *thou* by Marjory, they chatted to each other as any other girls might have done. But just then, for a few minutes, neither spoke.

"Well, Magot!" said Marjory, breaking the silence at last, "have we nought to say to each other? Thou art forgetting, I think, that I want a full account of all these three years since I came to see thee before. They have not been empty of events, I know."

Margaret's answer was a groan.

"Empty!" she said. "Fair Aunt, I would they had been, rather than full of such events as they were. Father Nicholas saith that the old Romans —or Greeks, I don't know which—used to say the man was happy who had no history. I am sure we should have been happier, lately, if we had not had any."

"'Don't know which!' What a heedless Magot!"

"Why, fair Aunt, surely you don't expect people

to recollect lessons. Did you ever remember yours?"

Marjory laughed. "Sufficiently so, I hope, to know the difference between Greeks and Romans. But, however,—for the last three years. Tell me all about them."

"Am I to begin with the Flood, like a professional chronicler?"

"Well, **no.** I think the Conquest would be soon enough."

"Delicious Aunt Marjory! How many weary centuries you excuse me!"

"*How* many, Magot?"

"Oh, please don't! How can I possibly tell? If you really want to know, I will send for Father Nicholas."

Marjory laughed, and kissed the lively face turned up to her.

"Idle Magot! Well, go on."

"I don't think I am idle, fair Aunt. But I do detest learning dates.—Well, now,—was it in April you left us? I know it was very soon after my Lady of Cornwall was married, but I do not remember exactly what month."

"It was in May," said Marjory, shortly.

"May, was it? Oh, I know! It was the eve of Saint Helen's Day. Well, things went on right enough, till my Lord of Canterbury took it into his head that my Lord and father had no business to detain Tunbridge Castle,—it all began with that. It was about July, I think."

"I thought Tunbridge Castle belonged to my Lord of Gloucester. What had either to do with it?"

"O Aunt Marjory! Have you forgotten that my young Lord of Gloucester is in ward to my Lord and father? The Lord King gave him first to my Lord the Bishop of Winchester, when his father died; and then, about a year after, he took him away from the Bishop, and gave him to my fair father. Don't you remember him?—such a pretty boy! I think you knew all about it at the time."

"Very likely I did, Magot. One forgets things, sometimes."

And Margaret, looking up into the fair face, saw, and did not understand, the hidden pain behind the smile.

"So my Lord of Canterbury complained of my fair father to the Lord King. (I wonder he could not attend to his own business.) But the Lord King said that as my Lord of Gloucester held in chief of the Crown, all vacant trusts were his, to give as it pleased him. And then—Aunt Marjory, do you like priests?"

"Magot, what a question!"

"But do you?"

"All priests are not alike, my dear child. They are like other people—some good, and some bad."

"But surely all priests ought to be good."

"Art thou always what thou oughtest to be, Magot?"

Margaret's answer was a sudden spring from the stool and a fervent hug of Marjory.

"Aunt Marjory," she said, when she had sat down again, "I just hate that Bishop of Winchester."[1]

"Shocking, Magot!"

"Oh yes, of course it is extremely wicked. But I do."

"I wish he were here, to set thee a penance for such a naughty speech. However, go on with thy story."

"Well, what do you think, fair Aunt, that my

[1] Peter de Rievaulx, always one of the two chief enemies of Margaret's father.

Lord's Grace of Canterbury[1] did? He actually excommunicated all intruders on the lands of his jurisdiction, and all who should hold communication with them, the King only excepted; and away he went to Rome, to lay the matter before the holy Father. Of course he would tell his tale from his own point of view."

"The Archbishop went to Rome!"

"Indeed he did, Aunt Marjory. My fair father was very indignant. 'That the head of the English Church could not stand by himself, but must seek the approbation of a foreign Bishop!' That was what he said, and I think my fair mother agreed with him."

Perhaps in this nineteenth century we scarcely realise the gallant fight made by the Church of England to retain her independence of Rome. It did not begin at the Reformation, as people are apt to suppose. It was as old as the Church herself, and she was as old as the Apostles. Some of her clergy were perpetually trying to force and to rivet the chains of Rome upon her: but the body of the laity, who are really the Church,[2] resisted this at-

---

[1] Richard Grant, consecrated in 1229.

[2] Any reader who is inclined to doubt this is requested to consult

tempt almost to the death. There was a perpetual struggle, greater or smaller according to circumstances, between the King of England and the Papacy. Pope after Pope endeavoured to fill English sees and benefices with Italian priests: King after King braved his wrath by refusing to confirm his appointments. Apostle, they were ready to allow the Pope to be: sovereign or legislator, never. Doctrine they would accept at his hands; but he should not rule over their secular or ecclesiastical liberties. The quarrel between Henry II. and Becket was entirely on this point. No wonder that Rome canonised the man who thus exalted her. The Kings who stood out most firmly for the liberties of England were Henry II., John, Edward I. and II., and Richard II. This partly explains the reason why history (of which monks were mainly the authors) has so little good to say of any of them, Edward I. only excepted. It is not easy to say why the exception was made, unless it were because he was too firmly rooted in popular admiration, and perhaps a little too munificent to

Acts xv. 4, 22. It is unquestionably the teaching of the New Testament. The clergy form part of the Church merely as individual Christians.

the monastic Orders, for much evil to be discreetly said of him. Cœur - de - Lion was a Gallio who cared for none of those things: Henry III. played into the hands of the Pope to-day, and of the Anglican Church to-morrow. Edward III. held the balance as nearly even as possible. The struggle revived faintly during the reign of Henry VI., but the Wars of the Roses turned men's minds to home affairs, and Henry VII. was the obedient servant of His Holiness. So the battle went on, till it cul-minated in the Reformation. Those who have never entered into this question, and who assume that all Englishmen were "Papists" until 1530, have no idea how gallantly the Church fought for her independent life, and how often she flung from off her the iron grasp of the oppressor. It was not probable that a Princess whose fathers had followed the rule of Columba, and lay buried in Protestant Iona, should have any Roman tendencies on this question. Marjory was as warm as any one could have wished her.

"Well, then," Margaret went on, "that horrid Bishop of Winchester"——

"Oh, fie!" said her aunt.

"—— Came back to England in August. Aunt

Marjory, it is no use,—he is horrid, and I hate him! He hates my fair father. Do you expect me to love him ? ”

“ Well done, Magot ! ” said another voice. “ When I want a lawyer to plead my cause, I will send for thee.—Christ save you, fair Sister ! I heard you were here, with this piece of enthusiasm.”

Both the girls rose to greet the Earl, Margaret courtesying low as beseemed a daughter.

It was very evident that, so far as outside appearance went, Margaret was “only the child of her mother.” Earl Hubert was scarcely so tall as his wife, and he had a bronzed, swarthy complexion, with dark hair. Though short, he was strongly-built and well-proportioned. His eyes were dark, small, but quick and exceedingly bright. He had, when needful, a ready, eloquent tongue and a very pleasant smile. Yet eloquent as undoubtedly he could be, he was not usually a man of many words; and capable as he was of very deep and lasting affection, he was not demonstrative.

The soft, caressing manners of the Princess Margaret were not in her husband's line at all. He was given to calling a spade a spade whenever he had occasion to mention the article : and if she preferred to allude to it as " an agricultural implement for the trituration of the soil," he was disposed to laugh good-humouredly at the epithet, though he dearly loved the silver voice which used it.

A thoroughly representative man of his time was Hubert de Burgh, Earl of Kent; and he was one of those persons who leave a deep mark upon their age. He was a purely self-made man. He had no pedigree: indeed, we do not know with absolute certainty who was his father, though modern genealogists have amused themselves by making a pedigree for him, to which there is no real evidence that he had the least claim. Yet of his wives—for he was four times married—the first was an heiress, the second a baron's widow, the third a countess in her own right and a divorced queen, and the last a princess. His public life had begun by his conducting a negotiation to the satisfaction of Cœur-de-Lion, in the first year of his reign, 1189, when in all probability Hubert was little over twenty years of age. From that moment he rose rapidly. Merely to enumerate all the titles he bore would almost take a page. He was by turns a very rich man and a very poor one, according as his royal and capricious master made or revoked his grants.

The religious character of Hubert is not a matter of speculation, but of certainty. It was—what his contemporaries considered elevated piety—a most singular mixture of the barest and basest superstition with some very strong plain common sense. The superstition was of the style set forth in the famous Spanish drama entitled " The Devotion of the Cross " —the true Roman type of piety, though to Protestant minds of the nineteenth century it seems almost inconceivable. The hero of this play, who is represented as tinctured with nearly every crime which humanity can commit, has a miracle performed in his favour, and goes comfortably to Heaven after it, on account of his devotion to the cross. The innocent reader must not suspect the least connection between this devotion and the atonement wrought upon the cross. It simply means, that whenever Eusebio sees the shape of a cross—in the hilt of his sword, the pattern of a woman's dress, two sticks thrown upon one another,—he stops in the midst of whatever sin he may be committing, and in some form, by word or gesture, expresses his " devotion."

Of this type was Hubert's religion. His notion of spirituality was to grasp the pix with one hand, and to hold the crucifix in the other. He kept a nicely-

balanced account at the Bank of Heaven, in which—
this is historical—the heaviest deposit was the fact
that he had many years before saved a large crucifix
from the flames. The idea that this action was not
most pious and meritorious would have been in
Hubert's eyes rank heresy. Yet he might have
known better. The Psalter lay open to him, which,
had he been acquainted with no other syllable of
revelation, should alone have given him a very
different conception of spiritual religion.

Athwart these singular notions of excellence,
Hubert's good common sense was perpetually gleaming, like the lightning across a dark moor. Whatever else this man was, he was no slave of Rome.
It was supported by him, and probably at his
instigation, that King John had sent his lofty message to the Pope, that—

> " No Italian priest
> Should tithe or toll in his dominions."

It was when the administration lay in his hands
that Parliament refused to comply with the demands
of the Pope till it was seen what other kingdoms
would do: and no Papal aggressions were successful
in England so long as Hubert was in power. To
reverse the famous phrase of Lord Denbigh, Hubert

was "a Catholic, if you please; but an Englishman first."

Truer Englishman, at once loyalist and patriot, never man was than he—well described by one of the English people as "that most faithful and noble Hubert, who so often saved England from the ravages of the foreigner, and restored England to herself." He stood by the Throne, bearing aloft the banner of England, in three especially dark and perilous days, when no man stood there but himself. To him alone, under Providence, we owe it that England did not become a vassal province of France. Most amply was his fidelity put to the test; most unspotted it emerged from the ordeal: most heavy was the debt of gratitude owed alike by England and her King.

That debt was paid, in a sense, to the uttermost farthing. In what manner of coin it was discharged, we are about to see.

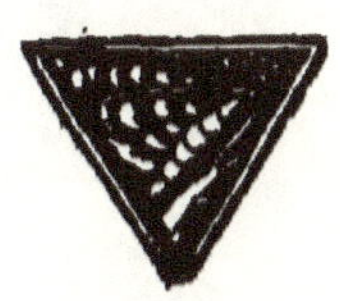

CHAPTER II.

" WHAT DO YOU LACK ?"

" If pestilence stalk through the land, ye say, This is God's doing.
Is it not also His doing, when an aphis creepeth on a rosebud ?"
—MARTIN F. TUPPER.

EARL HUBERT was far too busy a man to waste his time in lounging on velvet settles and exchanging sallies of wit with the ladies of his household. He had done little more than give a cordial welcome to Marjory, and pat Margaret on the head, when he again disappeared, to be seen no more until supper-time.

"Well, Magot," said Marjory, sitting down in the chair, while Margaret as before accommodated herself with a footstool at her feet, "let us get on with thy story. I want to know all about that affair two years ago. Thy fair father looks wonderfully well, methinks, considering all that he has gone through."

"Does he not? O Aunt Marjory, I scarcely know how I am to tell you about that. It was dreadful,—dreadful!"

And the tears stood in big drops on Margaret's eyelashes.

"Well, I will try," she said, with a deep sigh, as Marjory stroked her hair. "In the first place, the year ended all very well. My fair father had been created Justiciary of Ireland for life, and Constable of the Tower, and various favours had been granted to him. That he should be on the brink of trouble —and such trouble!—was the very last thing thought of by any one of us. And then that Bishop of Winchester came back, and before a soul knew anything about it, he was high in the Lord King's favour, and on the twenty-ninth of July—(I am not likely to forget *that* date !)—the blow fell."

"He was dismissed, then, was he not, from all his offices, without a word of warning ?"

"Dismissed and degraded, without a shadow of it !—and a string of the most cruel, wicked accusations brought against him—things that he never did nor dreamed of doing—Aunt Marjory, it makes my blood boil, only to remember them ! I am not going to tell you all : there was one too horrid to mention."

"I know, my maiden." Marjory interposed rather hastily. She had heard already of King Henry's delicate and affectionate assault upon the fair name of Margaret's mother, and she did not wish for a repetition of it.

"But beyond that, of what do you think he was accused?"

"I have not heard the other articles, Magot."

"Then I will tell you. First, of preventing the Lord King's marriage with the Duke of Austria's daughter, by telling the Duke that the King was lame, and blind, and deaf, and a leper, and "——

"Gently, Magot, gently!" said Marjory, laughing.

"I am not making a syllable of it, fair Aunt!— And that he was a wicked, treacherous man, not worthy of the love or alliance of any noble lady. *Pure foy!*—but I know what I should say, if I said just what I think."

"It is sometimes quite as well not to do that, Magot."

"Ha! Perhaps it is, when one may get into prison by it. It is a comfort one can always think. Neither Pope nor King can stop that."

"Magot, my dear child!"

"Oh yes, I know! You think I am horribly

imprudent, Aunt Marjory. But nobody hears me except you and Eva de Braose—she *is* the only person in the wardrobe, and there is no one in the ante-chamber. And as I have heard her say more than I did just now, I don't suppose there is much harm done.—Then, secondly,—they charged my fair father with stealing—only think, *stealing !*—a magical gem from the royal treasury which made the wearer victorious in battle, and sending it to the Prince of Wales."[1]

"Why should they suppose he would do that ?"

"*Pure foy*, Aunt Marjory, don't ask me ! Then, thirdly, they said it was "——

Margaret sprang from her footstool suddenly, and disappeared for a second through the door of the wardrobe. Marjory heard her say,—

"Eva ! I had completely forgotten, till this minute, to tell Marie that my Lady and mother desired her to finish that piece of tapestry to-night, if she can. Do go and look for her, and let her know, or she will not have time."

A slight rustle as of some one leaving the room was audible, and then Margaret dashed back to her footstool, as if she too had not a minute to lose.

[1] Llywelyn the Great, with whom King Henry was at war.

"You know, Aunt Marjory, I could not tell you the next thing with Eva listening. They said that it was by traitorous letters from my fair father that the Prince of Wales had caused Sir William de Braose to be hung."

" Eva's father, thou meanest ? "

"Yes. Then they accused him of administering poison to my Lord of Salisbury, of sending my cousin Sir Raymond to try and force the Lady of Salisbury into marrying him while her lord was beyond seas, of poisoning my Lord of Pembroke, Sir Fulk de Breaut, and my sometime Lord of Canterbury's Grace. He might have spent his life in poisoning every body ! Then, lastly, they said he had obtained favour of the Lord King by help of the black art."

Marjory smiled contemptuously. It was not because she was more free from superstition than other people, but simply because she knew full well that the only sorcery necessary to be used towards Henry III. was "the sorcery of a strong mind over a weak one."[1]

"It was rather unfortunate," she said, "that my

---

[1] This was the answer given to her judges, four hundred years later, by Leonora Galigai, when she was asked to confess what kind of magic she had employed to obtain the favour of Queen Maria de' Medici.

good Lord of Salisbury (whom God rest !) was seized with his last illness the very day after he had supped at my fair brother's table."

"Aunt Marjory!" cried her indignant niece. "Why, it is not a month since I was taken ill in the night, after I had supped likewise. Do you suppose he poisoned me?"

"It is quite possible that walnuts might have something to do with it, Magot. But did I say he poisoned any one?"

"Now, Aunt Marjory, you are laughing at me, because you know I like them. But don't you think it is absurd—the way in which people insist on fancying themselves poisoned whenever they are ill? It looks as if every human being were a monster of wickedness!"

"What would Father Warner say they are, Magot?"

"Oh, he would say it was perfectly true: and he would be right—so far as my Lord of Winchester and a few more are concerned.—Well, Eva, hast thou found Marie?"

"Yes, my dear. She is with the Lady, and she is busy with the tapestry."

"Oh, that is right! I am sorry I forgot."

"And the Lady bade me tell thee, *mignonne*, that she is coming to thy bower shortly, with a pedlar who is waiting in the court, to choose stuffs for thy Whitsuntide robes."

"A pedlar! Delightful! Aunt Marjory, I am sure you want something?"

Marjory laughed. "I want thy tale finished, Magot, before the pedlar comes."

"Too long, my dear Aunt Marjory, unless the pedlar takes all summer to mount the stairs. But you know my Lord and father fled into sanctuary at Merton Abbey, and refused to leave it unless the Lord King would pledge his royal word for his safety. I don't think I should have thought it made much difference. (I wonder if that pedlar has any silversmiths' work.) The Lord King did not pledge his word, but he ordered the Lord Mayor and the citizens to fetch my fair father—only think of that, Aunt Marjory!—dead or alive. Some of the nobler citizens appealed to the Bishop, who was everything with the King just then: but instead of interceding for my fair father, as they asked, he merely confirmed the order. So twenty thousand citizens marched on the Abbey; and when my fair father knew that, he fled to the high altar, and embraced the holy cross with one hand, holding the blessed pix in the other."

"Was our Lord in the pix?" inquired Marjory—meaning, of course, to refer to the consecrated wafer.

"I am not sure, fair Aunt. But however, things turned out better than seemed likely: for not only the Bishop of Chichester, but even my Lord of Chester—my fair father's great enemy—interceded with the Lord King in his behalf. We heard that my Lord of Chester spoke very plainly to him, and told him not only that he would find it easier to draw a crowd together than to get rid of it again, but also that his fickleness would scandalise the world."

"And the Lord King allowed him to say that?"

"Yes, and it had a great effect upon him. I think people who are fickle don't like others to see it—don't you? Do you think that pedlar will have any sendal[1] of India?"

"Thine eyes and half thy tongue are in the pedlar's pack, Magot. I cannot tell thee. But just let me know how it ended, and thy fair father was set free."

---

[1] A silk stuff of extremely fine quality.

"Oh, it did not end for ever so long! My Lord's Grace of Dublin got leave for him to come home and see my fair mother and me ; and after that, when he had gone into Essex, the King sent after him again, and Sir Godfrey de Craucumbe took him away to the Tower. They sent for a smith to put him in fetters, but the man would not do it when he heard who was to wear the fetters. He said he would rather die than be the man to put chains on 'that most faithful and noble Hubert, who so often saved England from the ravages of foreigners, and restored England to herself.' Aunt Marjory, I think he was a grand fellow! I would have kissed him if I had been there."

As the kiss was at that time the common form of greeting between men and women, for a lady to offer a kiss to a man as a token that she approved his words or actions, was not then considered more demonstrative than it would be to shake hands now. It was, in fact, not an unusual occurrence.

"And my fair father told us," pursued Margaret, "when he heard what the smith said, he could not help thinking of those words of our Lord, when He thanked God that His mission had been hidden from the wise, but revealed to the ignorant. 'For,' our

Lord said, 'to Thee, my God, do I commit my cause; for mine enemies have risen against me.'"[1]

"And they took him to the Tower of London?"

"Yes, but the Bishop of London was very angry at the violation of sanctuary, and insisted that my fair father should be sent back. He threatened the King with excommunication, and of course that frightened him. He sent him back to the church whence he was taken, but commanded the Sheriff of Essex to surround the church, so that he should neither escape nor obtain food. But my fair father's true friend, my good old Lord of Dublin—(you were right, Aunt Marjory; all priests are not alike)—interposed, and begged the Lord King to do to him what he had thought to do to my Lord and father. The Lord King then offered the choice of three things :—my Lord and father must either abjure the kingdom for ever, or he must be perpetually imprisoned, or he must openly confess himself a traitor."

" A fair choice, surely!"

" Horrid, wasn't it ?"

" He chose banishment, did he not ?"

[1] The Earl's quotation from Scripture was extremely free, combining Matt. xi. 25 with the substance, but not the exact words, of several passages in the Psalms. Nor did Friar Matthew Paris know much better, since he refers to it all as " that passage in the Gospels."

"He said, if the King willed it, he was content to go out of England for a time,—not for ever: but a traitor he would never confess himself, for he had never been one."

"The words of a true man!" said Marjory.

"Splendid!—and then (Eva!—is that pedlar never coming up?) the Lord King found out that my fair father had laid up treasure in the Temple, and he actually accused him of taking it fraudulently from the royal treasury, and summoned him to resign it. My fair father replied (I shouldn't have done!) that he and all he had were at the King's pleasure, and sent an order to the Master of the Temple accordingly. Then—O Aunt Marjory, it is too long a tale to tell!—and I want that pedlar. But I do think it was a shame, after all that, for the Lord King to profess to compassionate my Lord and father, and to say that he had been faithful to our Lord King John of happy memory,[1] and also to our Lord King Richard (whom God pardon!); therefore, notwithstanding the ill-usage of himself, and the harm he had done the kingdom, he would rather pardon my fair father than execute him. 'For,' he said, 'I

---

[1] King Henry was given to allusions of this class, to the revered memory of his excellent father.

would rather be accounted a remiss king than a man of blood.'"

"Well, that does not sound bad, Magot."

"Oh no! Words are very nice things, Aunt Marjory. And our Lord King Henry can string them very prettily together. I have no patience— I say, Eva! Do go and peep into the court and see what is becoming of that snail of a pedlar!"

"He is in the hall, eating and drinking, Margaret."

"Well, I am sure he has had as much as is good for him!—So then, Aunt Marjory, my fair father was sent to Devizes: and many nobles became sureties for him,—my Lord of Cornwall, the King's brother, among others. And while he was there, he heard of the death of his great enemy, my Lord of Chester. Then he said, 'The Lord be merciful to him: he was my man by his own doing, and yet he never did me good where he could work me harm.' And he set himself before the holy cross, and sang over the whole Psalter for my Lord of Chester. Well, after that,—I cannot go into all the ups and downs of the matter,—but after a while, by the help of some of the garrison, my fair father contrived to escape from Devizes, and joined the Prince of Wales. That was last November;

and he stayed in Wales until the King's journey to Gloucester. Last March the Lord King came here to the Abbey, and he granted several manors to my fair mother: and she took the opportunity to plead for my Lord and father. So when the Lord King went to Gloucester, he was met by my Lord's Grace of Canterbury, who had been to treat with the Prince of Wales, and by his advice all those who had been outlawed, and had sought refuge in Wales, were to be pardoned and received to favour. One of them, of course, was my fair father. So they met the Lord King at Gloucester, and he took them to his mercy. My Lord and father said the Lord King looked calmly on them, and gave them the kiss of peace. But my fair father himself was so much struck by the manner in which our Lord had repaid him his good deeds, that, as his varlet Adam told us, he clasped his hands, and looked up to Heaven, and he said,— 'O Jesus, crucified Saviour, I once when sleeping saw Thee on the cross, pierced with bloody wounds, and on the following day, according to Thy warning, I spared Thy image and worshipped it: and now Thou hast, in Thy favour, repaid me for so doing, in a lucky moment.'"

It did not strike either Marjory or Margaret, as perhaps it may the reader, that this speech presented a very curious medley of devotion, thankfulness, bare-faced idolatry, and belief in dreams and lucky moments. To their minds the mixture was perfectly natural. So much so, that Marjory's response was,—

"Doubtless it was so, Magot. It is always very unlucky to neglect a dream."

At this juncture Eva de Braose presented herself. She was one of three maidens who were alike—as was then customary—wards of the Earl, and wait-ing-maids of the Countess. They were all young ladies of high birth and good fortune, orphan heirs or co-heirs, whose usual lot it was, throughout the Middle Ages, to be given in wardship to some nobleman, and educated with his daughters. Eva de Braose, Marie de Lusignan, and Doucebelle de Vaux,[1] were therefore the social equals and constant companions of Margaret. Eva was a rather pretty, fair-haired girl, about two years older than our heroine.

"The pedlar is coming now, Margaret."

---

[1] Eva and Marie (but not Doucebelle) are historical persons.

"*Ha, jolife!*" [1] cried Margaret. "Is my Lady and mother coming?"

"Yes, and both Hawise and Marie."

Hawise de Lanvalay was the young wife of Margaret's eldest brother. Earl Hubert's family consisted, beside his daughter, of two sons of his first marriage, John and Hubert, who were respectively about eighteen and fifteen years older than their sister.

The Countess entered in a moment, bringing with her the young Lady Hawise,—a quiet-looking, dark-eyed girl of some eighteen years; and Marie, the little Countess of Eu, who was only a child of eleven. After them came Levina, one of the Countess's dressers, and two sturdy varlets, carrying the pedlar's heavy pack between them. The pedlar himself followed in the rear. He was a very respectable-looking old man, with strongly-marked aquiline features and long white beard; and he brought with him a lithe, olive-complexioned youth of about eighteen years of age.

The varlets set down the pack on the floor, and

---

[1] "Oh, delightful!" The modern schoolboy's "How jolly!" is really a corruption of this. The companion regret was "Ha, chétife!" —("Oh, miserable!")

departed. The old man unstrapped it, and opening it out with the youth's help, proceeded to display his goods. Very rich, costly, and beautiful they were. The finest lawn of Cambray (whence comes "cambric"), and the purest sheeting of Rennes, formed a background on which were exhibited rich diapered stuffs from Damascus, crape of all colours from Cyprus, golden baudekyns from Constantinople, fine sendal from India, with satins, velvets, silks, taffetas, linen and woollen stuffs, in bewildering profusion. Over these again were laid rich furs,—sable, ermine, miniver, black fox, squirrel, marten, and lamb; and trimmings of gold and silver, gimp and beads, delicate embroidery, and heavy tinsel.

"Here, Lady, is a lovely thing in changeable sendal," said the old man, hunting for it among his silks: "it would be charming for the fair-haired damsel—(lift off that fox fur, Cress),—blue and gold. Or here,—a striped tartaryn, which would suit the dark young lady,—orange and green. Then—(Cress, give me the silver frieze),—this, Lady, would be well for the little maid, for somewhat cooler weather. ·And will my Lady see the Cyprus? (Hand the pink one, Cress.) This would

make up enchantingly for the damsel that was in
my Lady's chamber."

"Where is Doucebelle?" asked the Countess,
looking round. "I thought she had come. Marie,
run and fetch her.—Hast thou any broidery-work
of the East Country, good man?"

"One or two small things, Lady.—Cress, give me
thy sister's scarves."

The young man unfolded a woollen wrapper, and
then a lawn one inside it, and handed to his father
three silken scarves, of superlatively fine texture,
and covered with most exquisite embroidery. Even
the Countess, accustomed as her eyes were to
beautiful things, was not able to suppress an ad-
miring ejaculation.

"This *is* lovely!" she said.

"Those are samples," remarked the pedlar, with
a gleam of pleasure in his eyes. "I have more, of
various patterns, if my Lady would wish to see
them. She has only to speak her commands."

"Yes. But — these are all imported, I suppose?"

"All imported, such as I have shown to my
Lady."

"I presume no broideress is to be found in Eng-

land, who can do such work as this?" said the
Countess in a regretful tone.

"Did my Lady wish to find one?"

" I wished to have a scarf in my possession copied,
with a few variations which I would order. But I
fear it cannot be done—it would be almost necessary
that I should see the broideress myself, to avoid
mistakes; and I would fain, if it were possible, have
had the work done under my own eye."

" That might be done, perhaps. It would be
costly."

" Oh, I should not care for the cost. I want the
scarf for a gift; and it is nothing to me whether I
pay ten silver pennies or a hundred."

"Would my Lady suffer her servant to see the
scarf she wishes to have imitated?"

"Fetch it, Levina," said the Countess; "thou
knowest which I mean."

Levina brought it, and the pedlar gave it very
careful inspection.

" And the alterations?" he asked.

"I would have a row of silver harebells and green
ferns, touched with gold, as an outer border," explained the Countess: "and instead of those ornaments in the inner part, I would have golden scrolls,

worked with the words 'Dieu et mon droit' in scarlet."

The pedlar shook his head. "The golden scrolls with the words can be done, without difficulty. But I must in all humility represent to my Lady that the flowers and leaves she desires cannot."

"Why?" asked the Countess in a surprised tone.

"Not in this work," answered the pedlar. "In this style of embroidery "—and he took another scarf from his pack—"it could be wrought: but not in the other."

"But that is not to be compared with the other!"

"My Lady has well said," returned the pedlar with a smile.

"But I do not understand where the difficulty lies?" said the Countess, evidently disappointed.

"Let my Lady pardon her servant. We have in our company—nay, there is in all England—one broideress only, who can work in this style. And I dare not make such an engagement on her behalf."

"Still I cannot understand for what reason?"

"Lady, these flowers, leaves, heads, and such representations of created things, are the work of Christian hands. That broidery which my Lady desires is not so."

" But why cannot Christians work this broidery ? "

" Ha ! They do not. My Lady's servant cannot speak further."

" Then what is she who alone can do this work ? What eyes and fingers she must have ! "

" She is my daughter," answered the pedlar, rather proudly.

" But I am sure the woman who can broider like this, is clever enough to make a row of harebells and ferns ! "

" Clever enough,—oh yes ! But—she could not do it."

" ' Clever enough,' but ' could not do it '—old man, I cannot understand thee."

" Lady, she would account it sin to imitate created things."

The Countess looked up with undisguised amazement.

" Why ? "

" Because the Holy One has forbidden us to make to ourselves any likeness of that which is in heaven above, or in the earth beneath."

" But I would pay her any sum she asked."

" If my Lady can buy Christian consciences with gold, not so a daughter of Israel."

The old man spoke proudly now, and his head was uplifted in a very different style from his previous subservient manner. His son's lip was curled, and his black eyes were flashing fire.

"Well! I do not understand it," answered the Countess, looking as much annoyed as the sweet Princess Margaret knew how to look. "I should have thought thy daughter might have put her fancies aside; for what harm can there be in broidering flowers? However, if she will not, she will not. She must work me a border of some other pattern, for I want the scarf wider."

"That she can do, as my Lady may command." The old Jew was once more the obsequious tradesman, laying himself out to please a profitable customer.

"What will be the cost, if the scarf be three ells in length, and—let me see—about half an ell broad?"

"It could not be done under fifteen gold pennies, my Lady."

"That is costly! Well, never mind. If people want to make rich gifts, they must pay for them. But could I have it by Whitsuntide?—that is, a few days earlier, so as to make the gift then."

The pedlar reflected for a moment.

“Let my Lady pardon her servant if he cannot give that answer at this moment. If my daughter have no work promised, so that she can give her time entirely to this, it can be done without fail. But it is some days since my Lady’s servant saw her, and she may have made some engagement since.”

“I am the better pleased thou art not too ready to promise,” said the Countess, smiling. “But what about the work being done under my eye? I will lodge thy daughter, and feed her, and give her a gold penny extra for it.”

The old Jew looked very grave.

“Let my Lady not be angered with the lowest of her servants! But—we are of another religion.”

“Art thou afraid of my converting her?” asked the Countess, in an amused tone.

“Under my Lady’s pardon—no!” said the old man, proudly. “I can trust my daughter. And if my noble Lady will make three promises on whatsoever she holds most holy, the girl shall come.”

“She should be worth having, when she is so hard to get at!” responded the Countess, laughing, as she took from her bosom a beautiful little silver crucifix, suspended by a chain of the same material from her neck, "Now then, old man, what am I to swear?"

" First, that my daughter shall not be required to work in any manner on the holy Sabbath,—namely, as my Lady will understand it, from sunset on Friday until the same hour on Saturday."

" That I expected. I know Jews are very precise about their Sabbaths. Very well,—so that the scarf be finished by Wednesday before Whitsuntide, that I swear."

" Secondly, by my Lady's leave, that she shall not be compelled to eat any thing contrary to our law."

" I have no desire to compel her. But what will she eat? I must know that I can give her something."

" Any kind of vegetables, bread, milk, and eggs."

" Lenten fare. Very well. I swear it."

" Lastly, that my Lady will appoint her a place in her own apartments, or in those of the damsel her daughter, and that she may never stir out of that tower while she remains in the Castle."

" Poor young prisoner! Good. If thou art so anxious to consign thy child to hard durance, I will swear to keep her in it."

" May my Lady's servant ask where she will be?"

The Countess laughed merrily. "This priceless treasure of thine! She might be a king's daughter. I will put her in my daughter's ante-chamber, just behind thee."

The pedlar walked into the ante-chamber, and inspected it carefully, to the great amusement of the ladies.

"It is enough," he said, returning. "Lady, my child is not a king's daughter, but she is the dearest treasure of her old father's heart."

The old man had well spoken, for his words, Jew as he was—a creature, according to the views of that day, born to be despised and ill-treated—went straight to the tender heart of the Princess Margaret.

"'Tis but nature," she said softly. "Have no fear, old man: I will take care of thy treasure. What is her name?"

"Will my Lady suffer her grateful servant to kiss her robe? I am Abraham of Norwich, and my daughter's name is Belasez."

Singular indeed were the Jewish names common at this time, beyond a very few Biblical ones, of which the chief were Abraham, Aaron, and Moses—the last usually corrupted to Moss or Mossy. They were, for men,—Delecresse ("Dieu le croisse"), Ursel,

Leo, Hamon, Kokorell, Emendant, and Bonamy: —for women, — Belasez ("Belle assez"), Floria, Licorice (these three were the most frequent), Esterote, Cuntessa, Belia, Anegay, Rosia, Genta, and Pucella. They used no surnames beyond the name of the town in which they lived.

"And what years has she?" asked the Countess.

"Seventeen, if it please my Lady."

"Good. I hope she will be clever and tractable.— Now, Madge, what do *you* want?"

The Princess Marjory wanted a silver necklace, a piece of green silk for a state robe, and some unshorn wool for an every-day dress, beside lamb's fur and buttons for trimming. Buttons were fashionable ornaments in those days, and it was not unusual to spend six or eight dozen upon one dress.

"Now, Magot, let me see for thee," said her mother. "Thy two woollen gowns must be shorn for winter, and thou wilt want a velvet one for gala days: but there is time for that by and bye. What thou needest now is a blue Cyprus[1] robe for thy best summer one, two garments of coloured thread for common, a silk hood, one or two lawn wimples,[2]

---

[1] Crape.

[2] The wimple covered the neck, and was worn chiefly out of doors.

and a pair of corsets.[1] Thou mayest have a new armilaus[2] if thou wilt."

"And may I not have a new mantle?" was Margaret's answer, in a coaxing tone.

"A new mantle? Thou unconscionable Magot! Somebody will be ruined before thy wants are supplied."

"And a red velvet gipcière, Lady? And I *did* so want a veil of sendal of Inde!"

"Worse and worse! Come, old man, prithee, measure off the Cyprus, and look out the wimples quickly, or this damsel of mine will leave me never a farthing in my pocket."

"And Eva wants a new gown," suggested Margaret.

"Oh yes!" said the Countess, laughing. "And so does Marie, and so does Doucebelle, I suppose,— and Hawise, I have no doubt. I shall be completely ruined among you!"

"But my Lady will give me the sendal of Inde? I will try to do without the gipcière."

A gipcière was a velvet bag dependent from the

Ladies from a queen to a countess wore it coming over the chin; women of less rank, beneath.

[1] Tight-lacing dates from about the twelfth century.

[2] A short cloak, worn by both sexes, ornamented with buttons.

waist, which served as a purse or pocket, as occasion required.

"Magot, hast thou no conscience? Come, then, old man, let this unreasonable damsel see thy gipcières. And if she must have some sendal of Inde, well,—fate is inevitable. What was the other thing, Magot? A new mantle? Oh, shocking! I can't afford that. What is the price of thy black cloth, old man?"

It was easy to see that Margaret would have all she chose to ask, without much pressure. Some linen dresses were also purchased for the young wards of the Earl,—a blue fillet for Eva, and a new barm-cloth [1] for Marie; and the Countess having chosen some sendal and lawn for her own use, the purchases were at last completed.

The old Jew, helped by Delecresse, repacked his wares with such care as their delicacy and costliness required, and the Countess desired Levina to summon the varlets to bear the heavy burden down to the gate.

"Peace wait on my Lady!" said the pedlar, bowing low as he took leave. "If it please the Holy One, my Belasez shall be here at my Lady's command before a week is over."

[1] Apron.

CHAPTER III.

BELASEZ.

" And, born of Thee, she may not always take
Earth's accents for the oracles of God."
—*Felicia Hemans.*

THE last word had scarcely left the pedlar's lips, when the door of the ante-chamber was flung open, and a boy of Margaret's age burst into the room.

He was fair-haired and bright-faced, with a slender, elegant figure, and all his motions were very agile. Beginning with—" I say, Magot !"—he stopped suddenly both tongue and feet as he caught sight of the Countess.

" Well, Sir Richard ? " suggested that lady.

" I cry you mercy, Lady. I did not know you were here."

" And if you had done—what then ? "

" Why, then," answered Richard, laughing but

colouring, "I suppose I ought to have come in more quietly."

"Ah! Did you ever read with Father Nicholas about an old man who said that the Athenians knew what was right, but the Lacedemonians did it?"

"Your pardon, Lady! I always forget what I read with Father Nicholas."

"I should suppose so. I am afraid there is Athenian blood in your veins, Sir Richard!"

"Lady, if it stand with your pleasure, there is none but true Christian blood in *my* veins!" was the proud reply.

"*Pure foy!* If you are so proud of your blood, I fear you will disdain to do what I was about to bid you."

"I shall never disdain to execute the commands of a fair lady."

"My word, Sir Richard, but you are growing a courtly knight! You see that Jew boy has left his cap behind. As there are none here but damsels, I was thinking I would ask you to call him back to fetch it."

"He shall have it—a Jew boy? I'll take the tongs, then!"

The next minute Delecresse, who was just turning

back to fetch the forgotten cap, heard a boyish voice calling to him out of a window, and looking up, saw his cap held out in the tongs.

"Here, thou cur of a Jew! What dost thou mean, to leave thy heathen stuff in the chamber of a noble damsel?"

And the cap was dropped into the courtyard, with such good aim that it first hit Delecresse on the head, and then lodged itself in the midst of a puddle.

Delecresse, without uttering a word, yet flushing red even through his dark complexion, deliberately stooped, recovered his wet cap, and placed it on his head, pressing it firmly down as if he wished to impart the moisture to his hair. Then he turned and looked fixedly at Richard, who was watching him with an amused face.

"That wasn't a bad shot, was it?" cried the younger lad.

"Thank you," was the answer of Delecresse. "I shall know you again!"

The affront was a boyish freak, perpetrated rather in thoughtlessness than malice: but the tone of the answer, however simple the words, manifestly breathed revenge. Richard de Clare was not an ill-natured boy. But he had been taught from his babyhood that a Jew was the scum of the earth, and that to speak contumeliously to such was so far from being wrong, that it absolutely savoured of piety. Jews had crucified Christ. To have aided one of them, or to have been over civil to him, would in a Christian have been considered as putting a slight upon his Lord. There was, therefore, some excuse for Richard, educated as he had been in this belief.

Delecresse, on the contrary, had been as carefully brought up in the opposite conviction. To him it was the Gentile who was the refuse of humanity, and it was a perpetual humiliation to be forced to cringe to, and wait upon, such contemptible creatures. Moreover, the day was coming when their positions should be reversed; and who could say how near it was at hand? Then the proud Christian noble would be the slave of the despised Jew pedlar, and—thought Delecresse, grinding his teeth—he at least would take care that the Christian slave should indulge no mistakes on that point.

To both the youths Satan was whispering, and by both he was obeyed. And each of them was positively convinced that he was serving God.

The vengeful words of Delecresse made no impression whatever on the young Earl of Gloucester.

He would have laughed with scorn at the mere idea that such an insect as that could have any power to hurt him. He danced back to Margaret's bower, where, in a few minutes, he, she, Marie, and Eva were engaged in a merry round game.

Beside the three girls who were in the care of the Countess, Earl Hubert had also three boy-wards—Richard de Clare, heir of the earldom of Gloucester; Roger de Mowbray, heir of the barony of Mowbray, now about fifteen years old; and John de Averenches (or Avranches), the son of a knight. With these six, the Earl's two sons, his daughter, and his daughter-in-law, there was no lack of young people in the Castle, of whom Sir John de Burgh, the eldest, was only twenty-nine.

The promise made by Abraham of Norwich was faithfully kept. A week had not quite elapsed when Levina announced to the Countess that the Jew pedlar and the maiden his daughter awaited her pleasure in the court. The Countess desired her to bring them up immediately to Margaret's bower, whither she would go herself to meet them.

Margaret and Doucebelle had just come in from a walk upon the leads—the usual way in which ladies took airings in the thirteenth century. Indeed, the leads were the only safe and proper place for a young girl's out-door recreation. The courtyard was always filled by the household servants and soldiers of the garrison: and the idea of taking a walk outside the precincts of the Castle, would never have occurred to anybody, unless it were to a very ignorant child indeed. There were no safe highroads, nor quiet lanes, in those days, where a maiden might wander without fear of molestation. Old ballads are full of accounts of the perils incurred by rash and self-sufficient girls who ventured alone out of doors in their innocent ignorance or imprudent bravado. The roadless wastes gave harbour to abundance of fierce small animals and deadly vipers, and to men worse than any of them.

Old Abraham, cap in hand, bowed low before the Princess, and presented a closely-veiled, graceful figure, as the young broideress whom he had promised.

"Lay thy veil aside, my maid," said the Countess, with most unusual kindness, considering that it was a Jewess to whom she spoke.

The maiden obeyed, and revealed to the eyes of the Princess and her damsels a face and figure of such extreme loveliness that she no longer wondered at the anxiety of her father to provide for her concealment. But the beauty of Belasez was of an entirely different type from that of the Christians around her. Her complexion was olive, her hair raven black, her eyes large and dark, now melting as if in liquid light, now brilliant and full of fire. And if Margaret looked two years beyond her real age, Belasez looked more like seven.

"Thou knowest wherefore thou art come hither?" asked the Countess, smiling complacently on the vision before her.

"To broider for my Lady," said Belasez, in a low, clear, musical voice.

"And wilt thou obey my orders?"

"I will obey my Lady in every thing not forbidden by the holy law."

"Well, I think we shall agree, my maid," returned the Countess, whose private views respecting religious tolerance were something quite extraordinary for the time at which she lived. "I would not willingly coerce any person's conscience. But as I do not know thy law, thou wilt have to tell me if I should desire thee to do some forbidden thing."

"My Lady is very good to her handmaiden," said Belasez.

"Margaret, take the maid into thy wardrobe for a little while, until she has dined; and after that I will show her what I require. She will be glad of rest after her journey."

Margaret obeyed, and a motion of her mother's hand sent Doucebelle after her. The daughter of the house sat down on the settle which stretched below the window, and Doucebelle followed her example: but Belasez remained standing.

"Come and sit here by me," said Margaret to the young Jewess. "I want to talk to thee."

Belasez obeyed in silence.

"Art thou very tired with thy journey?"

"Not now, damsel, I thank you. We have come but a short stage this morning."

"Art thou fond of broidery?"

"I love every thing beautiful."

"And nothing that is not beautiful?"

"I did not say that, damsel." Belasez's smile showed a perfect row of snow-white teeth.

"Am I fair enough to love?" asked Margaret laughingly. She had a good deal of her mother's easy tolerance of differences, and all her sweet affability to those beneath her.

"Ah, my damsel, true love regards the heart

rather than the face, methinks. I cannot see into my damsel's heart in one minute, but I should think it was not at all difficult to love her."

"I want every body to love me," said Margaret. "And I love every body."

"If my damsel would permit me to counsel her,—love every body by all means: but do not let her want every body to love her."

"Why not?"

"Because I fear my damsel will meet with disappointment."

"Oh, I hate to be disappointed. Hast thou brought thine image with thee?"

To Margaret this question sounded most natural. In the first place, she could not conceive the idea of prayer without something visible to pray to: and in the second, she had been taught that all Jews and Saracens were idolaters. She was surprised to see the blood rush to Belasez's dark cheek, and the fire flash from her eyes.

"Will my damsel allow me to ask what she means? I do not understand."

"Wilt thou not want to say thy prayers whilst thou art here?" responded Margaret, who was at least as much puzzled as Belasez.

"Most certainly! but not to an image!"

"Oh, do you Jews sometimes pray without images?"

"Does my damsel take us for idolaters?"

"Yes, I was always told so," said Margaret, looking astonished.

The fire died out of Belasez's eyes. She saw that Margaret had simply made an innocent mistake from sheer ignorance of the question.

"My damsel has been misinformed. We Israelites hold all images to be wicked, and abhorrent to the holy law."

"Then thou wilt not want to set up an idol for thyself anywhere?"

"Most assuredly not."

"I hope I have not vexed thee," said Margaret, ingenuously. "I did not know."

"My damsel did not vex me, as soon as I saw that she did not know."

"And wouldst thou not like better to be a Christian than a Jew?" demanded Margaret, who could not imagine the possibility of any feeling on Belasez's part regarding her nationality except those of regret and humiliation.

But the answer, though it came in a single syllable,

was unmistakable. Intense pride, passionate devotion to her own creed and people, the deepest scorn and loathing for all others, combined to make up the tone of Belasez's " No !"

" How very odd ! " exclaimed Margaret, looking at her, with an expression of great astonishment upon her own fair, open features.

" Is it odd to my damsel ? Does she know what her question sounded like, to me ?"

" Tell me."

" ' Would she not like better to be a villein scullion-maid, than to be the daughter of my noble Lord of Kent ?'"

" But Jews are not noble !" cried Margaret, gazing in bewilderment from Belasez to Doucebelle, as if she expected one of them to help her out of the puzzle.

" Not in the world's estimate," answered Belasez. " There is One above the world."

Before Margaret could reply, the deep bass " Dingdong !" of the great dinner-bell rang through the Castle, and Levina made her appearance at the door.

" My Lady has given me charge concerning thee, Belasez," she said, rather coldly addressing the Jewess. " Thou wilt come with me."

With a graceful reverence to Margaret, Belasez turned, and followed Levina.

At that date, no titles except those of nobility or office were usual in England. Any woman below a peer's daughter, was addressed by her Christian name or by that of her husband. That is to say, the unmarried woman was simply "Joan;" the married one was "John's Wife."

Belasez was gifted by nature with a large amount of that kind of intuition which has been defined as feeling the pressure of other people's atmosphere. It may be a gift which augurs delicacy and refinement, but it always brings discomfort to its possessor. She knew instinctively, and in a moment, that Levina was likely to be her enemy.

It was true. Levina was a prey to that green-eyed monster which sports itself with the miseries of humanity. She had been the best broideress in the Castle until that day. And now she felt herself suddenly supplanted by a young thing of barely more than half her age and experience, who was called in, forsooth, to do something which it was imagined that Levina could not do. What business had the Countess to suppose there was any thing she could not do?—or, to want something out of her power to provide? Was there the slightest likelihood, thought Levina, flaring up, that this scrap of a creature could work better than herself?—a mere chit of a child (Levina was past thirty), with a complexion like the fire-bricks (Levina's resembled putty), and hair the colour of nasty sloes (Levina's was nearer that of a tiger-lily), and great staring eyes like horn lanterns! The Countess was the most unreasonable, and Levina the most cruelly-outraged, of all the women that had ever held a needle since those useful instruments were originally invented.

Levina did not put her unparalleled wrongs into words. It would have been easier for Belasez to get on with her if she had done so. She held her head up, and snorted like an impatient horse, as she stalked through the door into the ante-chamber.

"This is where thou art to be," she snapped in a staccato tone.

Any amount of personal slight and scorn was merely what Belasez had been accustomed to receive from Christians ever since she had left her cradle. The disdain of Levina, therefore, though she could hardly enjoy it, made far less impression on her than the unaccountable kindliness of the royal ladies.

"The Lady bade me ask what thou wouldst eat?" demanded Levina in the same tone as before.

"I thank thee. Any thing that has not had life."

"What's that for?" came in shorter snaps than ever.

"It would not be *kosher.*"

"Speak sense! What does the vermin mean?"

"I mean, it would not be killed according to our law."

"Suppose it wasn't!—what then?"

"Then I must not eat it."

"Stupid, silly, ridiculous stuff! May I be put in a pie, if I know what the Lady was thinking about, when she brought in such road-dirt as this! And my damsel sets herself above us all, forsooth! She must have her meat served according to some law that nobody ever heard of, least of all the Lord King's noble Council: and she must have a table set for her all by herself, as though she were a sick queen. Pray you, my noble Countess, would you eat in gold or silver?—and how many varlets shall serve to carry your dainty meat?—and is your sweet Grace served upon the knee, or no? I would fain have things done as may pleasure my right noble Lady."

Belasez answered as she usually disposed of similar affronts,—by treating them as if they were offered in genuine courtesy, but with a faint ring of satire beneath her tone.

"I thank you. I should prefer wood, or pewter if it please you: and I should think one varlet might answer. I was never served upon the knee yet, and it will scarcely be necessary now."

Levina gave a second and stronger snort, and disappeared down the stairs. In a few minutes she made her reappearance, carrying in one hand a plate of broiled ham, and in the other a piece of extremely dry and rather mouldy bread.

"Here is my gracious damsel's first course! Fulk le Especer was so good as to tell me that folks of her sort are mighty fond of ham; so I took great care to bring her some. There'll be sauce with the next."

That there would be sauce—of one species—with every course served to her in that house, Belasez was beginning to feel no doubt. Yet however Levina chose to behave to her, the young Jewess maintained her own dignity. She quietly put aside the plate of ham, and, cutting off the mouldy pieces, ate the dry bread without complaint. Belasez's kindly and generous nature was determined that the Countess, who had been so much kinder to her than at that time Christians usually were to Jews, should hear no murmuring word from her unless it came to actual starvation.

Levina's sauce presented itself unmistakably with the second course, which proved to be a piece of apple-pie, swimming in the strongest vinegar. Though it must have set her teeth on edge, Belasez consumed the pie in silence, avoiding the vinegar so far as she could, and entertained while she did so by Levina's assurances that it delighted her to see how completely Belasez enjoyed it.

The third article, according to Levina, was cheese: but the first mouthful was enough to convince the persecuted Jewess that soft soap would have been a more correct epithet. She quietly let it alone.

"*Ha, chétife!* I am sadly in fear that my sweetest damsel does not like our Suffolk cheese?" said Levina in a most doleful tone.

"Is it manufactured in this county?" asked Belasez very coolly; for, in 1234, all soaps were of foreign importation. "I thought it tasted more like the French make."

Levina vanished down the stairs, but her suppressed laughter was quite audible. She came up again with two more plates, and informed Belasez that they constituted the last course. One of them was filled with chicken-bones, picked exceedingly clean: the other with a piece of sweet cake, over which had been poured some very hot saline compound which by no means harmonised with the cake, but set Belasez's throat on fire. She managed, however, to eat it, thinking that she would get little food of any kind if she did not: and Levina departed with the plates, remarking that it had done her good to see the excellent meal which Belasez had made. It was a relief to the girl to be left alone: for solitude had no terrors for her, and Levina was certainly not an enjoyable companion. After half-an-hour's quiet, Margaret and Eva entered the ante-chamber.

"Hast thou dined, Belasez?" asked Margaret, kindly.

"I thank my damsel, yes."

"Did Levina bring thee such dishes as thou mightest eat?"

"According to our law? Oh yes."

It was rather a relief to Belasez that the question took that form.

"Then that is all right," said Margaret, innocently, and passed on into her own room.

The Countess's step was heard approaching, but just before entering she stopped at the head of the stairs.

"Thou hast given the girl her dinner, Levina?"

"Oh yes, my Lady!"

"What had she?"

"I brought her apple-pie, if it please my Lady, and cheese, and gâteau de Dijon, and ham, and— a few other little things: but she would not touch the ham, and scarcely the cheese."

"Thou hast forgotten, Levina: I told thee no meat of any kind, nor fish; and I believe no Jew will touch ham. I did not know they objected to cheese. But had she enough? Apple-pie and gâteau de Dijon make but a poor dinner."

And without questioning Levina further, the Countess went on and addressed Belasez direct.

"My maid, hast thou fared well? I fear Levina did not bring thee proper things."

Belasez hesitated. She was very unwilling to say no: and how could she in conscience say yes?

"They were according to our law, I thank my

Lady,—all but the ham. That, under her gracious leave, I must decline."

"But thou didst not take the cheese?"

"No,—with my Lady's leave."

"Was it not in accordance with thy law, or didst thou not like it?"

"If my Lady will pardon me," said poor Belasez, driven into a corner, "I did not like it."

"What kind was it?"

"Levina said it was Suffolk cheese." Belasez's conscience rather smote her in giving this answer.

"Ah!" responded the unconscious Countess, "it is often hard, and everybody does not like it, I know."

Belasez was silent beyond a slight reverence to show that she heard the observation.

"But hast thou had enough?" pursued the Countess, still unsatisfied.

"I am greatly obliged to my Lady, and quite ready to serve her," was the evasive reply.

The Countess looked hard at Belasez, but she said no more. She despatched Levina for the scarf which was to be copied, and gave the young Jewess her instructions. The exquisite work which grew in Belasez's skilful hands evidently delighted the

Countess. She was extremely kind, and the reserved but sensitive nature of Belasez went out towards her in fervent love.

To Margaret, the Jewish broideress was an object of equal mystery and interest. She would sit watching her work for long periods. She noticed that Belasez ignored the existence of her private oratory, made no reverence to the gilded Virgin which stood on a bracket in her wardrobe, and passed the *bénitier* without vouchsafing the least attention to the holy water. Manifestly, Jews did not believe in gilded images and holy water. But then, in what did they believe? Had they any faith in any thing? Belasez had owned to saying her prayers, and she acknowledged the existence of some law which she felt herself bound to obey. But whose law was it?—and to whom did she pray? These thoughts seethed in Margaret's brain till at last, one afternoon when she sat watching the embroidery, they burst forth into speech.

"Belasez!"

"What would my damsel?"

"Belasez, what dost thou believe?"

The Jewess looked up in surprise.

"I am not sure that I understand my

damsel's question. Will she condescend to explain ?"

"I mean, what god dost thou worship ?"

"There is but one God," answered Belasez, solemnly.

"That I believe, too: but we do not worship the same God, do we ?"

"I think we do—to a certain extent."

"But there is a difference between us. What is the difference ?"

Belasez seemed to hesitate.

"Don't be afraid, but speak out!" said Margaret, eagerly.

"If I say what my Lady would not approve, would it be right in me ?"

"My Lady and mother will not mind. Go on !"

"Damsel, I think the difference touches Him who is the Sent of God, and the Son of the Blessed. We believe in Him, as well as you. But we believe that He is yet to come, and is to be the salvation of Israel. You believe"—Belasez's words came slowly, as if dragged from her—"that He is come, long ago ; and you think He will save all men."

"But that is our Lord Christ, surely ?" said Margaret.

"You call Him so," was Belasez's reply.

"But He did come!" said Margaret, in a puzzled tone.

"A man came, undoubtedly, who claimed to be the Man who was to come. But was the claim a true one?"

"I have always been told that it was!"

"And I have always been told that it was not."

"Then how are we to find out which is true?"

Belasez spread her hands out with a semi-Eastern gesture, which indicated hopeless incapacity, of some sort.

"Damsel, do not ask me. The holy prophets told our fathers of old time that so long as Israel walked contrary to the Holy One, so long should they wander over the earth, forsaken exiles, and be punished seven times for their sins. Are we not exiles? Is He not punishing us? Our holy and beautiful house is a desolation; our land is overthrown by strangers. Yet we are no idolaters; we are no Sabbath-breakers; we do not profane the name of the Blessed. Do you think I never ask myself for what sin it is that we are thus cast away from the presence of our King? In old days it was always for such sins as I have named: it cannot be

that now. Is it—O Abraham our father! can it be?
—that He has come, the King of Israel, and we
have not known Him? Damsel, there are thousands
of the sons of Israel that have asked that question!
And then "——

Belasez stopped suddenly.

"Go on!" urged Margaret. "What then?"

"I shall say what my damsel will not wish to hear,
if I do go on."

"But I wish very much to hear it."

"And then we look around on you, who call
yourselves servants of Him whom ye say is come.
We ask you to tell us what you have learned of
Him. And ye answer us with the very things which
the King of Israel solemnly forbade. Ye point us
to images of dead men, and ye hold up before us
a goddess, a fair dead woman, and ye say, These
are they whom ye shall serve! And we answer, If
these things be what ye have learned from him that
is come, then he never can be the Sent of God.
God forbade all idolatry, and all image-making:
if he taught it, can he be Messiah? This is why
in all the ages we have stood aloof. We might
have received him, we might have believed him,—
but for this."

"But I do not know," said Margaret, thoughtfully, "that holy Church lays much stress on images. I should think, if ye prefer to pray without them, she would allow you to do so. I cannot understand how ye can pray without them; for what is there to pray to? It is your infirmity, I suppose."

"Ah, Damsel," said Belasez with a sad smile, "this seems to you a very, very little matter! How shall a Jew and a Christian ever understand each other? For it is life or death to us. It is a question of obeying, or of disobeying—not of doing something we fancy, or do not fancy."

"Yes, but holy Church would decide it for you," urged Margaret, earnestly.

"Damsel, your words are strange to my ears. The Holy One (to whom be praise!) has decided it long ago. 'Ye shall *not* make unto you any graven image: ye shall *not* bow down to them, nor worship them.' The command is given. What difference can it make to us, that the thing you call the Church dares to disregard it? I scarcely understand what 'the Church' is. If I rightly know what my damsel means, it signifies all the Christians. And Christians are Gentiles. How can the sons of Israel take laws from them? And to speak as if they could abrogate the law of Him that sitteth in the heavens, before whom they are all less than nothing and vanity! It is a strange tongue in which my damsel speaks. I do not understand it."

Neither did Margaret understand Belasez. She sat and looked at her, with her mind in bewildered confusion. To her, the authority of the Church was paramount,—was the only irrefragable thing. And here was something which looked like another Church, setting itself up with some unaccountable and unheard-of claim to be older, truer, better!—something which denied that the Church—with horror be it whispered!—had any right to make laws!—which referred to a law, and a Legislator, so high above the Church that it scarcely regarded the Church as worth mention in the matter at all! Margaret felt stunned.

"But God speaks through the Church!" she gasped.

"If that were so, they would speak the same thing," was Belasez's unanswerable response.

Margaret felt pushed into a corner, and did not know what to say next. The difference between her point of view and that of Belasez was so vast, that considerations which would have silenced any one else at once passed as the idle wind by her. And Margaret could not see how to alter it.

"I must ask Father Nicholas to show thee how it is," she said at last in a kindly manner. "I am only an ignorant girl. But he can explain to thee."

"Can he?" said Belasez. "What explanations of his, or any one's, can prove that man may please himself about obeying his Maker? He will tell me—does my damsel think I have never listened to a Christian priest?—he will tell me to offer incense to yonder gilded image. Had I not better offer it to myself? I am a living daughter of Israel: is that not better than the stone image of a dead one?"

"Better than our blessed Lady!" cried the horrified Margaret.

"Perhaps, if she were here, a living woman, she might be the better woman of the two," said Belasez, coolly. "But a living woman, I am sure, is better than a stone image, which can neither see, nor hear, nor feel."

"Oh, but don't you know," said Margaret eagerly, as a bright idea occurred to her, "that we have the holy Father,—the Pope? He keeps the Church right; and our Lord commissioned Saint Peter, who was the first Pope, to teach every body and promised to guard him from all error."

Margaret was mentally congratulating herself on this brilliant solution of all difficulties. Belasez looked up thoughtfully.

"But did He promise to guard all the successors?"

"Oh, of course!"

"I wonder—supposing He were the Messiah—if He did," said Belasez. "Because I have sometimes thought that might explain it."

"What might explain it?"

"My damsel knows that the disciples of great teachers often corrupt their master's teaching, and in course of time they may come to teach doctrines quite different from his. It has struck me sometimes whether it might be so with you: that your Master was truly the Sent of God, and that you have so corrupted His doctrines that there is very little likeness left now. There must be very little, if He spoke according to the will of the Holy One."

"But the Church never changes," said Margaret.

"Then He could not be true," said Belasez.

"Oh, but Father Nicholas says the Church develops! She always teaches the truth, but she unfolds it more and more as time goes on."

"The truth is one, my damsel. It may be more. But it can never be different and contrary."

"But we change," urged Margaret, taking the last weapon out of her quiver. "We may need one thing to-day, and another to-morrow."

"We may. And if the original command had been even, 'Ye shall make no image *but one,*' I should think it might then, as need were, have been altered to, 'Ye may now make a thousand images.' But being, 'Ye shall make *none,*' it cannot be altered. That would be to alter His character who is in all His universe the only unchangeable One."

Margaret sat and watched the progress of the embroidery, but she said no more.

CHAPTER IV.

" I know that the thorny path I tread
 Is ruled with a golden line ;
And I know that the darker life's tangled thread,
 The brighter the rich design.

" For I see, though veiled from my mortal sight,
 God's plan is all complete ;
Though the darkness at present be not light,
 And the bitter be not sweet."

THE course of public events at that time was of decidedly a stirring character. The public considered that four mock suns which had been seen during the previous winter, two snakes fighting in the sea off the south coast, and fifteen days' continuous thunder in the following March, were portents sufficiently formidable to account for any succeeding political events whatever. The Church was busy introducing the Order of St. Francis into England. The populace were discovering how to manufacture cider, hitherto imported: and were, quite unknown to themselves, laying the foundation of their country's commercial greatness by breaking into the first vein of coal at Newcastle. In fact, the importance of this last discovery was so little perceived, that a hundred and fifty years were suffered to elapse before any advantage was taken of it.

Belasez's work was done, and entirely to the satisfaction of the Countess. So much, also, did the Princess Marjory admire it, that she requested another scarf might be worked for her, to be finished in time for her approaching marriage. She was now affianced to Gilbert de Clare, the new Earl of Pembroke. It was not without a bitter pang that Marjory had resigned her proud hope of wearing the crown of England, and had consented to become merely the wife of an English noble. But the crown was gone from her beyond recall. The fickle-hearted King, who had been merely attracted for a season by her great beauty, was now as eagerly pursuing a foreign Countess, Jeanne of Ponthieu, whom report affirmed to be equally beautiful: and perhaps Marjory was a little consoled, though she might not even admit it to herself, by the fact that Earl Gilbert was at once a much richer man than the King, and very much better-looking. She made him a good wife when the time came, and she grieved bitterly over his loss, when six years afterwards he was killed in a tournament at Hereford.

Marjory was not so particular as her sister about the work being done under her own eyes. She left pattern and colours to Belasez's taste, only expressing her wish that red and gold should predominate, as they were the tints alike of the arms of Scotland and of Clare. The Princess was to be married on the first of August, and Belasez promised that her father should deliver the scarf during his customary hawker's round in July.

The young Jewess had suffered less than might have been supposed from Levina. The Countess, without condescending to assign any reason, had quietly issued orders that Belasez's meals should be served in the ante-chamber, half an hour before the general repast was ready in the hall. In the presence of the young ladies, and not unfrequently of the Countess herself, Levina deemed it prudent to bring up apple-pie without sauce piquante, and to serve gateaux unmixed with pepper or anchovies.

Abraham became eloquent in his thanks for the

kindness shown to his daughter, and the tears were in Belasez's eyes when she took leave.

"Farewell, my maid," said the Countess, addressing the latter. "Thou art a fair girl, and thou hast been a good girl. I shall miss thy pretty face in Magot's ante-chamber. We shall meet again, I doubt not. Such work as thine is not to be lightly esteemed.—Wilt thou grudge thy treasure to me, if I ask for her again?" she added, turning to Abraham with a smile.

"Surely not, my Lady! My Lady has been as an angel of God to my darling."

"And remember, both of you, that if ye come into any trouble — as may be — and thou seekest safe shelter for thy bird, I will give it her at any time, in return for her lovely work."

This was a greater boon than it may appear. Troubles were only too likely to assail a Jewish household, and to know a place where Belasez could seek shelter and be certain of finding it, was a comfort indeed, and might at any hour be a most terrible necessity.

Abraham kissed the robe of the Countess, and poured out eloquent blessings on her. Belasez kissed her hand and that of Margaret: but the tears choked the girl's voice as she turned to follow her father.

The arguments against idolatry which Margaret had heard from Belasez were ghosts easily laid by Father Nicholas. A few vague platitudes concerning the supreme authority committed to the Apostle Peter, and through him to the Papacy (Father Nicholas discreetly left both points unencumbered by evidence),—the wickedness of listening to sceptical reasonings, and the happiness of implicit obedience to holy Church,—were quite enough to reduce Belasez's arguments, as they remained in Margaret's mind, to the condition of uncomfortable reminiscences, which, being also wicked, it was best to forget as soon as possible.

But there had been one listener to that conversation, of whom neither party took account, and who could not forget it. This was Doucebelle de Vaux. In her brain the words of the young Jewess took root and germinated, but so silently, that no one suspected it but herself. Father Nicholas had not the faintest idea of the importance of the question, when one morning, during the Latin lesson which he administered twice a week to the young ladies of the Castle, Doucebelle asked him the precise meaning of *adoro*.

"It means, in its original, to speak to or accost any one," said the priest; "but being now taken into the holy service of religion, it signifies to pray, to supplicate; and, thence derived—to worship, to bow one's self down."

"And,—if I do not trouble you too much, Father, —would you please to tell me the difference between *adoro* and *colo?*"

Father Nicholas was a born philologist, though in his day there was no appellation for the science. To be asked any question involving a derivation or comparison of words, was to him as a trumpet to a war-horse.

"My daughter, it is pleasure, not trouble, to me, to answer such questions as these. *Colo* is a word which comes from the Greek, but is now obsolete in that tongue, wherein it seems to have had the meaning of feed or tend. Transferred to the Latin, it signifies to cultivate, exercise, practise, or cherish,—say rather, in any sense, to take pains about a thing: hence, used in the blessed service of religion, it is to regard, venerate, respect, or worship. Therefore *cultus*, which is the noun of this verb, signifies, when referred to things inanimate, tending or cultivation; to things animate, education, culture; to God and the holy saints, reverence and worship. Dost thou now understand, my daughter?"

"I thank you very much, Father," said Doucebelle, quietly; "I understand now."

When she was alone, she put her information together, and thought it carefully over.

"*Non adorabis ea, neque coles.*"

Images, then, were not to be reverenced, either in heart or by bodily gesture. So said the version of Scripture made by Saint Jerome, and used and authorised by the Church. But how was it that the Church allowed these things to be done? Did she not know that Scripture forbade them? Or was she above all Scripture? Practically, it looked like it.

Yet how was it, if the Church were the mouth-piece of God, that the commands issued by the One were diametrically at variance with the recommendations given by the other? If God did not change,—if the Church did not change,—when had they been in accord, and how came they to differ?

Doucebelle had now reached a point where she could neither turn round nor go further. The more she cogitated on her problem, the more insoluble it appeared to her. Yet her instinctive feeling told her that to refer it to Father Nicholas would be of no service. He was one of the better class of priests,—a man of respectable character, with literary proclivities, which had in his case the effect of keeping him from vice on the one hand, and of deadening his spiritual sensibilities on the other. To him, the religion he taught, and had himself been taught, was sufficient for all necessities, and he could not understand any one wanting more. When a man's mind has never been disturbed by the question, it is no cause for wonder that he has never sought for the answer.

That Father Nicholas would have listened to her, Doucebelle knew; for he was by no means an unkind or disobliging man. But she had sense to perceive that he was incapable of understanding her, and that his only idea of dealing with such queries would be not to solve, but to suppress them.

Doucebelle passed in mental review every person in the Castle: and every one, in turn, she dismissed as unsuitable for her purpose. The other chaplain of the Earl, Father Warner, was a stern, harsh man, of whom she, in common with all the young people, was very much afraid; she could not think of putting such queries to him. The chaplain of the Countess, Father Elias, had just resigned his post, and his successor had not yet been appointed. Master Aristoteles, the household physician, was an excellent authority on the virtues of comfrey or frogs' brains, but a very poor resource on a theological question. The Earl was not at home. The Countess would be likely to enter into Doucebelle's perplexities little better than Father Nicholas, and would playfully chide her for entertaining them. All the young people were too young except Sir John de Burgh and Hawise. Sir John had not an idea beyond war, politics, and falconry; and Hawise was accustomed to decline mental investigations altogether. So Doucebelle was shut up to her thoughts and her Psalter. Perhaps she might have been worse situated.

On the 7th of February 1235, died Hugh, Bishop of Lincoln, "the enemy of all monks." He had not, however, by any means been the enemy of all superstition. He was remarkably easy to take in by young women who had sustained personal encounters with Satan, nuns who had been favoured with apparitions of the Virgin, and monks to whom Saint Peter or Saint Lawrence had made revelations. It is little wonder that he was canonised, and perhaps not much that a touch of his bones, or a shred of his chasuble, were asserted to be possessed of miraculous power. A very different man filled the see of Lincoln in his stead. On the 3rd of June following, Robert Grosteste was appointed to the vacant episcopal throne.

Grosteste was a man who had learned his life-lessons, not from priest or monk, from Fathers or Decretals, but direct from God. I do not presume to say that he held no false doctrine, or that he made no mistakes: but considering the time at which he lived, and the corruption all around him, his teaching was singularly free from "wood, hay, stubble"—singularly clear, evangelical, and true to the one Foundation. Especially he set himself in opposition to the most popular doctrine of the day—that which was termed grace of congruity. And for a man in such a position to set himself in entire and active opposition to popular taste and belief, and to persevere in it, requires supplies either of vast pride from Satan, or of great grace from God. Grace of congruity is simply a variety of the old heresy of human merit. It clad its proud self in the silver robe of humility, by professing to possess only an *imperfect* degree of qualification for the reception of God's grace. Grace of condignity, on the other hand, put itself on an equality with the Divine gift, by its pretension to possess that qualification to the uttermost.

The summer was chiefly occupied by pageants and feasts, for there were two royal marriages, that of the Princess Marjory of Scotland with Gilbert de Clare, and that of the Princess Isabel of England with the Emperor Frederic II. of Germany. The latter ceremony did not take place in England, but the gorgeous preparations did : for Henry III., who delighted in spending money even more than in acquiring it, provided his sister with the most splendid trousseau ever known even for a royal bride. Her very cooking-vessels were all of silver, and her reins and bridles were worked in gold. She was married at Worms, in June : the wedding of the Princess Marjory took place on the first of August. Abraham and Belasez were faithful to their promises, and the beautiful scarf, wrought in scarlet and gold, was delivered into Marjory's hands in time to be worn at the wedding. The young people of the Castle were naturally interested in the stereotyped rough and silly gambols which were then the invariable concomitants of a marriage: and the stocking, skilfully flung by Marie, hit Margaret on the head, to the intense delight of the merry group around her. The equally amusing work of cutting up the bridecake revealed Richard de Clare in possession of the ring, supposed to indicate approaching matrimony, Marie of the silver penny which denoted riches, and Doucebelle of the thimble which doomed her to celibacy.

"There, now! 'Tis as plain to be seen as the church spire!" said Eva, clapping her hands. "Margaret is destined by fate to wed with my cousin Sir Richard."

"Well, if 'fate' mean my wish and intention, so she is," whispered the Countess to her sister the bride.

"Doth thy Lord so purpose it?" asked Marjory.

"Oh, hush!" responded the Countess, laughing. "He knows nothing about it, and I don't intend that he shall, just yet. Trust me to bring things about."

"But suppose he should be angry?"

"*Pure foy!* He is never angry with me. Oh, thou dost not understand, my dear Madge,—at present. Men always want managing. When thou hast been wed a year, thou wilt know more about it."

"But can all women manage men ?" asked Marjory in an amused tone.

"*Ha, chétife!* No, indeed. And there are some men who can't be managed,—worse luck! But my Lord is not one of the latter, the holy saints be thanked."

"And thou art one of the women who can manage men," answered Marjory, laughing. "I wonder at thee, Magot, and have done so many times,—thou hast such a strange power of winning folks to thy will."

"Well, that some have, and some have not. I have it, I know," said the Countess, complacently. "But I will give thee a bit of counsel, Madge, which thou mayest find useful. First, have a will: let it be clear and distinct in thine own mind, what thou wouldst have done. And, secondly, let people see that thou takest quietly for granted that of course they will do it. There is a great deal in that, with some people. A weak will always bends to a strong."

"But when two strong ones come in collision, how then ?"

"Why, like wild animals,—fight it out, and discover which is the stronger."

"A tournament of wills !" said Marjory. "I should hardly care to enter those lists, I think."

The Countess laughed, and shook her head. She knew that among the strong-willed women Marjory was not to be reckoned.

A tournament of that class was being held all that summer between the regular priests and the newly-instituted Predicant Friars. The priests complained that the friars presumed to hear confessions in the churches, which it was the prerogative of the regularly appointed priests to do: and wrathfully alleged that the public were more ready to confess to these travelling mendicants than to the proper authorities. It is possible that the cause may be traced to that human proclivity which inclines a man to confide rather in a stranger whom he may never meet again, than in one who can remind him of uncomfortable facts at inconvenient times: but also it is possible that the people recognised in the teaching of the Minorite Friars, largely recruited as they were from the ranks of the Waldenses, somewhat more of that good news which Christ came to bring to men, than of the endless, unmeaning ceremonies which encumbered the doctrine of the regular priests.

The summer had given place to autumn. The courtyard of Bury Castle was strewn with golden and russet leaves; the Countess was preparing a new dress for the feast of St. Luke. A foggy day had ended in a dark night, and Eva threw down her work and rethreaded her needle with a long-drawn sigh.

"Tired of sewing, Eva?"

"Very tired, Lady. I almost wish buttons grew on robes, and required no sewing."

"Lazy maiden!" said the Countess playfully.

"Then I am lazy too," interposed Margaret; "for I do hate sewing."

"If it please the Lady," said Levina's voice at the door, "an old man and woman entreat the honour of laying a petition before her."

"An old man and woman?—such a night as this! Do they come from the town?"

"If it please the Lady, I do not know."

"Very well. If the warder thinks them not suspicious persons, they can come into the hall. I shall be down shortly."

When the Countess descended, followed by Margaret and Doucebelle, she found her petitioners awaiting her. Most unsuspicious, harmless, feeble creatures they looked. The old man had tottered in as if barely able to stand; the old woman walked with a stout oaken staff, and was bent nearly double.

"Well, good people!—what would ye have?" asked the Countess.

In answer, the old man lifted his head, pulled away a mass of false grey hair and a wax mask from his face, and the old Jew pedlar, Abraham of Norwich, stood before the astonished ladies.

"I am come," he said in a voice broken by emotion, "to claim my Lady's promise."

"What promise, old man?"

"My Lady was pleased to say, that if the robbers broke into the nest, or the hawk hovered over it, the young bird should be safe in her care."

"Thy daughter? I remember, I did say so. Where is she?"

At a signal from Abraham, the aged woman at his side suddenly straightened herself, and the removal of another wax mask and some false white hair revealed the beautiful face of Belasez.

"Welcome, my maiden," said the Countess kindly. "And what troubles have assailed thee, old Abraham, which made this disguise and flight necessary?"

"My Lady is good to her poor servants,—may the Blessed One bind her in the bundle of life! But not all Christians are like her. Lady, there is this day sore trouble, and great rebuke and blasphemy, against the sons of Israel that dwell in Norwich. They accuse us of having kidnapped and crucified a Christian child. They lay too much to us, Lady,— too much! We have never done such a thing, nor thought of it. But the house of my Lady's servant is despoiled, and his son ill-treated, and his brother in the gaol at Norwich for this cause: and to save his beautiful Belasez he has brought her to his gracious Lady. Will she give his bird shelter in her nest, according to her word?"

"Indeed I will," answered the Countess. "Margaret, take the maid up to thine ante-chamber, and bid Levina bring her food. She must stay here a while. And thou, sit thou down, old Abraham, and rest and refresh thee."

"Truly, my Lady is as one of the angels of the Holy One to her tried servants!" said Abraham thankfully.

Belasez kissed the hand of the Countess, and then turned and followed Margaret to the ante-chamber.

"Art thou very tired, Belasez?"

"Very, very weary, my Damsel. We have come fourteen miles on foot since yesterday."

Very weary Belasez looked. Now that the momentary excitement of her arrival and reception was over, the light had died out of the languid eyes, and her head drooped as if she could scarcely hold it up.

"Go to bed," said Margaret; "that is the best place for over-tired people.—Levina! My Lady and mother wills thee to bring the maid some food."

Levina appeared at the door, with an expression of undisguised annoyance.

"*Ha, chétife!*—if here is not my Lady Countess Jew come again! What would it please her sweetest Grace to take?"

But Levina had forgotten, as older people sometimes do, that Margaret was no longer a child to be kept in silent subjection. Girls of fifteen—and she was nearly that now—were virtually women in the thirteenth century. Margaret turned to the scoffing Levina, with an air of dignified displeasure which rather startled the latter.

"Levina! thou hast forgotten thyself. Do as thou art bid."

And Levina disappeared without venturing a reply.

"What have they done to thy brother, Belasez?" asked Margaret.

"They beat him sorely, Damsel, and turned him forth into the street."

"Where did he go?"

"That is known to the Blessed One. Out in the fields somewhere. It is not the first time that a Jew hath lain hidden for a night or more, until the fury of the Christians should pass away."

Doucebelle de Vaux was a grave and thoughtful girl, beyond her years. She sat silent now, trying to recall, from the stores of a memory not too well furnished, whether Christ, whom these Christians professed to follow, had ever treated people in such a manner as this. At length she remembered that she had seen a picture at Thetford of His driving sundry people out of the Temple with a scourge. But was that because they were Jews? Doucebelle thought not. She was too ignorant to be sure, but she fancied they had been doing something wrong.

"I should think," said Margaret warmly, "that you Jews must hate us Christians."

"Christians are not all alike," said Belasez with a faint smile.

"But do you not hate us?" persisted Margaret.

"Delecresse does, I am afraid," replied Belasez, colouring.

"But thyself?"

"No. O my Damsel, no!" She warmed into vivid life for an instant, to make this reply; then she sank back against the wall, apparently overpowered by utter weariness.

"I am glad of that," said Margaret, with her usual outspoken earnestness.—"What can Levina be doing? Doucebelle, do go and see.—And hast thou been hard at work at Norwich all the summer, Belasez?"

"No, if it please my Damsel. I have dwelt all this summer at Lincoln, with my mother's father."

"'The Devil overlooks Lincoln,' they say," remarked Margaret, laughingly. "I hope he did thee no mischief, Belasez. But, perhaps Jews do not believe in the Devil?"

"Ah! We have good cause to believe in the Devil," answered Belasez gravely. "Nay, Damsel, he did me no mischief. Yet—what know I? The Holy One knoweth all things."

Belasez's tone struck Margaret as hinting at some one thing in particular. But she did not explain further. Perhaps she was too tired.

Doucebelle returned at this point, followed by Levina, who carried a plate of manchet-bread and a bowl of milk. And though Belasez did not know it, she owed thanks to Doucebelle that it was not skim milk. The young Jewess ate as if she were very faint as well as weary.

"Then hast thou come here all the way from Lincoln?" inquired Margaret when the bowl was emptied.

"If it please my Damsel, no. I had returned home only two days before the riot."

"Is thy mother living?" asked Margaret abruptly.

"Yes. She abode at Lincoln with my grandfather. He is very old, and will not in likelihood live long. When he dies, my mother will come back to us."

"Do go to bed, Belasez. Thou canst scarcely hold thine head up, nor thine eyes open," said Margaret compassionately: and Belasez accepted the invitation with thanks. Doucebelle went with her, and silently noticed two facts: that Belasez stood for a few minutes in silent prayer, with her face turned to the wall, before she offered to undress; and that she was fast asleep almost as soon as her head had touched the pillow.

Doucebelle stood still and looked at the sleeping girl. Why was it so wicked to be a Jew? Had Belasez been a Christian of noble birth, or even of mean extraction, she would have been regarded as an ornament of any Court in Christendom. Some nobleman or knight would very soon have found that lovely face, and her refined and dignified manners were fit for any lady in the land. Why must she be regarded as despicable, and treated with abuse and loathing, merely because she had been born a Jewess? Of course Doucebelle knew the traditionary reason—because the Jews had crucified Christ. But Belasez had not been one of them. Why must she bear the shame of others' sins? Did none of my ancestors, thought Doucebelle, ever do some wicked deed?   Yet people do not despise me on that account.   Why do they scorn her?

Belasez stirred in her sleep, and one or two broken words dropped from her unconscious lips. Greatly interested, and a little startled, Doucebelle bent over her. But she could make out nothing connected from the indistinct utterances. It sounded as if Belasez were dreaming about somebody whose face she could not see. "Hid faces," Doucebelle heard her murmur. It was probably, she thought, some reminiscence connected with the tumults which had brought her to seek shelter at the Castle. Doucebelle drew the coverlet higher over the weary sleeper, and went to seek rest in her own bed.

CHAPTER V.

NOT WISELY.

"I love but one, and only one,—
O Damon, thou art he ;
Love thou but one, and only one,
And let that one be me." [1]

THE pedlar, Abraham, declined to remain at the Castle. There were plenty of places, he said, where an old man could be safe: it was quite another thing for a young girl. If his gracious Lady would of her bounty give his bird shelter until the riot and its consequences were over, and every thing peaceable again, Abraham would come and fetch her as soon as he deemed it thoroughly prudent. Meanwhile, Belasez could work for the Lady.

The Countess was only too pleased to procure

---

[1] These lines are (or were) to be seen, written with a diamond upon a pane of glass in a window of the Hôtel des Pays-Bas, Spa, Belgium, with the date 1793. I do not know whether they are to be found in the writings of any poet.

such incomparable embroidery on such easy terms. She set Belasez to work on the border of an armilaus, intended as a present for the new Queen: for the hitherto unmarriageable King had at last found a Princess to accept him. She was the second daughter of a penniless Provençal Count; but she was a great beauty, though an extremely young girl; and her eldest sister was Queen of France. She proved a costly bargain. Free from all visible vices except two, which, unfortunately, were two cultivated by Henry himself—unscrupulous acquisition and reckless extravagance—she nevertheless contrived to do terrible mischief, by giving her husband no advice in general, and bad advice whenever she gave it in particular. His ivy-like nature wanted a strong buttress upon which to lean; and Eléonore of Provence was neither stronger nor more stable than himself. Her one idea of life was to enjoy herself to the utmost. When she wanted a new dress, she had not the slightest notion of waiting till she had money to pay for it. What were the people of England in her eyes, but machines for making it—things to be taxed—a vast and inexhaustible treasury, of which you did but turn the handle, and coins came showering out?

So the tax-gatherers went grinding on, and the land cried to God, and the Court heard no sound. The man who was to be God's avenger upon them was an obscure foreigner as yet. And the English noble who above all others was to aid him in that vengeance, was still only a fair-haired youth of fifteen, whose thoughts were busy with a very different subject. But out of the one, the other was to grow, watered by tears and blood.

He was standing—young Richard de Clare— in one of the recessed windows of the great hall, with Margaret beside him. They were talking in very low tones. Richard's manner was pleading and earnest, while Margaret's eyes were cast down, and she was diligently winding round her finger a shred of green sewing-silk, as though her most important concern were to make it go round a certain number of times.

It was the old story, so many times repeated in this world, sometimes to flow smoothly on like waters to their haven, sometimes to end in stormy wreckage and bitter disappointment.

They were very young lovers. We should term them mere boy and girl, and count them unfit to consider the matter at all. But in the thirteenth century, when circumstances forced men and women early to the front, and sixty years was considered ripe old age, fifteen was equivalent at least to twenty now.

In this instance, the course of true love—for it was on both sides very true—seemed likely to be smooth enough. The King had granted the marriage of Richard to Earl Hubert; and, as was then well understood, the person to whom he would most probably marry his ward was his own daughter. The only irregular item of the matter was that the pair should fall in love, or should broach the subject at all to each other. But human hearts are unaccountable articles; and even in those days, when matrimony was an affair of rule and compasses, those irregular things did occasionally conduct themselves in a very irregular manner, leading young people to fall in love (and sometimes to run away) with the wrong person, but happily and occasionally, as in this instance, with the right one.

Half an hour later, Margaret was kneeling on a velvet cushion at the feet of the Countess, who was (with secret delight) receiving auricular confession concerning the very point on which she had set her heart.

This mother and daughter were great friends,—
a state of things too infrequent at any time, and
particularly so in the Middle Ages. Margaret, the
only one of her mother, was an unusually cherished
and petted child. The result was that she had no
fear of the Countess, and looked upon her as her
natural confidante. Perhaps, if more daughters
would do so, there might be fewer unhappy marriages. At the same time it must be admitted,
that some mothers by no means invite confidence.

The Countess of Kent, sweet as she was, had
one great failing,—a fault often to be found in
very gentle and amiable natures. She was not
sufficiently straightforward. Instead of honestly
telling people what she wanted them to do, she
liked to manage them into it; and this managing
involved at most times more or less dissimulation.
She dearly loved to conduct her affairs by a series
of little secrets. This is a temperament which
usually rests on a mixture of affection and want of
courage. We cannot bear to grieve those whom
we love, and we shrink from calling down their
anger on ourselves, or even from risking their disapprobation of our conduct, past or proposed.
Now, it had been for some years the dearest wish

of the Countess's heart that her Margaret should marry Richard de Clare. But she never whispered her desire to any one,—least of all to her husband, with whom, humanly speaking, it lay mainly to promote or defeat it. And now, when Margaret's blushing confession was whispered to her, the Countess privately congratulated herself on her excellent management, and thought how much better it was to pull unseen strings than to blaze one's wishes abroad.

"And, Lady, will you of your grace plead for us with my Lord and father?" said Margaret in a coaxing tone at last.

"Oh, leave it all to me," replied her mother. "I will manage him into it. Never tell a man anything, my dove, if thou wouldst have him do it. Men are such obstinate, perverse creatures, that as often as not they will just go the other way out of sheer wilfulness. Thou must always contrive to manage them into it."

Margaret, who had inherited her father's honesty with her mother's amiability, was rather puzzled by this counsel.

"But how do you manage them?" said she.

"There is an art in that, my dear. It takes brains.

Different men require very different kinds of management. Now thy father is one who will generally consent to a thing when it is done, though he would not if it were suggested to him at first. He rather likes his own way; still, he is very good when he is well managed"— for instance after instance came floating back to the wife's mind, in which he had against his own judgment given way to her. "So that is the way to manage him. Now our Lord King Henry requires entirely different handling."

That was true enough. While Earl Hubert always had a will of his own, and knew what it was (though he did not always get it), King Henry had no will, and never knew what it was until somebody else told him.

"I am afraid, Lady, I don't understand the management of men," said Margaret, with a little laugh and blush.

"Thou wilt learn in time, my dear. Thou art rather too fond of saying all thou meanest. That is not wise—for a woman. Of course a man ought to tell his wife every thing. But there is no need for a wife always to be chattering to her husband : she must have her little secrets, and he ought to respect them. Now, as to Sir Richard, I can see as well as possible the kind of management he will require; thou must quietly suggest ideas to him, gently and diffidently, as if thou wert desirous of his opinion: but whenever he takes them up, mind and always let him think he is getting his own way. He has a strong will, against which a foolish woman would just run full tilt, and spoil every thing. A wise one will quietly get her own way, and let him fancy he has got his. That is thy work, Magot."

Margaret shook her bright head with a laugh. Such work as that was not at all in her line.

It took only a day for the girls to discover that the Belasez who had come back to them in October was not the Belasez who had gone away from them at Whitsuntide. She seemed almost a different being. Quite as amiable, as patient, as refined, as before, there was something about her which they instantly perceived, but to which they found it hard to give a name. It was not exactly any one thing. It was not sadness, for at times she seemed more bright and lively than they remembered her of old: it was not ill-temper, for her patience was proof against any amount of teasing. But her moods were far more variable than they used to be. A short time after she had been playing with little Marie, all smiles and sunshine, they would see tears rush to her eyes, which she seemed anxious to conceal. And at times there was an expression of distress and perplexity in her face, evidently not caused by any intricacy in the pattern she was working.

Indirect questions produced none but evasive answers. Each of the girls had her own idea as to the solution of the enigma. Margaret, very naturally, pronounced Belasez in love. Eva, one of whose sisters had been recently ill, thought she was anxious about her brother. Marie suggested that too much damson tart might be a satisfactory explanation,— that having been the state of things with herself a few days before. Hawise, who governed her life by a pair of moral compasses, was of opinion that Belasez thought it proper to look sorrowful in her circumstances, and therefore did so except in an emergency. Doucebelle alone was silent: but her private thought was that no one of the four had come near the truth.

When Belasez had been about a week at the Castle, one afternoon she and Doucebelle were working alone in the wardrobe. The Countess and Margaret were away for the day, on a visit to the Abbess of Thetford; Eva and Marie were out on the leads; Hawise was busy in her own apartments. Belasez had been unusually silent that morning. She worked on in a hurried, nervous way, never speaking nor looking up, and a lovely arabesque pattern grew into beauty under her deft fingers. Suddenly Doucebelle said,—

"Belasez, does life never puzzle thee?"

Belasez looked up, with almost a frightened expression in her eyes.

"Can anything puzzle one more?" she said: "unless it were the perplexity which is hovering over my soul."

"Is that anything in which I could help thee?"

"It is something in which no human being could help me—only He before whom the inhabitants of the earth are as grasshoppers."

There was silence for a moment. Then, in a low, hushed tone, Belasez said,—

"Doucebelle, didst thou ever do a thing which must be either very right, or very wrong, and thou hadst no means whereby to know which it was?"

"No," answered Doucebelle slowly. "I can scarcely imagine such a thing."

"Scarcely imagine the thing, or the uncertainty?"

"The uncertainty. Because I should ask the priest."

"The priest!—where is he?"

Doucebelle looked up in surprise at the tone, and saw that Belasez was in tears.

"We had priests," said the young Jewess. "We had sons of Aaron, and a temple, and an altar, and a holy oracle, whereby the Blessed One made known His will in all matters of doubt and perplexity to His people. But where are they now? The mountains of Zion are desolate, and the foxes walk upon them. The light has died out of the sacred gems, even if they themselves were to be found. We have walked contrary to Him,—ah! where is the unerring prophet that shall tell us how we did it?—and He walks contrary to us, and is punishing us seven times for our sins. We are in the desert, in the dark. And the pillar of fire has gone back into Heaven, and the Angel of the Covenant leadeth us no more."

Doucebelle was almost afraid to speak, lest she should say something which might do more harm than good. She only ventured after a pause to remark—

"Still there are priests."

"Yours? I know what they would tell me." Belasez's fervent voice had grown constrained all at once.

"Yes, thou dost not believe them, I suppose," said Doucebelle, with a baffled feeling.

"I want a prophet, Doucebelle, not a priest. Nay, He knows, the Holy One, that we want a priest most bitterly; that we have no sacrifice wherewith to stand before Him,—no blood to make atonement. But we want the prophet to point us to the priest. Let us know, by revelation from Heaven, that this man, or that man, is the accepted Priest of the Most High, and trust us to bring our fairest lambs in sacrifice."

"Belasez, I believe that the Lamb was offered, twelve hundred years ago, and the sacrifice which alone God will accept for the sins of men is over for ever, and is of everlasting efficacy."

"I know." Belasez's face was more troubled than before.

"If thou canst not trust His priests, couldst thou not trust Him?"

"Trust whom?" exclaimed Belasez, with her eyes on fire. "O Doucebelle, Doucebelle, I know not how to bear it! I thought I was so strong to stand up against all falsehood and error,—and here, one man, with one word,—Let me hold my peace. But O that Thou wouldst rend the heavens, that

Thou wouldst come down! Hast Thou but one blessing, O Thou that art a Father unto Israel? Or are we so much worse off than our fathers in the desert? Nay, are we not in the desert, with no leader to guide us, no fiery pillar to bid us rest here, or journey thither? Why hast Thou given the dearly beloved of Thy soul into the hands of her enemies? Is it — is it, because we hid our faces—from Him!"

And to Doucebelle's astonishment, Belasez covered her face with her apron, and sobbed almost as if her heart were breaking.

"Poor Belasez!" said Doucebelle, gently. "It is often better to tell out what troubles us, than to keep it to ourselves."

"If thou wert a daughter of Israel, I should tell it thee, and ask thy counsel. I need some one's counsel sorely."

"And canst thou not trust me, Christian though I am?"

"Oh no, it is not that. Thou dost not understand, Doucebelle. Thou couldst not enter into my difficulty unless thou wert of my faith. That is the reason. It is not indeed that I mistrust thee."

"Hast thou told thy father?"

"My father? No! He would be as much horrified to hear that such thoughts had ever entered
my head, as the Lady would be if thou wert to
tell her thou didst not believe any longer in thy
Christ."

"Then what canst thou do? Could thy mother
help thee, or thy brother?"

"My mother would command me to dismiss such
ideas from my mind, on pain of her curse. But I
cannot dismiss them. And for Delecresse—I think
he would stab me if he knew."

"What sort of thoughts are they?"

"Wilt thou keep my secret, if I tell thee?"

"Indeed, I will not utter them without thy leave."

Belasez cut off her silk, laid down the armilaus,
and clasped both hands round her knee.

"When your great festivals draw nigh," she said,
"four times in every year, we Israelites are driven
into your churches, and forced to listen to a discourse
from one of your priests. Until that day, I have
never paid any attention to what I deemed blasphemy. I have listened for a moment, but at the
first word of error, or the first repetition of one of
your sacred names, I have always stopped my ears,
and heard no more. But this last Midsummer, when

we were driven into Lincoln Cathedral, the new Bishop was in the pulpit. And he spake not like the other priests. I could not stop my ears. Why should I, when he read the words of one of our own prophets, and in the holy tongue, rendering it into French as he went on? And Delecresse said it was correctly translated, for I asked him afterwards. He saw nothing in it different from usual. But it was terrible to me! He read words that I never knew were in our Scriptures—concerning One whom it seemed to me must be—*must* be, He whom you call Messiah. 'As a root out of a dry ground'—'no form nor comeliness'—'no beauty that we should desire Him,'—'despised and rejected of men'—and lastly, 'we hid our faces from Him.' For we did, Doucebelle,—we did! I could think of nothing else for a while. For we did not hide them from others. We welcomed Judas of Galilee, and Barchocheba, and many another who rose up in our midst, claiming to be sent of God. But He, who claimed to be The Sent One,—we crucified Him. We did not crucify them. We hid our faces from Him, and from Him alone. And then I heard more words, for the Bishop kept reading on. 'We all like sheep have gone astray; we have turned every one to his own way'—

ah, was that not true of the dispersed of Judah?—
'and the Lord hath made to meet upon Him the
iniquities of us all.' Doucebelle, it was like carrying
a lamp into a dark chamber, and beholding every
thing in it suddenly illuminated. Was that what it
all meant? Was the Bishop right, when he said
afterwards, that it was not possible that the blood
of bulls and goats could take away sin? Were they
all not realities, as I had always thought them, but
shadows, pointing forward through the ages, to the
One who was to come, to the Blood which could take
away sin? Did our own Scripture say so? 'The
Man that is My Fellow'—he read it, from one of our
very own prophets. And 'we hid our faces from
Him!' If He from whom we hid our faces—for
there was but one such—if He were the Sent of God,
the Man that is His Fellow, the Lamb whose blood
maketh atonement for the soul,—why then, what
could there be for us but tribulation and wrath and
indignation from before the Holy One for ever?
Was it any marvel that we were punished seventy
times for our sins, if we had done that?"

Belasez drew a long breath, and altered her position.

"And, if we had not done that, what had we done?
The old perplexity came back on me, worse than

ever. What had we done? We were not idolaters any more; we were not profane; we kept the rest of the holy Sabbath. Yet the Blessed One was angry with us,—He hid His face from us: and the centuries went on, and we were exiles still,—still under the displeasure of our heavenly King. And what had we done?—if we had not hidden our faces from Him who was the Man that is His Fellow. And then,"—

Belasez paused again, and a softer, sadder expression came into her eyes.

"And then the Bishop read some other words,—I suppose they were from your sacred books: I do not think they came from ours. He read that 'because this Man continueth to eternity, untransferable hath He the priesthood.' He read that 'if any man sin, we have an Advocate with the Father, and He is the propitiation for our sins.' And again he read some grand words, said by this Man Himself,—'I am the First and the Last, and the Living One: and I was dead, and am alive for evermore; and with Me are the keys of Sheol and of death.' Oh, it was so different, Doucebelle, from your priests' sermons generally! There was not a word about that strange thing you call the Church,—not a word about the maiden whom you worship. It was all about Him

who was to be the Sent of God. And I thought—
may I be forgiven of the Holy One, if it were wicked!
—I thought this was the Priest that would suit me:
this was the Prophet that could teach me: this was
the Man, who, if only I knew that to do it was truth
and not error, was light and not darkness, was life
and not death, I could be content to follow to the
world's end. And how am I to know it?"

Doucebelle looked up earnestly, and the girls'
eyes met. One of them was groping in the darkness in search of Christ. The other had groped
her way through the darkness, and had caught hold
of Him. She did not see His Face very clearly,
but enough so to be sure that it was He.

"Belasez, dear maid, He said one other thing.
'Come unto Me, all ye that labour and are heavy
laden, and I will give you rest.' Trust me, the
surest way to find out who He is, is to come to
Him."

"What meanest thou? He is not on earth."

"He is where thy need is," answered Doucebelle
gently. "In any labyrinth out of which we know
not the way,—over any grave where our hearts lie
buried,—we can meet Him."

"But how? Thy words are a riddle to me."

"Call Him, and see if He do not come to thee. And if He and thou do but meet, it does not much matter by which track thou camest thither."

Belasez was silent, and seemed to be thinking deeply.

"Doucebelle," she said at last, "are there two sorts of Christians? Because thy language is like the Bishop of Lincoln's. All the priests, and other Christians, whom I have heard before, spoke in quite another strain."

"There are live Christians, and dead ones. I know not of any third sort."

"The dead ones must be fearfully in the majority!" said Belasez: "I mean, if thou and the Bishop are live ones."

"That may be true, I am afraid," replied Doucebelle.

"It must be the breathing of the Holy One that makes the difference," observed Belasez, very thoughtfully. "For it is written, that Adonai formed man of the dust of the earth, and breathed into his nostrils the neshama of life; and man became a living soul. Thus He breathed the life into man at first, in the day of the creation of Adam. Surely, in the day when the soul of man becomes alive to the will of the Holy One, He must breathe into him the second time, that he may live."

"Belasez, what are your sacred books? You seem to have some."

"We gave them to you," was Belasez's reply. "But ye have added to them."

"But the Scriptures were given to the Church!" remonstrated Doucebelle with some surprise.

"I know not what ye mean by the Church," answered the Jewess. "They were ours,—given to our fathers, revealed to them by the Holy One. We gave them to you,—or ye filched them from us,— I scarcely know which. And ye have added other books, which we cannot recognise."

The flash of fervent confidence had died away, and Belasez was once more the reserved, impenetrable Jewish maiden, to whom Gentile Christians were unclean animals, and their doctrines to be mentioned only with scorn and abhorrence. And as Marie came dancing in at that moment, the conversation was not renewed. But it made a great impression upon Doucebelle, who ever afterwards added to her prayers the petition,—"Fair Father,[1] Jesu Christ, teach Belasez to know Thee."

[1] "Bel Père"—then one of the common epithets used in prayer.

But to every one in general, and to Doucebelle in particular, Belasez seemed shut up closer than ever.

The January of 1236 came, and with it the royal marriage. The ceremonial took place at Canterbury, and Earl Hubert was present, as his office required of him. The Countess excused herself on the ground of slight illness, which would make it very irksome for her to travel in winter. Her "intimate enemies" kindly suggested that she was actuated by pique, since a time had been when she might have been herself Queen of England. But they did not know Margaret of Scotland. Pique and spite were not in her. Her real motive was something wholly different. She was not naturally ambitious, nor did she consider the crown of England so highly superior to the gemmed coronal of a Scottish Princess; and she had never held King Henry in such personal regard as to feel any regret at his loss. Her true object in remaining at Bury was to "manage" the marriage of Margaret with Richard de Clare. It was to be a clandestine match, except as concerned a few favoured witnesses; and Earl Hubert was to be kept carefully in the dark till all was safely over. The wedding was to be one "*per verba de presenti*," then as sacred by the canon law as if it had been performed by a priest in full canonicals; and as a matter of absolute necessity, no witness was required at all. But the Countess thought it more satisfactory to have one or two who could be trusted not to chatter till the time came for revelation. She chose Doucebelle along with herself, as the one in whose silence she had most confidence. Thus, in that January, in the dead of the night, the four indicated assembled in the bedchamber of the Countess, and the bride and bridegroom, joining hands, said simply,—

"In the presence of God and of these persons, I, Richard, take thee, Margaret, to my wedded wife:" and, "In the same presence I, Margaret, take thee, Richard, to my wedded husband."

And according to canon and statute law they were legally married, nor could anything short of a divorce part them again.

"Now then, go to bed," said the Countess, addressing Doucebelle: "and beware, every soul of you, that not a word comes out till I tell you ye may speak."

"Belasez, when wilt thou be wed?" inquired Margaret, the next morning. If the thoughts of the bride ran upon weddings, it was not much to be wondered.

"Next summer," said Belasez, as coolly as if the question had been when she would finish her embroidery. There was no shadow of emotion of any kind to be seen.

"Oh, art thou handfast?" replied Margaret, interested at once.

"I was betrothed in my cradle," was the answer of the Jewish maiden.

"To a Jew, of course?"

"Of course! To Leo the son of Hamon of Norwich, my father's greatest friend.

"Is he a nice young man?"

"I never saw him."

"Why, Belasez!"

"The maidens of my people are strictly secluded. It is not so with Christians."

Yet it was less strange to these Christian girls than it would be to the reader. They lived in times when the hand of an heiress was entirely at the disposal of her guardian, who might marry her to some one whom she had never seen. As to widows, they were in the gift of the Crown, unless they chose (as many did) to make themselves safe by paying a high price for "liberty to marry whom they would." Even then, such a thing was known as the Crown disregarding the compact. Let it be added, since much good cannot be said of King John, that he at least was careful to fulfil his engagements of this description. His son was less particular.

Margaret looked at Belasez with a rather curious expression.

" And how dost thou like the idea," she asked, " of being wife to one whom thou hast never seen ? "

" I do not think about it," said Belasez, in the same tone as before. " What is to be will be."

" But what is to be," said Margaret, " may be very delightful, or it may be very horrid."

" Yes, no doubt," was the cool answer. " I shall see when the time comes."

Margaret turned away, with a shrug of her shoulders and a comic look in her eyes which nearly upset the gravity of the rest.

CHAPTER VI.

THE NEW CONFESSOR.

"Had the knight looked up to the page's face,
    No smile the word had won ;
Had the knight looked up to the page's face,
    I ween he had never gone :
Had the knight looked back to the page's geste,
    I ween he had turned anon,—
For dread was the woe in the face so young,
And wild was the silent geste that flung
Casque, sword, to earth as the boy down-sprung,
    And stood—alone, alone !"
        —*Elizabeth Barrett Browning.*

NOBODY enjoyed the spring of the year 1236. Rain poured down, day after day, as if it were the prelude to a second Deluge. The Thames overflowed its banks to such an extent that the lawyers had to return home in boats, floated by the tide into Westminster Hall. There was no progress, except by boat or horse, through the streets of the royal borough.

Perhaps the physical atmosphere slightly affected the moral and political, for men's minds were much unsettled, and their tempers very captious. The King, with his usual fickleness and love of novelty, had thrown himself completely into the arms of the horde of poor relations whom the new Queen brought over with her, particularly of her uncle, Guglielmo of Savoy, the Bishop of Valentia, whom he constituted his prime minister. By his advice new laws were promulgated which extremely angered the English nobles, who complained that they were held of no account in the royal councils. The storms were especially violent in the North, and there people took to seeing prophetic visions of dreadful import. Beside all this, France was in a very disturbed state, which boded ill to the English provinces across the sea. The Counts of Champagne, Bretagne, and La Marche, used strong language concerning the disgraceful fact that "France, the kingdom of kingdoms, was governed by a woman," Queen Blanche of Castilla being Regent during the minority of her son, St. Louis. It is a singular fact that while the name of Blanche has descended to posterity as that of a woman of remarkable wisdom, discretion, and propriety of life, the popular estimate of her during her regency was almost exactly the reverse.

Meanwhile, the royal marriage festivities went on uproariously at Canterbury. There was not a pea-cock-pie the less on account either of the black looks of the English nobles, or of the very shallow condition of the royal treasury. To King Henry, who had no intention of paying any bills that he could help, what did it signify how much things cost, or whether the sum total were twenty pence or twenty thousand pounds?

The feasts having at last come to an end, King Henry left Canterbury for Merton Abbey, and Earl Hubert accompanied him. What became of the Queen is not stated: nor are we told whether His Majesty thus went "into retreat" to seek absolution for his past transgressions, or from the lamentable necessity of paying his debts.

On the 20th of January, the royal penitent emerged from his retreat, to be crowned with his bride at Westminster. Earl Hubert of course was present; and the Countess thought proper to feel well enough to join him for the occasion. The ceremony was a most splendid one,—very different from that first hurried coronation of the young Henry on his father's death, when, all the regalia having been lost in fording the Wash, he was crowned with a gold collar belonging to his mother. The Archbishop of Canterbury was the officiating priest. The citizens of London, hereditary Butlers of England, presented three hundred and sixty cups of gold and silver, at which the eyes of the royal and acquisitive pair doubtless glistened, and which, in all probability, were melted down in a month to pay for the coronation banquet. King Henry paid a bill just often enough to prevent his credit from falling into a hopelessly disreputable condition. The Earl of Chester—one of Earl Hubert's two great enemies—bore Curtana, "the sword of St. Edward," says the monk of St. Albans, "to show that he is Earl of the Palace, and has by right the power of restraining the King if he should commit an error." Either Earl Ranulph de Blundeville was very neglectful of his office, or else he must have found it anything but a sinecure. The Constable of Chester attended the Earl; his office was to restrain not the King, but the people, by keeping them off with his wand when they pressed too close. The Earl of Pembroke, husband of Princess Marjory of Scotland, carried a wand before the King, cleared the way, superintended the banquet, and arranged the guests. The basin was presented by a handsome young foreigner, Simon de Montfort, youngest son of the Count de Montfort, and cousin of the Earl of Chester, to whose good offices in the first instance he probably owed his English preferment. He had not yet become the most powerful man in the kingdom, the darling of the English people, the husband of the King's sister, the man whom, on his own testimony,—much as he feared a thunderstorm,— Henry feared "more than all the thunder and lightning in the world!" The Earl of Arundel should have been the cupbearer; but being too young to discharge the office, his kinsman the Earl of Surrey officiated for him. The citizens of Winchester were privileged to cook the banquet; and the Abbot of Westminster kept every thing straight by sprinkling holy water.

Once more, the banquet over, the King returned into retreat at Merton to get rid of his additional shortcomings. Never was man so pious as this Monarch,—if piety consisted of tithing mint, anise, and cummin, and of neglecting the weightier matters of the law, judgment, mercy, and faith.

It was a sharp frosty morning in February. Margaret, Doucebelle, and Belasez were at work in the bower, while Father Nicholas was hearing Marie read Latin in the ante-chamber. The other chaplains were also present, — Father Warner, who, with Nicholas, belonged to the Earl; and Father Bruno, the chaplain of the Countess. Also present was Master Aristoteles, the reverend physician of the household. Fortunately for herself, Marie was by no means shy, and she feared the face of no human creature unless it were Father Warner, who, Margaret used to say, had eyes in the back of his head, and could hear what the cows were thinking about in the meadow. He was an extremely strict disciplinarian when on duty, but he never interfered with the proceedings of a brother tutor.

Father Bruno was a new inmate of the household. He had come from Lincoln, with a recommendation from the recently-appointed Bishop, but had been there too short a time to show his character, since he was a silent man, who appeared to see everything and to say nothing.

"Very well, my daughter. Thou hast been a good, attentive maiden this morning," said Father Nicholas, when the reading was finished.

"Then, Father, will you let me off my sums?" was Marie's quick response.

Marie hated arithmetic, which was Doucebelle's favourite study.

"Nay, my child," said Father Nicholas, in an amused tone; "that is not my business. Thou must ask Father Warner."

"Please, Father Warner, will you let me off my sums?" pleaded Marie, but in a more humble style.

"Certainly not, daughter. Fetch them at once."

Marie left the room with a grieved face.

"No news abroad, I suppose, my brethren?" suggested Master Aristoteles, in his brisk, simple, innocent manner.

"Nay, none but what we all knew before," said Father Nicholas.

"Methinks the world wags but slowly," said Master Aristoteles.

"Much too fast," was the oracular reply of Father Warner.

"The pace of the world depends mainly on our own wishes, I take it," said Father Nicholas. "He who would fain walk thinks the world is at a gallop; while he who desires to gallop reckons the world but jogging at a market-trot."

"There has been a great massacre of Jews in Spain," said Father Bruno, speaking for the first time.

All the conversation was plainly audible to the girls in the next room. When Father Bruno spoke, Belasez's head went up suddenly, and her work stood still.

"Amen and Alleluia!" said Father Warner, who probably little suspected that he was using Hebrew words to express his abhorrence of the Hebrews.

"Nay, my brother!" answered Father Bruno, gravely. "Shall we thank God for the perdition of human souls?"

"Of course not,—of course not!" interposed Father Nicholas, quickly. "I am sure our Brother Warner thanked God for the vindication of the Divine honour."

"And is not the Divine honour more fully vindicated by far," demanded Father Bruno, "when a soul is saved from destruction, than when it is plunged therein?"

"Yes, yes, no doubt, no doubt!" eagerly assented Father Nicholas, who seemed afraid of a *fracas*.

"Curs!" said Father Warner, contemptuously. "They all belong to their father the Devil, and to him let them go. I would not give a farthing for a Jew's soul in the market."

Belasez's eyes were like stars.

"Brother," said Father Bruno, so gravely that it was almost sadly, "our Master was not of your way of thinking. He bade His apostles to begin at Jerusalem when they preached the good tidings of His kingdom. Have we done it?"

Master Aristoteles' "Ah!" might mean anything, as the hearer chose to take it.

"Of course they did so. The Church was first at Jerusalem, before St. Peter transferred it to Rome," snapped Father Warner.

"Pardon me, my brother. I did not ask, Did they do so? I said, Have we done so?" explained Bruno.

"How could we?" responded Father Nicholas in a perplexed tone. "I never came across any of the evil race—holy Mary be my guard!—and if I had done, I should have crossed over the road, lest they should cast a spell on me."

Belasez's smile was one of contemptuous amusement.

"*Pure foy!* If I ever came across one, I should spit in his face!" cried Warner.

"Two might play at that game," was the cool observation of Bruno.

"I'd have him hung on the new machine if he did!" exclaimed Warner.

The new machine was the gibbet, first set up in England in this year.

"Brethren," said Bruno, "we are verily guilty, one and all. For weeks this winter, and I hear also last summer, there has been in this house a maiden of the Hebrew race, who has never learned the faith of Christ the Lord, has probably never heard His name except in blasphemy. Which of us four of His servants shall answer to God for that child's soul?"

Margaret expected Belasez's eyes to flash, and her lip to curl in scorn. To her great surprise, the girl caught up her work and went on with it hastily. Doucebelle, watching her with deep yet concealed interest, fancied she saw tears glistening on the samite.

"Really, I never—you put it so seriously, Brother Bruno!—I never looked at the matter in that way. I did not think"——, and Father Nicholas came to a full stop. "You see, I have been so very busy illuminating that missal for the Lady. I really never ——never considered the thing so seriously."

"Brother Nicholas," answered Bruno, "the Devil was serious enough when he tempted our mother Eva. And Christ was serious when He bore away your sins and mine, and nailed them to His cross.

And the angels of God are serious, when they look down and see us fighting with sin in the dark and weary day. What! God is serious, and Satan is serious, and the holy angels are serious,—and can we not be serious? Will the great Judge take that answer, think you? 'Lord, I was so busy illuminating and writing, that I let the maiden slip into perdition, and Thou wilt find her there.'"

Belasez's head was bowed lower than before.

"Brother Bruno! You are unreasonable," interposed Warner. "We all have our duties to our Lord and Lady. And as to that contemptible insect in the Lady's chamber,—well, I do not know what you think, but I would not scorch my fingers pulling her out of Erebus."

The dark brows of the young Jewess were drawn close together.

"Ah, Brother Warner!" said Bruno. "Christ my Master scorched His fingers so much with me, that I cannot hesitate to burn mine in His service."

Marie and her arithmetic seemed forgotten by all parties.

"I am afraid, Brother Bruno," faltered Father Nicholas, "really afraid, I may have been too remiss. The poor girl!—of course, though she is a Jew—and they are very bad people, very—yet she has a soul to be saved; yes, undoubtedly. I will see what I can do. There are only about a dozen leaves of the missal,—and then that treatise on grace of congruity that I promised the Abbot of Ham—and,—let me see! I believe I engaged to write something for the Prior of St. Albans. What was it, now? Where are my tables? Oh, here!—yes,—ah! that would not take long: a week might do it, I think. I will see,—I really will see, Brother Bruno,—when these little matters are disposed of,—what I can do for the girl."

"Do! Give her ratsbane!" sneered Warner laconically.

Bruno's reply was a quotation.

"'While thy servant was busy here and there, he was gone.'"

Then he rose and left the room.

"Dear, dear!" said Father Nicholas. "Our brother Bruno means well,—very well indeed, I am sure: but those enthusiastic people like him—don't you think they are very unsettling, Brother Warner? Really, he has made me feel quite uncomfortable. Why, the world would have to be turned upside down! We could never write, nor paint, nor cultivate letters,—

we should have to be incessantly preaching and confessing people."

"Stuff! The fellow's an ass!" was Father Warner's decision. "*Ha, chétife!*—what has become of that little monkey, Damsel Marie? I must go and see after her."

And he followed his colleague. Father Nicholas gathered his papers together, and from the silence that ensued, the girls gathered that the ante-chamber was deserted.

"Belasez," said Doucebelle that night, as she was brushing her hair—the two slept in the wardrobe—"wert thou very angry with Father Bruno, this morning?"

Belasez looked up quickly.

"With *him*? No! I thought"——

But the thought progressed no further till Doucebelle said,—"Well?"

"I thought," said Belasez, combing out her own hair very energetically, "that I had at last found even a Christian priest who was worthy of him of whom the Bishop of Lincoln preached,—him whom you believe to be Messiah."

"Then," said Doucebelle, greatly delighted, "thou wilt listen to Father Bruno, if he talks to thee?"

"I would not if I could help it," was Belasez's equivocal answer.

"Belasez, I cannot quite understand thee. Sometimes thou seemest so different from what thou art at other times."

"Because I am different. Understand me! Do I understand myself? The Holy One—to whom be praise!—He understands us all."

"But sometimes thou art willing to hear and talk, and at others thou art close shut up like a coffer."

"Because that is how I feel."

"I wish thou wouldst tell thy feelings to Father Bruno."

"I shall wait till he asks me, I think," said Belasez a little drily.

"Well, I am sure he will."

"I am not sure that he will—twice."

"Why, what wouldst thou say to him?"

"He will hear if he wants to know."

And Belasez thereupon "shut up like a coffer," and seemed to have lost her tongue for the remainder of the night.

Doucebelle determined that, if she could possibly contrive it, without wounding the feelings of Father

Nicholas, her next confession should be made to Father Bruno. He seemed to her to be a man made of altogether different metal from his colleagues. Master Aristoteles kept himself entirely to physical ailments, and never heard a confession, except from the sick in emergency. Father Nicholas was a very easy confessor, for his thoughts were usually in his beloved study, and whatever the confession might be, absolution seemed to follow as a matter of course. If his advice were asked on any point outside philology in all its divisions, he generally appeared to be rather taken by surprise, and almost as much puzzled as his penitent. His strongest reproof was,—

" Ah, that was wrong, my child. Thou must not do that again."

So that confession to Father Nicholas, while eminently comfortable to a dead soul, was anything but satisfying to a living one.

Father Warner was a terrible confessor. His minute questions penetrated into every corner of soul and body. He took nothing for granted, good nor bad. Absolution was hard to get from him, and not to be had on any terms but those of severe penance. And yet it seemed to Doucebelle that there was an inner sanctuary of her heart from which he never even tried to lift the veil, a depth in her nature which he never approached. Was it because there was no such depth in his, and therefore he necessarily ignored its existence in another?

In one way or another, they were all miserable comforters. She wished to try Father Bruno.

Most unwittingly, Father Nicholas helped her to gain her end by requesting a holiday. He had heard a rumour that a Latin manuscript had been discovered in the library of St. Albans' Abbey, and Father Nicholas, in whose eyes the lost books of Livy were of more consequence than any thing else in the world except the Order of St. Benedict, was unhappy till he had seen the MS.

The Countess, in the Earl's absence, readily granted his request, and Doucebelle's fear of hurting the feelings of her kind-hearted though careless old friend were no longer a bar in the way of consulting Father Bruno.

Father Warner, who was confessing the other half of the household, growled his disapprobation when Doucebelle begged to be included in the penitents of Father Bruno.

"Something new always catches a silly girl's fancy!" said he.

But Doucebelle had no scruple about hurting his feelings, since she did not believe in their existence. So when her turn came, she knelt down in Bruno's confessional.

At first she wondered if he were about to prove like Father Nicholas, for he did not ask her a single question till she stopped of herself. Then, instead of referring to any thing which she had said, he put one of weighty import.

"Daughter, what dost thou know of Jesus Christ?"

"I know," said Doucebelle, "that He came to take away the sins of the world, and I humbly trust that He will take away mine."

"That He will?" repeated Bruno. "Is it not done already?"

"I thought, Father, that it would be done when I die."

"What has thy dying to do with that? If it be done at all, it was done when He died."

"Then where are my sins, Father?" asked Doucebelle, feeling very much astonished. This was a new doctrine to her. But Bruno was an Augustinian, and well read in the writings of the Founder of his Order.

"They are where God cannot find them, my child. Therefore there is little fear of thy finding them. Understand me,—if thou hast laid them upon Christ our Lord."

"I know I have," said Doucebelle in a low voice.

"Then on His own authority I assure thee that He has taken them."

"Father! may I really believe that?"

"May! Thou must, if thou wouldst not make God a liar."

"But what, then, have I to do?"

"What wouldst thou do for me, if I had rescued thee from a burning house, and lost my own life in the doing of it?"

"I could do nothing," said Doucebelle, feeling rather puzzled.

"Wouldst thou love or hate me?"

"O Father! can there be any question?"

"And supposing there were some thing left in the world for which thou knewest I had cared—a favourite dog or cat—wouldst thou leave it to starve, or take some care of it?"

"I think," was Doucebelle's earnest answer, "I

should care for it as though it were my own child."

"Then, daughter, see thou dost that for Him who did lose His own life in rescuing thee. Love Him with every fibre of thine heart, and love what He has loved for His sake. He has left with thee those for whom on earth He cared most,—the poor, the sick, the unhappy. Be they unto thee as thy dearest, and He the dearest of all."

This was very unlike any counsel which Doucebelle had ever before received from a confessor. There was something here of which she could take hold. Not that Father Bruno had suggested a new course of action so much as that he had supplied a new motive power. To do good, to give alms, to be kind to poor and sick people, Doucebelle had been taught already: but the reason for it was either the abstract notion that it was the right thing to do, or that it would help to increase her little heap of human merit.

To all minds, but in particular to an ignorant one, there is an enormous difference between the personal and the impersonal. Tell a child that such a thing must be done because it is right, and the motive power is faint and vague, not unlikely to be overthrown by the first breath of temptation. But let the child understand that to do this thing will please or displease God, and you have supplied a far stronger energising power, in the intelligible reference to the will of a living Person.

Doucebelle felt this—as, more or less, we all do.

"Father," she said, after a momentary pause, "I want your advice."

"State thy perplexity, my daughter."

"I hope, Father, you will not be angry; but a few days ago, when you and the other priests were talking in the ante-chamber about Belasez, the door was open, and we heard every word in the bower."

"Did Belasez hear what was said?"

"Yes."

"Ha! What did she say?"

"I asked her, at night, whether what you had said had wounded her. And she said, No: but she thought there was one Christian priest who was like what the Scripture described Christ to be."

"Did she say that?" There was a tone of tender regret in the priest's voice.

"She did. But, Father, I want to know how to deal with Belasez. Sometimes she will talk to me quite freely, and tell me all her thoughts and feelings : at other times I cannot get a word out of her."

"Let her alone at the other times. What is the state of her mind ?"

"She seems to have been very much struck, Father, with a sermon from your Bishop, wherein he proved out of her own Scriptures, she says, that our Lord is the Messiah whom the Jews believe. But I do not know if she has reached any point further than that. I think she hardly knows what to believe."

"Only those sermons do good which God preaches," said Bruno. Perhaps he spoke rather to himself than to Doucebelle. "Whenever the maiden will speak to thee, do not repulse her. Lead her, to the best of thy power, to see that Christ is God's one cure for all evil. Yet He must teach it first to thyself."

"I think He has done so—a little," answered Doucebelle. "But, Father, will you not speak to her ? "

"My child, we will both wait upon God, and speak the words He gives us, at the time He will. And remember,—whatever blunders men make,— Belasez is, after the flesh, nearer akin to Him than thou art. She is the kinswoman of the Lord Jesus.

Let that thought spur thee on, if thou faint by the way."

"Father! Our Lord was not a Jew?"

"He was a Jew, my daughter."

Hardly any news could more have amazed Doucebelle.

"But why then do people use them so harshly?"

"Thou hadst better ask the people," answered Bruno, drily.

"Father, is it right to use Jews so?"

"Thou hadst better ask the Lord."

"What does He say, Father?"

"He said, speaking to Abraham, the father of them all, 'I will bless him that blesseth thee, and curse him that curseth thee.'"

"Oh, I am so glad!" cried Doucebelle. "If you please, Father, I could not help loving Belasez: but I tried hard not to do so, because I thought it was wicked. It cannot be wrong to love a Jew, if Christ Himself were one."

Bruno did not reply immediately. When he did, it was with a slight quiver in his voice which surprised Doucebelle.

"It can never be wrong to love," he said. "But, daughter, let not thy love stop at liking the maid's company. Let it go on till thou canst take it into Heaven."

The strangest of all strange ideas was this to Doucebelle. She had been taught that love was always a weakness, and only too frequently a sin. That so purely earthly a thing could be taken into Heaven astonished her beyond measure.

"Father!" she said, in a tone of mingled amazement and inquiry.

"What now, my daughter?"

"People always speak of love as weak, if not wicked."

"People often talk of what they do not understand, my child. 'God is love.' Think not, therefore, that God resembles a worldly fancy which springs to-day, and fades away to-morrow. His is the heavenly love which can never die, which is ready to sacrifice all things, which so looks to the true welfare of the beloved that it will give thee any earthly suffering rather than see thee sink into perdition by thy sins. This is real love, daughter: and thou canst not sin in giving it to Belasez or to any other."

"Yet, Father," said Doucebelle in a puzzled tone, "the religious give up love when they go into the cloister. I do not understand. A Sister of St.

Ursula may not leave her convent, even if her own mother lies dying, and pleads hard to see her. And though some priests do wed"—this had not yet, in England, ceased to be the case—"yet people always seem to think the celibate priests more holy, as if that were more in accordance with the will of God. Yet God tells us to love each other. I cannot quite understand."

If Doucebelle could have seen, as well as spoken, through the confessional grating, assuredly she would have stopped sooner. For the agony that was working in every line of Father Bruno's face would have been terrible to her to see. But she only thought that it was a long while before he answered her, and she wondered at the hard, constrained tone in his voice.

"Child!" he said, "does any one but God 'quite understand'? Do we understand ourselves?—and how much less each other? It is only love that understands. He who most loves God will best understand men. And for the rest,—O Lord who hast loved us, pardon the blunders and misunderstandings of Thy people, and save Thy servants that trust in Thee!—Now go, my child,—unless thou hast more to say. *Absolvo te.*"

Doucebelle rose and retired. But she did not know that Father Bruno heard no more confessions. She only heard that he was not at home when dinner was served; and when he appeared at supper, he looked very worn and white, as if after a weary journey.

CHAPTER VII.

THE SHADOW OF LONG AGO.

SO faithfully had the Countess adhered to her plighted word that Belasez should be seen by no one, that not one of the priests had yet beheld her except Father Nicholas, and the meeting in that case had been accidental and momentary. But when Father Bruno announced to his brother priests his intention of seeking an interview with the Jewish maiden, Father Nicholas shook his head waggishly.

"Have a care of the toils of Satan, Brother Bruno!" said he. "The maiden may have the soul of a fiend, for aught I wot, yet hath she the face of an angel."

"I thank thee. There is no fear!" answered Bruno, with a smile which made him look sadder.

The Countess had not returned from the coronation festivities, and the girls were alone in Margaret's bower, when Father Bruno entered, with " God save all here!"

Belasez rose hastily, and prepared to withdraw.

"Wait, my child," said the priest, gently: " I would speak with thee."

But when she turned in answer, and he saw her face, some strange and terrible emotion seemed to convulse his own.

"*Domine, in Te speravi,*" fell from his trembling lips, as if he scarcely realised what he was saying.

Belasez looked at him with an astonished expression. Whatever were the cause of his singular emotion, it was evidently neither understood nor shared by her.

With a manifest effort of self-control, Bruno recovered himself.

"Sit down, daughters," he said : for all had risen in reverence to the priest : and he seated himself on the settle, whence he had a full view of Belasez.

"And what is thy name, my daughter ? "

" Belasez, at your service."

L

"And thy father's name?"

"Abraham of Norwich, if it please you."

"Abraham—of Norwich! Not—not the son of Ursel of Norwich?"

"The same."

Again that look of intense pain crossed Bruno's face.

"No wonder!" he said, speaking not to Belasez. "The very face—the very look! No wonder!—And thy mother?"

"My mother is Licorice, the daughter of Kokorell of Lincoln."

Bruno gave a little nod, as if he had known it before.

"Hast thou any brethren or sisters?"

"One brother only; his name is Delecresse."

The reply seemed to extinguish Bruno's interest. For a moment, as if his thoughts were far elsewhere, he played with a morsel of sewing silk which he had picked up from the floor.

"The Lord is wiser than men," he said at last, as if that were the conclusion to which his unseen thoughts had led him.

"Yes; and better," answered the young Jewess.

"And better," dreamily repeated the priest. "We

shall know that one day, when we wake up to see His Face."

"Amen," said Belasez. "'When we awake up after Thy likeness,' saith David the Prophet, 'we shall be satisfied with it.'"

"'Satisfied!' echoed Bruno. Art thou satisfied, my daughter?"

The answering "No!" appeared to come from the depths of Belasez's heart.

"Shall I tell thee wherefore? There is but one thing that satisfies the soul of man. Neither in earth nor in Heaven is any man satisfied with aught else. My child, dost thou know what that is?"

Belasez looked up, her own face working a little now.

"You mean," she said, "the Man whom ye call Christ."

"I mean Him."

"I know nothing about Him." And Belasez resumed her embroidery, as if that were of infinitely greater consequence.

"Dost thou know much about happiness?"

"Happiness!" exclaimed the girl. "I know what mirth is. Do you mean that? Or, I know what it is to feel as if one cared for nothing. Is that your meaning ?"

"Happiness," said Bruno, "is what thy King meant when he said, 'I shall be satisfied with it.' Dost thou know that ?"

Belasez drew a long breath, and shook her head sadly.

"No," she said. "I have never known that."

"Because thou hast never known Jesus Christ."

"I know He said, 'I am the life,'" responded the girl slowly. "And life is not worth much. Perhaps it might be,—if one were satisfied."

"Poor child! Is life not worth much to thee?" answered the priest in a pitying tone. "And thou art very young—not much over twenty."

"I am under twenty. I am just eighteen."

Once more Bruno's face was convulsed.

"Just eighteen !" he said. "Yes—Licorice's child! *Yet* she had no pity. Aye me—just eighteen !"

"Do you know my mother ?" said Belasez in accents of mingled surprise and curiosity.

"I did—eighteen years ago."

And Bruno rose hastily, as if he wished to dismiss the subject. Margaret dropped on her knees and requested his blessing, which he gave as though his thoughts were far away: and then he left the room slowly, gazing on Belasez to the last.

This was the first, but not by any means the last, interview between Father Bruno and the Jewish maiden. A month later, Doucebelle asked Belasez how she liked him.

"I do not like him; I love him," said Belasez, with more warmth than usual.

"What a confession!" answered Doucebelle, playfully.

"Oh, not that sort of love!" responded Belasez with a tinge of scorn. "I think it must be the sort that we can take into Heaven with us."

The next morning, Levina announced to the Countess, in a tone of gratified spite, that two persons were in the hall—an old man, unknown to her, and the young Jew, Delecresse. He had come for his sister.

Belasez received the news of her recall at first with a look of blank dismay, and then with a shower of passionate tears. Her deep attachment to her Christian friends was most manifest. She kissed the hand of the Countess and Margaret, warmly embraced Doucebelle, and then looked round as if something were wanting still.

"What is it, my maid?" kindly asked the Countess.

"Father Bruno!" faltered Belasez through her tears. "Oh, I must say farewell to Father Bruno!"

The Countess looked astonished, for she knew not that Bruno and Belasez had ever met. A few words from Doucebelle explained. Still the Countess was extremely dissatisfied.

"My maid," she said, "thy father may think I have not kept my word. I ought to have told Father Bruno. I never thought of it, when he first came. I am very sorry. Has he talked with thee on matters of religion at all?"

"Yes." Belasez explained no further.

"Dear, dear!" said the Countess. "He meant well, I suppose. And of course it is better thy soul should be saved. But I wish he had less zeal and more discretion."

"Lady," said Belasez, pausing for an instant, "if ever I enter the kingdom of the Blessed One above, I think I shall owe it to the Bishop of Lincoln and to Father Bruno."

"That is well, no doubt," responded the Countess, in a very doubtful tone. "Oh dear! what did make Father Bruno think of coming up here?"

As Belasez passed down towards the hall, Father Bruno himself met her on the stairs.

"Whither goest thou, my child?" he asked in some surprise.

"I am going—away." Belasez's tears choked her voice.

"To thy father's house?"

She bowed.

"Without Christ?"

"No, Father, not without Him," sobbed the girl. "Nor,—if you will grant it to me at this moment—without baptism."

"Dost thou believe that Jesus Christ is the Son of God?"

"I do."

Bruno hesitated a minute, while an expression of deep pain flitted over his face.

"I cannot do it, Belasez."

"O Father! do you reject me?"

"God forbid, my child! I do not reject thee in any wise: I only reject myself. Belasez, long years ago, Licorice thy mother did me a cruel wrong. If I baptize thee, I shall feel it to be my revenge on her. And I have no right thus to defile the snow-white robe of thy baptism because my hands are not clean, nor to mingle the revenge of earth with the innocence of Heaven.   Wait a moment."

And he turned and went rapidly down the stairs. Belasez waited till he came back.   He was accompanied by Father Warner.   She trembled at the ordeal which she guessed to await her, and soon found that she was not far wrong.   Father Warner took her into the empty chapel, and required her to repeat the Creed (which of course she could not do), to tell him which were the seven deadly sins, and what the five commandments of the Church.   Belasez had never heard of any of them.   Warner shook his head sternly, and wondered what Brother Bruno could possibly mean by presenting this ignorant heathen as a fit candidate for baptism.

Belasez felt as if God and man alike would have none of her.   Warner recommended her to put herself under the tuition of some priest at Norwich— which was to her a complete impossibility—and perhaps in a year or thereabouts, if she were diligent and obedient in following the orders of her director, she might hope to receive the grace of holy baptism.

She went out sobbing, and encountered Bruno at the head of the stairs.

"O Father Bruno!" faltered the girl. "Father Warner will not do it!"

"I was afraid so," said Bruno, sadly. "I should not have thought of asking him had my Brother Nicholas been at home. Well, daughter, this is no fault of thine. Remember, we baptize only with water: but He whose ministers we are can baptize thee with the Holy Ghost and with fire. Let Him be thy Shepherd to provide for thee; thy Priest to absolve thee; thy King to command thine heart's allegiance. So dwell thou to Him in this world now, that hereafter thou mayest dwell with Him for ever."

Belasez stooped and kissed his hand. He gave her his blessing in fervent tones, bade her a farewell which gave him unmistakable pain, and let her depart. Belasez drew her veil closely over her face, and joined Delecresse and her father's old friend Hamon in the hall.

"What a time thou hast been!" said Delecresse, discontentedly. "Do let us go now. I want to be outside this accursed Castle."

But to Belasez it seemed like stepping out of the sunlit fold into the dreary wilderness beyond.

As they passed the upper end of the hall, Belasez

paused for an instant to make a last reverence to Margaret, who sat there talking with her unacknowledged husband, Sir Richard de Clare. The black scowl on the face of her brother drew her attention at once.

"Who is that young Gentile?" he demanded.

"Sir Richard de Clare, Lord of Gloucester."

"What hast thou against him?" asked old Hamon.

"That is the youth that threw my cap into a pool, a year ago, and called me a Jew cur," said Delecresse, between his teeth.

"Pooh, pooh!" said old Hamon. "We all have to put up with those little amenities. Never mind it, child."

"I'll never mind it—till the time come!" answered Delecresse, in an undertone. "Then—I think I see how to wipe it off."

Belasez found her mother returned from Lincoln. She received a warm welcome from Abraham, a much cooler one from Licorice, and was very glad, having arrived at home late, to go to bed in her own little chamber, which was inside that of her parents. She soon dropped asleep, but was awoke ere long by voices in the adjoining room, distinctly audible through the curtain which alone separated the chambers. They spoke in Spanish, the language usually employed amongst themselves by the English Sephardim.

"*Ay de mi,*[1] that it ever should have been so!" said the voice of Licorice. "What did the shiksah[2] want with her?"

"I told thee, wife," answered Abraham, in a slightly injured tone, "she wanted the child to embroider a scarf."

"And I suppose thou wert too anxious to fill thy saddle-bags to care for the danger to her?"

"There was no danger at all, wife. The Countess promised all I asked her. And I made thirteen gold pennies clear profit. Thou canst see the child is no worse—they have been very kind to her: she said as much."

"Abraham, son of Ursel, thou art a very wise man!"

"What canst thou mean, Licorice?"

"'Kind to her!' If they had starved her and beaten her, there might have been no harm done. Canst thou not see that the girl's heart is with her

---

[1] Woe is me!

[2] The feminine singular of the Hebrew word rendered, in the A. V., "creeping things." Dr. Edersheim tells us that this flattering term is commonly employed in speaking of a Gentile.

Christian friends? Why, she had been crying behind her veil, quietly, all the journey."

"Well, wife? What then?"

"'What then?' Abraham, Isaac, and Jacob! 'What then?' Why, then—she will do like Anegay."

"The God of our fathers forbid it!" cried Abraham, in tones of horror and distress.

"It is too late for that," said Licorice, with a short, contemptuous laugh. "Thou shouldst have said that a year ago, and have kept the child at home."

"We had better marry her at once," suggested Abraham, still in a voice of deep pain.

"'There are no birds in last year's nest,' old man," was the response. "Marry her or let it alone, the child's heart is gone from us. She has left behind her in yonder Castle those for whom she cares more than for us, and, I should not wonder also, a faith dearer to her than ours. It will be Anegay over again. Ah, well! Like to like! What else could we expect?"

"Can she hear us, Licorice?"

"Not she! She was fast asleep an hour ago."

"Wife, if it be so, have we not deserved it?"

"Abraham, don't be a fool!" cried Licorice, so

very snappishly that it sounded as if her conscience might have responded a little to the accusation.

"I cannot but think thou didst evil, Licorice,—thou knowest how and when."

"I understand thee, of course. It was the only thing to do."

"I know thou saidst so," answered Abraham in an unconvinced tone. "Yet it went to my heart to hear the poor child's sorrowful moan."

"Thy heart is stuffed with feathers."

"I would rather it were so than with stones."

"Thanks for the compliment!"

"Nay, I said nothing about thee. But, Licorice, if it be as thou thinkest, do not let us repeat that mistake."

"I shall repeat no mistakes, I warrant thee."

The conversation ceased rather suddenly, except for one mournful exclamation from Abraham,—"Poor Anegay!"

Anegay! where had Belasez heard that name before? It belonged to no friend or relative, so far as she knew. Yet that she had heard it before, and that in interesting connection with something, she was absolutely certain.

Belasez dropped asleep while she was thinking. It seemed to her that hardly a minute passed before she woke again, to hear her mother moving in the next room, and to see full daylight streaming in at the window.

And suddenly, just as she awoke, it rushed upon her when and how she had heard of Anegay.

She saw herself, a little child, standing by the side of Licorice. With them was old Belya, the mother of Hamon, and before them stood an enormous illuminated volume at which they were looking. Belasez found it impossible to remember what had been said by Belya; but her mother's response was as vivid in her mind as if the whole scene were of yesterday.

"Hush! The child must not know. Yes, Belya, thou art right. That was taken from Anegay's face."

What was it that was taken? And dimly before Belasez's mental eyes a picture seemed to grow, in which a king upon his throne, and a woman fainting, were the principal figures. Esther before Ahasuerus!

That was it, of course. And Belasez sprang up, with a determination to search through her father's books, and to find the picture which had been taken from Anegay's face.

But, after all, who was Anegay?

Licorice was in full tide of business and porridge-making, in her little kitchen, when Belasez presented herself with an apology for being late.

"Nay, folks that go to bed at nine may well not rise till five," said Licorice, graciously. "Throw more salt in here, child, and fetch the porringers whilst I stir it. Call thy father and Delecresse,—breakfast will be ready by the time they are."

Breakfast was half over when Licorice inquired of her daughter whom she had seen at Bury Castle.

"Oh! to speak to, only the Countess and her daughter, Damsel Margaret, and the other young damsels, Doucebelle, Eva, and Marie; and Levina, the Lady's dresser. They showed me some others through the window, so that I knew their names and faces."

Belasez quietly left out the priests.

"And what knights didst thou see there?"

"Through the window? Sir Hubert the Earl, and Sir Richard of Gloucester, and Sir John the Earl's son, and Sir John de Averenches. Oh! I forgot Dame Hawise, Sir John's wife; but I never saw much of her."

"There was no such there as one named Bruno de

Malpas, I suppose?" asked Licorice, with assumed carelessness.

"No, there was no knight of that name."

But in her heart Belasez felt that the name belonged to the priest, Father Bruno.

A few more questions were asked her, of no import, and then they rose. When Licorice set her free from household duties, Belasez took her way to the little closet over the porch which served as her father's library. He was the happy possessor of eleven volumes,—a goodly number at that date. Eight she passed by, knowing them to contain no pictures. The ninth was an illuminated copy of the Brut, which of course began, as all chronicles then did, with the creation; but Belasez looked through it twice without finding any thing to satisfy her. Next came the Chronicle of Benoît, but the illuminations in this were merely initials and tail-pieces in arabesque. There was only one left, and it was the largest volume in the collection. Belasez could not remember having ever opened it. She pulled it down now, just missing a sprained wrist in the process, and found it to be a splendid copy of the Hagiographa, with full-page pictures, glowing with colours and gold. Of course, the illuminations had been executed by Christian hands; but all these books had come to Abraham in exchange for bad debts, and he was not so consistent as to refuse to look at the representations of created things, however wicked he might account it to produce them. Belasez turned over the stiff leaves, one after another, till she reached the Book of Esther. Yes, surely that was the picture she remembered. There sat the King Ahasuerus on a curule chair, wearing a floriated crown and a mantle clasped at the neck with a golden fibula; and there fainted Queen Esther in the arms of her ladies, arrayed in the tight gown, the pocketing sleeve, the wimple, and all other monstrosities of the early Plantagenet era. A Persian satrap, enclosed in a coat of mail and a surcoat with a silver shield, whereon an exceedingly rampant red lion was disporting itself, appeared to be coming to the help of his liege lady; while a tall white lily, in a flower-pot about twice the size of the throne, occupied one side of the picture. To all these details Belasez paid no attention. The one thing at which she looked was the face of the fainting Queen, which was turned full towards the spectator.

It was a very lovely face of a decidedly Jewish

type. But what made Belasez glance from it to the brazen mirror fixed to the wall opposite? Was it Anegay of whom Bruno had been thinking when he murmured that she was so like some one? Undoubtedly there was a likeness. The same pure oval face, the smooth calm brow, the dark glossy hair: but it struck Belasez that her own features, as seen in the mirror, were the less prominently Jewish.

And, once more, who was Anegay?

How little it is possible to know of the innermost heart of our nearest friends! Belasez went through all her duties that day, without rousing the faintest suspicion in the mind of her mother that she had heard a syllable of the conversation between her parents the night before. Yet she thought of little else. Her household work was finished, and she sat in the deep recess of the window at her embroidery, when Delecresse came and stood beside her.

"Belasez, who was that damsel that sat talking with my Lord of Gloucester in the hall when we passed through?"

"That was the Damsel Margaret, daughter of Sir Hubert the Earl."

"What sort of a maiden is she?"

"Very sweet and gentle. I liked her extremely. She was always most kind to me."

" Is she attached to my Lord of Gloucester ?"

It was a new idea to Belasez.

" Really, I never thought of that, Cress. But I should not at all wonder if she be. She is constantly talking of him."

" Does he care for her ? "

" I fancy he does, by the way I have seen him look up at her windows."

" Yes, I could tell that from his face."

The tone of her brother's voice struck Belasez unpleasantly.

" Cress! what dost thou mean ? "

" It is a pity that the innocent need suffer with the guilty," answered Delecresse, contemptuously. " But it mostly turns out so in this world."

Belasez grasped her brother's wrists.

" Cress, thou hast no thought of revenging thyself on Sir Richard of Gloucester for that boyish trick he once played on thee ? "

" I'll be even with him, Belasez. No man—least of all a Christian dog—shall insult me with impunity."

" O Cress, Cress! Thou must not do it. Hast

thou forgotten that vengeance belongeth to the Holy One, to whom be glory? And for such a mere nothing as that!"

"Nothing! Dost thou call it nothing for a son of Abraham to be termed a Jew cur by one of those creeping things of Gentiles? Is not the day at hand when they shall be our ploughmen and vine-dressers?"

"Well, then," answered Belasez, assuming a playfulness which she was far from feeling, "when Sir Richard is thy ploughman, thou canst knock his cap off."

"Pish! They like high interest, these Christians. I'll let them have it, the other way about."

"Cress, what dost thou mean to do?"

"I mean that he shall pay me every farthing that he owes," said Delecresse through his clenched teeth. "I cannot have it in gold coins, perhaps. It will suit me as well in drops of blood,—either from his veins or from his heart."

"Delecresse, thou *shalt not* touch the Damsel Margaret, if that be the meaning of those terrible words."

"I am not going to touch her," replied Delecresse, scornfully, "even with the tongs he took to my cap.

I would not touch one of the vile insects for all the gold at Norwich!"

"But what dost thou mean?"

"Hold thou thy peace. I was a fool to tell thee."

"What art thou going to do?" persisted Belasez.

"What thou wilt hear when it is done," said Delecresse, walking away.

He left poor Belasez in grief and terror. Some misery, of what sort she could not even guess, was impending over her poor friend Margaret. How was it possible to warn her?—and of what was she to be warned?

A few minutes were spent in reflection, and then Belasez's work was hastily folded, and she went in search of her father. Abraham listened with a perplexed and annoyed face.

"That boy always lets his hands go before his head! But what can I do, daughter? In good sooth, I would not willingly see any injury done to the Christians that have been so kind to thee. Where is Cress?"

"He went into the kitchen," said Belasez.

Abraham shuffled off in that direction, in the loose yellow slippers which were one of the recognised signs of a Jew.

"Delecresse is just gone out," he said, coming back directly. "I will talk to him when he comes in."

But twelve days elapsed before Delecresse returned.

"Cress, thou wilt not do anything to Sir Richard of Gloucester?" earnestly pleaded Belasez, when she found him alone.

"No," said Delecresse, with a glitter in his eyes which was not promising.

"Hast thou done any thing?"

"All I mean to do."

"O Cress, what hast thou done?"

"Go to bed!" was the most lucid explanation which all the eager entreaties of Belasez could obtain from her brother.

CHAPTER VIII.

IN THE DARK.

"I trust Thee, though I cannot see
  Thy light upon my pathway shine:
However dark, Lord, let it be
  Thy way, not mine!"

"IF it stand with your good liking, may a man have speech of Sir Piers de Rievaulx?"

It was a tall youth who asked the question, and he stood under the porch of a large Gothic house, on the banks of the Thames near Westminster. The night was wet and dark, and it was the second of April 1236.

"And who art thou, that would speak with the knight my master?"

"What I have to say to him is of consequence. Who I may be does not so much matter."

"Well said, my young cockerel! Thou crowest

fairly." The porter laughed as he set down the lantern which he had been holding up to the youth's face, and took down a large key from the peg on which it hung. "What shall I say to my master touching thee ? "

" Say, if it please you, that one would speak with him that hath important tidings, which closely concern the King's welfare."

" They were rash folks that trusted a slip like thee with important tidings."

" None trusted me."

" Eavesdropping, eh ? Well, thou canst keep thine own counsel, lad as thou art. I will come back to thee shortly."

It was nearly half an hour before the porter returned ; but the youth never changed his position, as he stood leaning against the side of the porch.

"Come in," said the porter, holding the wicket open. " Sir Piers will see thee. I told him, being sent of none, thou wert like to have no token."

The unknown visitor followed the porter in silence through the paved courtyard, up a flight of stone steps, and into a small chamber, hung with blue. Here, at a table covered with parchments, sat one of King Henry's ministers, Sir Piers de Rievaulx, son

of the Bishop of Winchester, the worst living foe of
Earl Hubert of Kent. He was on the younger side
of middle age, and was only not quite so bad a man
as the father from whom he inherited his dark
gleaming eyes, lithe quick motions, intense prejudices, and profound artfulness of character.

"Christ save you ! Come forward," said Sir Piers.
"Shut the door, Oliver, and let none enter till I bid
it.—Now, who art thou, and what wouldst thou with
me ?"

" I am Delecresse, son of Abraham of Norwich."

"Ha ! A Jew, of course. Thy face matches thy
name. Now, thy news ?"

"Will my noble knight be pleased to tell his
unworthy servant if he likes the taste of revenge ?"

Delecresse despised himself for the words he used.
A son of Israel to humble himself thus to one of the
Goyim ! But it was expedient that the "creeping
thing" should be flattered and gratified, in order to
induce him to act as a tool.

"Decidedly ! " replied Sir Piers, looking fixedly
at Delecresse.

"Your Honour hates Sir Hubert of Kent, or I am
mistaken ?"

" Ha, *pure foy !* Worse than I hate the Devil."

The Devil was very near to both at that moment.

"If I help you to be revenged on him, will you pay me by giving me my revenge on another?"

Delecresse had dropped alike his respectful words and subservient manner, and spoke up now, as man to man.

"'Turn about is fair play,' I suppose," said Sir Piers. "If thou seek not revenge on any friend of mine, I will."

"I seek it on Sir Richard de Clare, the young Earl of Gloucester."

"*He* is no friend of mine!" said Sir Piers, between his teeth. "His father married the woman I wanted. I should rather enjoy it than otherwise."

"The Lady his mother yet lives."

"What is that to me? She is an old hag. What do I care for her now?"

Delecresse felt staggered for a moment. Bad as he was in one respect, he was capable of personal attachment as well as of hatred; and Sir Piers' delicate notions of love rather astonished him. But Sir Piers was very far from being the only man who was—or is—incapable of entertaining any others. Delecresse soon recovered himself. He was too anxious to get his work done, to quarrel with his tools. It was gratifying, too, to discover that Sir Piers was not a likely man to be troubled by any romantic scruples about breaking the heart of the young Margaret. Delecresse himself had been unpleasantly haunted by those, and had with some difficulty succeeded in crushing them down and turning the key on them. Belasez's pleading looks, and Margaret's bright, pretty face, persisted in recurring to his memory in a very provoking manner. Sir Piers was evidently the man who would help him to forget them.

"Well!—go on," said the Minister, when Delecresse hesitated.

"I have good reason to believe that Sir Richard is on the point of wedding the Damsel Margaret de Burgh; nay, I am not sure if they are not married clandestinely. Could not this be used as a handle to ruin both of them ?"

The two pairs of eyes met, and a smile which was anything but angelic broke over the handsome countenance of Sir Piers.

"Not a bad idea for one so young," he remarked. "Is it thine own ?"

"My own," answered Delecresse, shortly.

"I could make some use of thee in the King's service."

"Thank you," said Delecresse, rather drily. "I do not wish to have *more* to do with the Devil and his angels than I find necessary."

Sir Piers broke into a laugh. "Neat, that! I suppose I am one of the angels? But I am surprised to hear such a sentiment from a Jew."

Nothing is more inconsistent than sin. In his anxiety to gratify his revenge, Delecresse was enduring patiently at the hands of Sir Piers far worse insults than that over which he had so long brooded from Richard de Clare. He kept silence.

"It really is a pity," observed Sir Piers, complacently surveying Delecresse, "that such budding talent as thine should be cast away upon trade. Thou wouldst make far more money in secret service. It would be easy to change thy name. Keep thy descent quiet, and be ready to eat humble-pie for a short time. There is no saying to what thou mightest rise in this world."

"And the other?" Delecresse felt himself an unfledged cherub by the side of Sir Piers.

"Ba—h!" Sir Piers snapped his fingers. "What do such as we know about that? There is no other world. If there were, the chances are that both of us would find ourselves very uncomfortable there. We had better stay in this as long as we can."

"As you please, Sir Knight. I am not ready to sell my soul for gold."

"Only for revenge, eh? Well, that's not much better. There are a few scruples about thee, my promising lad, which thou wouldst find it necessary to sacrifice in the service. Some soft-hearted mother or sister, I imagine, hath instilled them into thee. Women are always after some mischief. I wish there were none."

What did Delecresse know of the momentary pang of sensation which had pricked that hard, seared heart, as for one second memory brought before him the loving face of a little child, over whose fair head for thirty years the churchyard daisies had been blooming? Could he hear the tender, pleading voice of the baby sister, begging dear Piers not to hurt her pet kitten, and she would give him all the sweetmeats Aunt Theffania sent her? Such moments do come to the hardest hearts: and they usually leave them harder. Before Delecresse had found an answer, Sir Piers was himself again.

"Thou hast done me a service, boy: and I will take care that thy friend Sir Richard feels the goad as well as my beloved Earl Hubert. Take this piece of gold. Nay, it will not burn thee. 'Tis only earthly metal. Thou wilt not? As thou list. The saints keep thee! Ah,—I forgot! Thou dost not believe in the saints. Bah! no more do I. Only words, lad,—all words. Fare thee well."

A few minutes later Delecresse found himself in the street. He was conscious of a very peculiar and highly uncomfortable mixture of feelings, as if one part of his nature were purely angelic, and the other absolutely diabolical. He felt almost as if he had come direct from a personal interview with Satan, and his spirit had been soiled and degraded by the contact. Yet was he any better than Sir Piers, except in lack of experience and opportunity? He leaned over the parapet as he passed, and watched the dark river flowing silently below.

"I wish I had not done it!" came in muttered accents from his lips at last. "I do almost, really, wish I had not done it!"

And then, as the reader knows, he went home and snubbed his sister.

Abraham could get nothing out of his son except some scornful platitudes concerning the "creeping creatures." Not a shred of information would

Delecresse give. He was almost rude to his father —a very high crime in the eyes of a Jew : but it was because he was so intensely dissatisfied with himself.

"O my son, light of mine eyes, what hast thou done !" mournfully ejaculated old Abraham, as he resigned the attempt to influence or reason with Delecresse.

"Done?—made those vile Gentiles wince, I hope !" retorted Licorice. "I hate every man, woman, and child among them. I should like to bake them all in the oven !"

And she shut the door of that culinary locality with a bang. Belasez looked up with saddened eyes, and her mother noticed them.

"Abraham, son of Ursel," she said that night, when she supposed her daughter to be safely asleep in the inner chamber, "when dost thou mean to have this maiden wedded ? "

"I do not know, wife. Would next week do ?"

Next week was always Abraham's time for doing every thing.

"If thou wilt. The gear has all been ready long ago. There is only the feast to provide."

"Then I suppose I had better speak to Hamon," said Abraham, in the tone of a man who would have been thankful if allowed to let it alone. "It is time, I take it?"

"It is far past the time, husband," said Licorice. "That girl's heart, as I told thee, is gone after the creeping things. Didst thou not see the look in her eyes to-night? Like to like—blood to blood! It made mine boil to behold it."

"Forbid it, God of our fathers!" fervently ejaculated Abraham. "Licorice, dost thou think the child has ever guessed "——

"Hush, husband, lest she should chance to awake. Guessed! No, and she never shall."

Belasez's ears, it is unnecessary to say, were strained to catch every sound. What was she not to guess?

"Art thou sure that Genta knows nothing?"

Genta was the daughter of Abraham's brother Moss.

"Nothing that would do much harm," said Licorice, but in rather a doubtful tone. "Beside, Genta can hold her peace."

"Aye, if she choose. But suppose she did not? She knows, does she not, about—Anegay?"

"Hush! Well, yes — something. But not what would do most mischief."

"What, about her marriage with "——

"Man! do, for pity's sake, give over, or thou wilt blurt all out! Do only think, if the child were to hear! Trust me, she would go back to that wasp's nest to-morrow. No, no! Just listen to me, son of Ursel. Get her safely married before she knows anything. Leo may be relied upon to keep her in safe seclusion: and when she has a husband and half-a-dozen children to tie her down, heart and soul, to us, she will give over pining after the Gentiles."

Belasez was conscious of a rising repugnance, which she had never felt before, to this marriage about to be forced upon her. Not personally to Leo, of whom she knew nothing; but to this tie contemplated for her, which was to be an impassable barrier between her and all her Christian friends.

"Well!" sighed Abraham. He evidently did not like it. "I suppose, then, I must let the Cohen[1] know about it."

"If it be not already too late," responded Licorice, dubiously. "If only this second visit had not happened! There was less harm done the first time, and I do not quite understand it. Some stronger

---

[1] Priest. All Jews named Cohen are sons of Aaron.

feeling has taken possession of her now. Either her faith is shaken "——

"May the All-Merciful defend us from such horror!"

"Well, it is either that, or there is love in her heart—a deeper love than for the Gentile woman, and the girls of whom she talks. She likes them, I do not doubt; but she would never break her heart after them. There is somebody else, old man, of whom we have not heard; and I counsel thee to try and find out him or her. I am sadly afraid it is *him*."

"But, Licorice, she has not seen any one. The Lady passed her word that not a soul should come near her."

"Pish! Did the shiksah keep it? Even if she meant to do—and who can trust a Gentile?—was she there, day and night? Did Emendant not tell thee that he saw her at the Coronation?"

"Well, yes, he did," admitted Abraham, with evident reluctance.

"And had she Belasez there, tied to her apron-string, with a bandage over her eyes? Son of Ursel, wilt thou never open thine? Who knows how many young gallants may have chattered to her then?

'When the cat is away—' thou knowest. Not that the shiksah was much of a cat when she was there, I'll be bound. Dost thou not care if the child be stolen from us? And when they have stolen her heart and her soul, they may as well take her body. It won't make much difference then."

" Licorice "——

Belasez listened more intently than ever. There was a world of tender regret in Abraham's voice, and she knew that it was not for Licorice.

" Licorice "—— he said, and stopped.

" Go on," responded her mother sharply, " unless thou wert after some foolery, as is most likely."

" Licorice, hast thou forgotten that Sabbath even, when thou broughtest home "——

" I wish thou wouldst keep thy tongue off names. I have as good a memory as thou, though it is not lined like thine with asses' skin."

" And dost thou remember what thou toldest me that she said to thy reproaches?"

" Well, what then?"

" 'What then?' O Licorice!"

" I do wish thou wouldst speak sense!—what art thou driving at?"

" Thou art hard to please, wife. If I speak

plainly thou wilt not hear me out, and if I only hint thou chidest me for want of plainness. Well! if thou canst not see 'what then,' never mind. I thought those sorrowful words of my poor child might have touched thy heart. ﹥I can assure thee, they did mine, when I heard of them. They have never been out of mine ears since."

It seemed plain to Belasez that her mother was being rebuked for want of motherly tenderness, and, as she doubted not, towards Anegay. This mysterious person, then, must have been a sister of whom she had never heard,—probably much older than herself.

"What a lot of soft down must have been used up to make thine heart!" was the cynical reply of Licorice.

"I cannot help it, Licorice. I have her eyes ever before me—hers, and his. It is of no use scolding me—I cannot help it. And if it be as thou thinkest, I cannot break the child's heart. I shall not speak to Hamon, nor the Cohen."

"Faint-hearted Gentile!" blazed forth Licorice.

"Get it over, wife," said Abraham, quietly. "I will try to find out if thou hast guessed rightly; though it were rather work for thee than me, if—

well, I will do my best. But suppose I should find that she has given her maiden heart to some Gentile, —what am I to do then?"

"Do! What did Phinehas the son of Eleazar the priest unto Zimri and Cozbi? Hath not the Blessed One commanded, saying, 'Thy daughter thou shalt not give unto his son'? What meanest thou? Do! Couldst thou do too much, even if they were offered upon the altar before the God of Sabaoth?"

"Where is it?" responded Abraham, desolately. "But, Licorice,—*our* daughter?"

"What dost thou mean?" said Licorice, fiercely. "Perhaps we might shed tears first. But they must not pollute the sacrifice. Do not the holy Rabbins say that a tear dropped upon a devoted lamb washeth out all the merit of the offering?"

"I believe they do," said Abraham; "though it is not in the Thorah. But I did not mean exactly that. Dost thou not understand me?"

"I understand that thou art no true son of Abraham!" burst out his wife. "I say she is, and she shall be!"

"Who ever heard of such reckoning in the days of the fathers?" answered Abraham. "Licorice, I am doubtful if we have done well in keeping back the truth so much. Doth not the Holy One love and require truth in all His people? Yet it was thy doing, not mine."

"Oh yes, thou wouldst have told her at once!" sneered Licorice. "She would stay with us meekly then, would she not? Go to sleep, for mercy's sake, I entreat thee, and hold thy tongue, before any worse mischief be done. My doing! yes, it is well it was. Had I listened to thee, that girl would have been worshipping idols at this moment."

"'Blessed is the man that trusteth in Adonai,'" softly said Abraham. "He could have helped it, I suppose."

"Aye, and happy is that woman that hath a wise man to her husband!" responded Licorice, irreverently. "Go to sleep, for the sake of Jael the wife of Heber the Kenite, or I shall get up and chop thy head off, for thou art not a whit better than Sisera!"

Perhaps Abraham thought it the wisest plan to obey his incensed spouse, for no word of response reached Belasez.

That damsel lay awake for a considerable time. She soon made up her mind to get as much as she could out of her cousin Genta. It was evident that a catechising ordeal awaited her, to the end of discovering a supposed Christian lover; but feeling her conscience quite clear on that count, Belasez was only disturbed at the possible revelation of her change of faith. She could, however, honestly satisfy Abraham that she had not received baptism. But two points puzzled and deeply interested her. How much had she better say about Bruno?—and, what was this mysterious point which they were afraid she might guess—which seemed to have some unaccountable reference to herself? If Anegay were her sister, as she could no longer doubt, why should her conduct in some way reflect upon Belasez? Suppose Anegay had married a Christian—as she thought most likely from the allusions, and which she knew would be in her parents' eyes disgrace of the deepest dye—or even if Anegay had herself become a Christian, which was a shade worse still,—yet what had that to do with Belasez, and why should it make her so anxious to go back to the Christians?

Then, as to Bruno,—Belasez was conscious in her heart that she loved him very dearly, though her affection was utterly unmingled with any thoughts of matrimony. She would have thought old Hamon as eligible for a husband, when he patted her on the head with a patriarchal benediction. It was altogether a friendly and daughterly class of feeling with which she regarded Father Bruno. But would Abraham enter into that? Was it wise to tell him?

Thinking and planning, Belasez fell asleep.

The ordeal did not come off immediately. It seemed to Belasez as if her father would gladly have avoided it altogether; but she was tolerably sure that her mother would not allow him much peace till it was done.

"Delecresse," she said, the first time she was alone with her brother, "had we ever a sister?"

"Never, to my knowledge," said Delecresse, looking as if he wondered what had put that notion into her head.

Evidently he knew nothing.

Genta, who was constantly coming in and out, for her home was in the same short street, dropped in during the evening, and Belasez carried her off to her own little bed-chamber, which was really a good-sized closet, on the pretext of showing her some new embroidery.

"Genta," she said, " tell me when my sister died."

"Thy sister, Belasez?" Genta's expression was

one of most innocent perplexity. "Hadst thou ever
a sister?"

"Had I not?"

"I never heard of one.

"Think, Genta! was she not called Anegay?"

Genta's shake of the head was decided enough to
settle any question, but Belasez fancied she caught a
momentary flash in her eyes which was by no means
a negation.

But Belasez did not hear a few sentences that were
uttered before Genta left the house.

"Aunt Licorice, what has Belasez got in her
head?"

"Nay, what has she, Genta?"

"I am sure some one has been telling her something. She has asked me to-night if she had not
once a sister, and if her name were not Anegay."

The exclamation in reply was more forcible than
elegant. But that night, as Belasez lay in bed,
through half-closed eyes she saw her mother enter
and hold the lantern to her face. I am sorry to add
that Belasez instantly counterfeited profound sleep;
and Licorice retired with apparent satisfaction.

"Husband!" she heard her mother say, a few
minutes later, "either some son of a Philistine has

told that child something, or she has overheard our words."

"What makes thee think so?" Abraham's tone was one of great distress, if not terror.

"She has been asking questions of Genta. But she has got hold of the wrong pattern—she fancies Anegay was her sister."

"Does she?" replied Abraham, in a tone of sorrowful tenderness.

"There's less harm in her thinking that, than if she knew the truth. Genta showed great good sense: she professed to know nothing at all about it."

"Dissimulation again, Licorice!" came, with a heavy sigh, from Abraham.

"Hold thy tongue! Where should we be without it?"

Abraham made no answer. But early on the following morning he summoned Belasez to the little porch-chamber, and she went with her heart beating.

As she suspected, the catechism was now to be gone through. But poor Abraham was the more timid of the two. He was so evidently unwilling to speak, and so regretfully tender, that Belasez's heart warmed, and she lost all her shyness. Of course, she told him more than she otherwise would have done.

Belasez denied the existence of any Christian lover, or indeed of any lover at all, with such clear, honest eyes, that Abraham could not but believe her. But, he urged, had she ever seen any man in the Castle, to speak to him?

"Yes," said Belasez frankly. "Not while the Lady was there. But during her absence, Sir Richard de Clare had been three times in the bower, and the priests had given lessons to the damsels in the ante-chamber."

"Did any of these ever speak to thee?"

"Sir Richard never spoke to me but twice, further than to say 'Good morrow.' Once he admired a pattern I was working, and once he asked me, when I came in from the leads, if it were raining."

"Didst thou care for him, my daughter?"

"Not in the least," said Belasez, "nor he for me. I rather think Damsel Margaret was his attraction."

Her father seemed satisfied on that point.

"And these priests? How many were there?"

Belasez told him. "Master Aristoteles the physician, and Father Nicholas, and Father Warner, chaplains of my Lord the Earl; and the chaplain of the Lady."

She hardly knew what instinct made her unwilling to utter Father Bruno's name; and, most unintentionally, she blushed.

"Oh!" said Abraham to himself, "the Lady's chaplain is the dangerous person.—Are they old men, my child?"

"None of them is either very old or very young, Father."

"Describe them to me, I pray thee."

"Master Aristoteles I cannot describe, for I have only heard his voice. Father Nicholas is about fifty, I should think: a kindly sort of man, but immersed in his books, and caring for little beside. Father Warner is not pleasant; all the girls were very much afraid of him."

"And the chaplain of the Lady?"

"He is forty or more, I should suppose: tall and slender, eyes and hair dark; a very pleasant man to speak with."

"I am afraid so!" was Abraham's internal comment.—"And his name, daughter?"

"Father Bruno."

"*What?*" Abraham had risen, with outspread

hands, as though he would fain push away some unwelcome and horrible thing.

Belasez repeated the name.

" Bruno !—de Malpas ? "

" I never heard of any name but Bruno."

" Has he talked with thee ? " Abraham's whole manner showed agitation.

" Much."

" Upon what subjects ? "

Belasez would gladly have avoided that question.

" Different subjects," she said, evasively.

" Tell me what he said when he first met thee."

" He seemed much distressed, I knew not at what, and murmured that my face painfully reminded him of somebody."

" Ah !—Belasez, didst thou know whom ? "

" Not till I came home," she said in a low tone.

" *Ay de mi !* What hast thou heard since thy coming home ? "

Belasez resolved to speak the truth. She had been struck by her father's hints that some terrible mischief had come from not speaking it ; and she thought that perhaps open confession on her part might lead to confidence on his.

" I overheard you and my mother talking at

night," she said. "I gathered that the somebody whom I was like was my sister, and that her name was Anegay; and I thought she had either become a Christian, or had wedded a Christian. Father, may I know?"

"My little Belasez," he said, with deep feeling, "thou knowest all but the one thing thou must not know. There was one called Anegay. But she was not thy sister. Let the rest be silence to thee."

It seemed to cost Abraham immense pain to say even so much as this. He sat quiet for a moment, his face working pitifully.

"Little Belasez," he said again, "didst thou like that man?"

"I think I loved him," was her soft answer.

Abraham's gesture, which she thought indicated despair and anguish, roused her to explain.

"Father," she said hastily, "I do not mean anything wrong or foolish. I loved Father Bruno with a deep, reverential love—such as I give you."

"Such as thou givest me—O Belasez!"

Belasez thought he was hurt by her comparison of her love for him to that of her love for a mere stranger.

"Father, how shall I explain? I meant"——

"My poor child, I need no explanation. Thou hast been more righteous than we. Belasez, the truth is hidden from thee because thou art too near it to behold it. My poor, poor child!" And suddenly rising, Abraham lifted up his arms in the attitude of prayer. "O Thou that doest wonders, Thou hast made the wrath of man to praise Thee. How unsearchable are Thy judgments, and Thy ways past finding out!" Then he laid his hand upon Belasez's head.

"It is Adonai," he said. "Let Him do what seemeth Him good. He said unto Shimei, Curse David. Methinks He hath said to thee, Love Bruno. The Holy One forbid that I should grudge the love of—of our child, to the desolate heart which we made desolate. Adonai knows, and He only, whether we did good or bad. Pray to Him, my Belasez, to forgive that one among us who truly needs His forgiveness!"

And Abraham hurried from the room, as if he were afraid to trust himself, lest if he stayed he should say something which he might afterwards regret bitterly.

CHAPTER IX.

PAYING THE BILL.

> " 'Tis hard when young heart, singing songs of to-morrow,
>   Is suddenly met by the old hag, Sorrow."
>
> *—Leigh Hunt.*

FATHER BRUNO was walking slowly, with his hands one in the other behind him, about a mile from Bury Castle. It was a lovely morning in April, and, though alone, he had no fear of high-waymen; for he would have been a bold sinner indeed who, in 1236, meddled with a priest for his harm. An absent-minded man was Father Bruno, at all times when he was free to indulge in medita-tion. For to him

> " The future was all dark,
>   And the past a troubled sea,
> And Memory sat in his heart
>   Wailing where Hope should be."

He was given to murmuring his thoughts half aloud when in solitude; and he was doing it now. They oscillated from one to the other of two subjects, closely associated in his mind. One was Belasez: the other was a memory of his sorrowful past, a fair girl-face, the likeness to which had struck him so distressingly in hers, and which would never fade from his memory "till God's love set her at his side again."

"What will become of the maiden?" he whispered to himself. "So like, so like!—just what my Beatrice might have been, if—nay, Thou art wise, O Lord! It is I who am blind and ignorant. Aye, and just the same age! She must be the infant of whom Licorice spoke: she was then in the cradle, I remember. She said that if Beatrice had lived, they might have been like twin sisters. Well, well! Aye, and it is well. For Anegay has found her in Heaven, safe from sin and sorrow, from tempest and temptation, with Christ for evermore.

"'*O mea, spes mea, O Syon aurea, ut clarior oro!*'

"And what does it matter for me, during these few and evil days that are left of this lower life? True, the wilderness is painful: but it will be over soon. True, my spirit is worn and weary: but the rest of the New Jerusalem will soon restore me. True, I am weak, poor, blind, ignorant, lonely, sorrowful : but my Lord is strength, wealth, light, wisdom, love, and joyfulness. Never canst thou be loveless, Bruno de Malpas, while the deathless love of Christ endureth ; never canst thou be lonely and forlorn, whilst thou hast His company who is the sunlight of Heaven. Perhaps it would not have been good for me, had my beloved stayed with me. Nay, since He saw it good, it can be no perhaps, but a certainty. I suppose I should have valued Him less, had my jewel-casket remained full. Aye, Thou hast done well, my Lord ! Pardon Thy servant if at times the journey grows very weary to his weak human feet, and he longs for a draught of the sweet waters of earthly love which Thou hast permitted to dry up. Grant him fresh draughts of that Living Water whereof he that drinketh shall thirst no more. Hold Thou me up, and I shall be safe !

"Was I right in refusing to baptize the maiden ? Verily, it would have been rich revenge on Licorice. I had no right, as I told her, to suffer the innocence of her chrism to be soiled with the evil passions which were sin in me. Yet had I any right to deny her the grace of holy baptism, because I was not free from evil passions? Oh, how hard it is to find the straight road!

"Poor little maiden! What will become of her now? I fear the impressions that have been made on her will soon be stifled in the poisonous atmosphere into which she is gone. And I cannot bear to think of her as a lost soul, with that face so like my Anegay, and that voice——

"Now, shame upon thee, Bruno de Malpas! Is Belasez more to thee than to Him that died for her? Canst thou not trust Him who giveth unto His sheep eternal life, not to allow this white lamb to be plucked out of His hand? O Lord, increase my faith!—for it is very low. I am one of the very weakest of Thy disciples. Yet I am Thine. Lord, Thou knowest all things; Thou knowest that I love Thee!"

During the time occupied by these reflections, Bruno had been instinctively approaching the Castle, and he looked up suddenly as he was conscious of a clang of arms and a confused medley of voices, not in very peaceful tones, breaking in upon his meditations. He now perceived that the drawbridge was thronged with armed men, the portcullis drawn up, and the courtyard beyond full of soldiers in mail.

"What is the matter, friend William?" asked Bruno of the porter at the outer gate.

"Nay, the saints wot, good Father, not I: but of this am I very sure, that some mischance is come to my Lord. You were a wise man if you kept away."

"Not so," was Bruno's answer, as he passed on: "it is the hireling, not the shepherd, that fleeth from the wolf, and leaveth the sheep to be scattered."

He made his way easily into the hall, for no one thought of staying a priest. The lower end was thronged with soldiers. On the daïs stood Sir Piers de Rievaulx and half-a-dozen more, confronting Earl Hubert, who wore an expression of baffled amazement. Just behind him stood the Countess, evidently possessed by fear and anguish; Sir John de Burgh, with his hand upon his sword; Doucebelle, very white and frightened; and furthest in the background, Sir Richard de Clare, who clasped in his arms the fainting form of Margaret, and bent his head over her with a look of agonised tenderness.

"Words are fine things, my Lord of Kent," was the first sentence distinguishable to Father Bruno, and the spokesman was Sir Piers. "But I beg you to remember that it is of no earthly use talking to *me* in this strain. If you can succeed in convincing my Lord the King that you had no hand in this business, well!"— and Sir Piers' shoulders went up towards his ears, in a manner which indicated that result to be far from what he expected. "But those two young fools don't attempt to deny it, and their faces would give them the lie if they did. As for my Lady"——

The Countess sprang forward and threw herself on her knees, clinging to the arm of her husband, while she passionately addressed herself to both.

"Sir Piers, on my life and honour, my Lord knew nothing of this! It was done while he was away with the Lord King at Merton.—It was my doing, my Lord, mine! And it is true, what Sir Piers tells you. My daughter has gone too far with Sir Richard de Clare, ever to be married to another."[1]

Sir Piers stood listening with a rather amused set of the lips, as if he thought the scene very effective. To him, the human agony before his eyes was no more than a play enacted for his entertainment. Of course it was in the way of business; but Sir Piers' principle was to get as much diversion out of his business as he could.

---

[1] The confession of the Countess is historical. She took the whole blame upon herself.

"Very good indeed, Lady," said that worthy Minister. "Your confession may spare you some annoyance. But as to your Lord, it will do nothing. You hardly expect us to swallow this pretty little fiction, I suppose? If you do, I beg you will undeceive yourself.—Officers, do your duty." The officers had evidently received previous instructions, for they at once laid their hands on the shoulders of Earl Hubert and Sir Richard. The half-insensible Margaret was roused into life by the attempt to take her bridegroom from her. With a cry that might have touched any heart but that of Sir Piers de Rievaulx, she flung her arms around him and held him close.

Apparently the officers were touched, for they stopped and looked at their chief for further orders.

"Coward loons as ye are!—are ye frightened of a girl?" said Sir Piers with a harsh laugh, and he came forward himself. "Lady Margaret, there is no need to injure you unless you choose. Please yourself. I am going to arrest this young knight."

But for one second, Sir Piers waited himself. Those around mistook it for that knightly courtesy of which there was none in him. They did not know that suddenly, to him, out of Margaret's pleading eyes looked the eyes of the dead sister, Serena de Rievaulx, and it seemed to him as though soft child-fingers held him off for an instant. He had never loved any mortal thing but that dead child.

With one passionate, pleading gaze at Sir Piers, Margaret laid her head on the breast of Sir Richard, and sobbed as though her heart were breaking.

"My Lord, my Lord!" came, painfully mixed with long-drawn sobs, from the lips of the young bride. "My own, own Richard! And only two months since we were married!—Have you the heart to part us?" she cried, suddenly turning to Sir Piers. "Did you never love any one?"

"Never, Madam." For once in his life, Sir Piers spoke truth. Never—except Serena: and not much then.

"Brute!" And with this calumnious epithet—for brutes can love dearly—Margaret resumed her former attitude.

"Lady Margaret, I must trouble you," said Sir Piers, in tones of hardness veneered with civility.

"My darling, you must let me go," interposed the young Earl of Gloucester, who seemed scarcely less miserable than his bride.

"Magot, my child, we may not stay justice," said the distressed tones of her father.

Yet she held tight until Sir Piers tore her away.

"Look to the damsel," he condescended to say, with a glance at Doucebelle and Bruno. "Oh, ha!—where is the priest that blessed this wedding? I must have him."

"There was no priest," sobbed the Countess, lifting her head from her husband's arm, where she had let it sink: "it was *per verba de presenti.*"

"That we will see," was the cool response of Sir Piers. "Take all the priests, Sir Drew.—Now, my Lady!"

"Fare thee well, my jewel," said Earl Hubert, kissing the brow of the Countess. "Poor little Magot! —farewell, too."

"Sir Hubert, my Lord, forgive me! I meant no ill."

"Forgive thee?" said the Earl, with a smile, and again kissing his wife's brow. "I could not do otherwise, my Margaret.—Now, Sir Piers, we are your prisoners."

"These little amenities being disposed of," sneered Sir Piers. "I suppose women must cry over something:—kind, I should think, to give them something to cry about.—March out the prisoners."

Father Nicholas had been discovered in his study, engaged in the deepest meditation on a grammatical crux; and had received the news of his arrest with a blank horror and amazement very laughable in the eyes of Sir Piers. Master Aristoteles was pounding rhubarb with his sleeves turned up, and required some convincing that he was not wanted professionally. Father Warner was no where to be found. The three priests were spared fetters in consideration of their sacred character: both the Earls were heavily ironed. And so the armed band, with their prisoners, marched away from the Castle.

The feelings of the prisoners were diverse. Father Nicholas was simply astonished beyond any power of words to convey. Master Aristoteles was convinced that the recent physical disturbances in the atmosphere were more than enough to account for the whole affair. Earl Hubert felt sure that his old enemy, the Bishop of Winchester, was at the bottom of it. Earl Richard was disposed to think the same. Father Bruno alone looked upwards, and saw God.

But assuredly no one of them saw the moving cause in that tall, stern, silent Jewish youth, and the last idea that ever entered the mind of Richard de Clare was to associate this great grief of his life with the boyish trick he had played on Delecresse two years before.

For the great grief of Richard's life this sorrow was. Through the six-and-twenty years which remained of his mortal span, he never forgot it, and he never forgave it.

It proved the easiest thing in the world to convince King Henry that he had not intended Richard to marry Margaret. Had his dearly-beloved uncle, the Bishop of Valentia, held up before him a black cloth, and said, "This is white," His Majesty would merely have wondered what could be the matter with his eyes.

The next point was to persuade that royal and most deceivable individual that he had entertained an earnest desire to see Richard married to a Princess of Savoy, a cousin of the Queen. This, also, was not difficult. The third lesson instilled into him was that, Richard having thought proper to render this impossible by choosing for himself, he, King Henry, was a cruelly-injured and unpardonably insulted man. His Majesty swallowed them all as glibly as possible. The metal being thus fused to the proper state, the prisoners were brought before their affronted Sovereign in person.

They were tried in inverse order, according to importance. Father Bruno could prove, without much difficulty, that the obnoxious marriage had taken place, on the showing of the prosecution itself, before he had entered the household. His penalty was the light one of discharge from the Countess's service. That he deserved no penalty at all was not taken into consideration. The Crown could not so far err as to bring a charge against an entirely innocent man. The verdict, therefore, in Father Bruno's case resembled that of the famous jury who returned as theirs, " Not Guilty, but we hope he won't do it again."

Master Aristoteles was next placed in the dock, and had the honour of amusing the Court. His asseverations of innocent ignorance were so mixed up with dissertations on the virtues of savin and betony, and lamenting references to the last eclipse, which might have warned him of what was coming on him, that the Court condescended to relax into a smile, and let the simple man go with the light sentence of six months' imprisonment. At a subsequent period in his life, Master Aristoteles was wont to say that this sentence was the best thing that ever happened to him, since the enforced meditation and idleness had enabled him to think out his grand discovery that the dust which gathered on beams of chestnut wood was an infallible specific for fever. He had since treated three fever patients in this manner, and not one of them had died. Whether the patients would have recovered without the dust, and with being so much let alone, Master Aristoteles did not concern himself.

Next came Father Nicholas. A light sentence also sufficed for him, not on account of his innocence, but because his friend the Abbot of Ham was a friend of the Bishop of Winchester.

Earl Hubert of Kent was then tried. The animus of his accusers was plainly shown, for they brought up again all the old hackneyed charges on account of which he had been pardoned years before—for some of them more than once. The affront offered to the King by the Earl's marriage with Margaret of Scotland, the fact that she and his third wife were within the forbidden degrees, and that no dispensation had been obtained ; these were renewed, with all the other disproved and spiteful accusations of old time. But the head and front of the offending, in this instance, was of course the marriage of his daughter. It did not make much difference that

Hubert calmly swore that he had never known of the marriage, either before or after, except what he had learned from the simple statement of the Countess his wife, to the effect that it had been contracted at Bury St. Edmund's, during his absence at Merton. The fervent intercession of Hubert's friends, moved by the passionate entreaties of the Countess, did not make much difference either; but what did make a good deal was that the Earl (who knew his royal master) offered a heavy golden bribe for pardon of the crime he had not committed. King Henry thereupon condescended to announce that in consideration of the effect produced upon his compassionate heart by the piteous intercession of the prisoner's friends,

> ——" His fury should abate, and he
> The crowns would take."

Earl Hubert therefore received a most gracious pardon, and was permitted to return (minus the money) to the bosom of his distracted family.

But the heaviest vengeance fell on the young head of Richard de Clare, and through him on the fair girl with the cedar hair, whose worst crime was that she had loved him. It was not vengeance that could be weighed like Hubert's coins, or told on the clock like the imprisonment of his physician. It was counted out, throb by throb, in the agony of two human hearts, one fiercely stabbed and artificially healed, and the other left to bleed to death like a wounded doe.

The King's first step was to procure a solemn Papal sentence of divorce between Richard and Margaret. Their consent, of course, was neither asked nor thought needful. His Majesty's advisers allowed him — and Richard — a little rest then, before they thought it necessary to do any thing more.

The result of the trial was to leave Father Bruno homeless. He returned to his monastery at Lincoln, and sought the leave of his Superior to be transferred to the Convent of the Order at Norwich. His heart still yearned over Belasez, with a tenderness which was half of Heaven and half of earth. Yet he knew that in all probability he would never find it possible to cross her path. Well! let him do what he could, and leave the rest with God. If He meant them to meet, meet they must, though Satan and all his angels combined to bar the way.

"Wife!"

"May thy beard be shaven! I was just dropping off. Well?"

It had taken Abraham a long while to summon up his courage to make what he felt would be to Licorice an unwelcome communication. He was rather dismayed to find it so badly received at the first step.

"Do go on, thou weariest of old jackdaws! I'm half asleep."

"I have spoken to the child, Licorice."

"As if thou couldst not have said that half an hour ago! Well, how do matters stand?"

"There is one person in particular whom she is sorry to leave."

"Of course there is! I saw that as plain as the barber's pole across the street. Didn't I tell thee so? Is it some young Christian gallant, and who is he? Blessed be the memory of Abraham our father!—why did we ever let that girl go to Bury?"

"It is not as thou art fearing, wife. But—it is worse."

"Worse!" Licorice seemed wide awake enough now. "Why, what could there be worse, unless she had married a Christian, or had abjured her faith?"

"Wife, this is worse. She has seen—him."

"De Malpas?" The name was almost hissed from the lips of Licorice.

"The same. It was to be, Licorice. Adonai knows why! But it is evident they were fated to meet."

"What did the viper tell her?"

"I do not gather that he told her any thing, except that she brought a face to his memory that he had known of old. She fancies—and so of course does he—that it was her sister."

A low, peculiar laugh from her mother made Belasez's blood curdle as she lay listening. There seemed so much more of the fiend in it than the angel.

"What an ass he must be, never to guess the truth!"

"She wants to know the truth, wife. She asked me if she might not."

"Thou let it alone. I'll cook up a nice little story, that will set her mind at rest."

"O Licorice!—more deception yet?"

"Deception! Why, wouldst thou tell her the truth? Just go to her now, and wake her, and let her know that she is "——

Belasez strained her ears to their utmost, but the

words which followed could not be heard from her mother's dropped tones.

"What would follow—eh?" demanded Licorice, raising her voice again.

"Adonai knows!" said Abraham, sadly. "But I suppose we could not keep her long."

"I should think not! Thou canst go and tell the Mayor, and see what he and his catchpolls will say. Wouldn't there be a pretty ferment? Old man, it would cost thee thy life, and mine also. Give over talking about lies as if thou wert one of the cherubim (I'll let thee know when I think there's any danger of it), and show a little spice of prudence, like a craftsman of middle earth as thou art. More deception! Of course there is more deception. A man had better keep off a slide to begin with, if he does not want to be carried down it."

"The child fancies, Licorice, that Anegay was her sister, and that she either became a Christian or married one. She has no idea of any thing more."

"Who told her Anegay's name?"

"I cannot imagine. It might be Bruno."

"We have always been so careful to keep it from her hearing."

There was a pause.

"Didst thou find the Christian dog had tampered with her faith?"

"I don't know, Licorice. I could not get that out of her."

"Then he has, no doubt. I'll get it out of her."
Belasez trembled at the threat.

"Any thing more, old man? If not, I'll go to sleep again."

"Licorice," said Abraham in a low voice, "the child said she loved him—as she loves me."

"May he be buried in a dunghill! What witch-craft has he used to them both?"

"It touched me so, wife, I could hardly speak to her. She did not know why."

"Abraham, do give over thy sentimental stuff! Nothing ever touches me!"

"I doubt if it do," was Abraham's dry answer.

"Such a rabbit as thou art!—as frightened as a hare, and as soft as a bag of duck's down. I'm going to sleep."

And Belasez heard no more. She woke, however, the next morning, with that uncomfortable conviction of something disagreeable about to happen, with which all human beings are more or less familiar. It gradually dawned upon her that

Licorice was going to "get it out of her," and was likewise about to devise a false tale for her especial benefit. She had not heard two sentences which passed between her parents before she woke, or she might have been still more on her guard.

"Licorice, thou must take care what thou sayest to that child. I told her that Anegay was not her sister."

"Just what might have been expected of thee, my paragon of wisdom! Well, never mind. I'll tell her she was her aunt. That will do as well."

When the daily cleaning, dusting, cooking, and baking were duly completed, Licorice made Belasez's heart flutter by a command to attend her in the little porch-chamber.

"Belasez," she began, in tones so amiable that Belasez would instantly have suspected a trap, had she overheard nothing,—for Licorice's character was well known to her—"Belasez, I hear from thy father that thou hast heard some foolish gossip touching one Anegay, that was a kinswoman of thine, and thou art desirous of knowing the truth. Thou shalt know it now. Indeed, there was no reason to hide it from thee further than this, that the tale being a painful one, thy father and I have not cared to talk about it. This Anegay was the sister of Abraham thy father, and therefore thine aunt."

Belasez, who had been imagining that Anegay might have been her father's sister, at once mentally decided that she was not. She had noticed that Abraham's references to the dead girl were made with far more indication of love and regret than those of Licorice: and she had fancied that this might be due to the existence of relationship on his part and not on hers. She now concluded that it was simply a question of character. But who Anegay was, was a point left as much in the dark as ever.

"She was a great friend of mine, daughter, and I loved her very dearly," said Licorice, applying one hand to her perfectly dry eyes—a proceeding which imparted to Belasez, who knew that such terms from her were generally to be interpreted by the rule of contrary, a strong impression that she had hated her. "And at that time thy father dwelt at Lincoln—it was before we were married, thou knowest—and Anegay, being an only and motherless daughter, used to spend much of her time with me. I cannot quite tell thee how, for indeed it was a puzzle to myself, but Anegay became acquainted with a Christian maiden whose name was Beatrice"—

A peculiar twinkle in the eyes of Licorice caused Belasez to feel especially doubtful of the truth of this part of the story.

"And who had a brother," pursued Licorice, "a young Christian squire, but as thou shalt hear, a most wicked and artful man."

Belasez at once set down the unknown squire as a model of all the cardinal virtues.

"Thou art well aware, Belasez, my child, that these idolaters practise the Black Art, and are versed in spells which they can cast over all unfortunate persons who are so luckless as to come within their influence."

There had been a time when Belasez believed this, and many more charges brought against the Christians, just as they in their turn believed similar calumnies against the Jews. But the months spent at Bury Castle, unconsciously to herself till it was done, had shaken and uprooted many prejudices, leaving her with the simple conviction that Jews and Christians were all fallible human beings, very much of the same stamp, some better than others, but good and bad to be found in both camps. Licorice, however, was by no means the person to whom she chose to impart such impressions. There had never been any confidence or communion of spirit between them. In fact, they were cast in such different moulds that it was hardly possible there should be any. Licorice was a sweeping and cooking machine, whose intellect was wholly uncultivated, and whose imagination all ran into cunning and deceit. Belasez was an article of much finer quality, both mentally and morally. The only person in her own family with whom she could exchange thought or feeling was Abraham; and he was not her equal, though he came the nearest to it.

It had often distressed Belasez that her mother and she seemed to have so little in common. Many times she had tried hard to scold herself into more love for Licorice, and had found the process a sheer impossibility. She had now given it up with a sorrowful recognition that it was not to be done, but a firm conviction that it was her own fault, and that she ought to be very penitent for such hardness of heart.

"It seems to me," continued Licorice, "that this bad young man, whose name was De Malpas, must have cast a spell on our poor, unhappy Anegay. For how else could a daughter of Israel come to love so vile an insect as one of the accursed Goyim?

"For she did love him, Belasez; and a bitter grief and disgrace it was to all her friends. Of course I need not say that the idea of a marriage between them was an odious impossibility. The only resource was to take Anegay away from Lincoln, where she would learn to forget all about the creeping creatures, and return to her duty as a servant of the Living and Eternal One. It was at that time that I and thy father were wedded; and we then came to live in Norwich, bringing Anegay with us."

Licorice paused, as if her tale were finished. It sounded specious : but how much of it was true ?

"And did she forget him, Mother ? "

"Of course she did, Belasez. It was her duty."

Belasez privately thought that people did not always do their duty, and that such a duty as this would be extremely hard to do.

"Was she ever married, Mother, if you please ? "

"She married a young Jew, my dear, named Aaron the son of Leo, and died soon after the birth of her first child," said Licorice, glibly.

"And was she really happy, Mother ? "

"Happy ! Of course she was. She had no business to be any thing else."

Belasez was silent, but not in the least convinced.

"Thou seest now, my Belasez, why I was so much afraid of thy visits to Bury. I well know thou art a discreet maiden, and entirely to be trusted so far as thine ability goes : but what can such qualities avail thee against magic ? I have heard of a grand-aunt of mine, whom a Christian by this means glued to the settle, and for three years she could not rise from it, until the wicked spell was dissolved. I do not mistrust thee, good daughter: I do but warn thee."

And Licorice rose with a manner which indicated the termination of the interview, apparently thinking it better to reserve the religious question for another time.

"May I ask one other question, Mother ?—what became of the maiden Beatrice and her brother ? "

Licorice's eyes twinkled again. Belasez listened for the answer on the principle of the Irishman who looked at the guide-post to see where the road did not lead.

"The squire was killed fighting the Saracens, I believe. I do not know what became of the maiden."

Licorice disappeared.

"The squire was not killed, I am sure," said Belasez to herself. "It is Father Bruno."

Left alone, Belasez reviewed her very doubtful information. Anegay was not her sister, and probably not her aunt. That she had loved Bruno was sure to be true; and that she had been forcibly separated from him was only too likely. But her subsequent marriage to Aaron, and the very existence of Beatrice, were in Belasez's eyes purely fictitious details, introduced to make the events dovetail nicely. Why she doubted the latter point she could hardly have told. It was really due to that gleam in her mother's eyes, which she invariably put on when she was launching out rather more boldly than usual into the sea of fiction. Yet there seemed no reason for the invention of Beatrice, if she were not a real person.

But was the story which Belasez had heard sufficient to explain all the allusions which she had overheard? She went over them, one by one, as they recurred to her memory, and decided that it was. She had heard nothing from her parents, nothing from Bruno, which contradicted it in the least. Why, then, this uncomfortable, instinctive feeling that something was left behind which had not been told her?

Belasez was lying awake in bed when she reached

that point: and a moment after, she sprang to a sitting posture.

Yes, there was something behind!

What had she heard that, if it were known, would cost Abraham and Licorice their lives? What had she heard which explained those mysterious allusions to herself as personally concerned in the story? Why would she leave them instantly if she knew all? What was that one point which Abraham had distinctly told her she must not know,—which Licorice expressed such anxiety that she should not even guess?

There was not much sleep for Belasez that night.

CHAPTER X.

"Guardami ben'! Ben' son', ben' son' Beatrice."
—*Dante.*

"WELL, now, this is provoking!"

"What is the matter, wife?" And Abraham looked up from a bale of silk which he was packing.

"Why, here has Genta been and taken the fever; and there is not a soul but me to go and nurse her."

"There is Esterote, her brother's wife."

"There isn't! Esterote has her baby to look to. Dost thou expect her to carry infection to him?"

"What is to be done?" demanded Abraham, blankly. "Could not Pucella be had, or old Cuntessa?"

"Old Cuntessa is engaged as nurse for Rosia the wife of Bonamy the rich usurer, and Pucella would be no good,—she's as frightened of the fever as a chicken, and she has never had it."

" Well, thou hast had it."

"I ? Oh, I'm not frightened a bit—not of that. I am tremendously afraid of thee."

"Of me ? I shall not hinder thee, Licorice. I do not think it likely thou wouldst take it."

"*Ay de mi*, canst thou not understand ? I might as well leave a thief to take care of my gold carcanet as leave thee alone with Belasez. I shall come back to find the child gone off with some vile dog of a Christian, and thee tearing thy garments, like a blind, blundering bat as thou art."

" Bats don't tear their garments, wife."

"They run their heads upon every stone they come across. And so dost thou."

"Wife, dost thou not think we might speak out honestly like true men, and trust the All-Merciful with the child's future ?"

" Well, if ever I did see a lame, wall-eyed, broken-kneed old pack-ass, he was called Abraham the son of Ursel ! "

And Licorice stood with uplifted hands, gazing on her lord and master in an attitude of pitying astonishment.

"I do believe, thou moon-cast shadow of a man, if Bruno de Malpas were to walk in and ask for her, thou wouldst just say, 'Here she is, O my Lord: do what thou wilt with thy slave.'"

"I think, Licorice, it would break my heart. But we have let him break his for eighteen years. And if it came to breaking hers—What wicked thing did he do, wife, that we should have used him thus?"

"What! canst thou ask me? Did he not presume to lay unclean hands on a daughter of Israel, of whom saith the Holy One, 'Ye shall not give her unto the heathen'?"

"I do not think De Malpas was a heathen."

"Hast thou been to the creeping thing up yonder and begged to be baptized to-morrow?"

This was a complimentary allusion to that Right Reverend person, the Bishop of Norwich.

"Nay, Licorice, I am as true to the faith as thou."

"*Ay de mi!* I must have put on my gown wrong side out, to make thee say so." And Licorice pretended to make a close examination of her skirt, as if to discover whether this was the case.

"Licorice, is it not written, 'Cursed be their wrath, for it was cruel?' Thine was, wife."

"Whatever has come to thy conscience? It quietly

went to sleep for eighteen years; and now, all at once, it comes alive and awake!"

Abraham winced, as though he felt the taunt true.

"'Better late than never,' wife."

"That is a Christian saying."

"May be.   It is true."

"Well!"   And Licorice's hands were thrust out from her, as if she were casting off drops of water. "I've done my best.   I shall let it alone now.   Genta must be nursed: and I cannot bring infection home. And after all, the girl is thine, not mine.   Thou must take thine own way.   But I shall bid her good-bye for ever: for I have no hope of seeing her again."

Abraham made no answer, unless his troubled eyes and quivering lips did so for him.   But the night closed in upon a very quiet chamber, owing to the absence of Licorice.   Delecresse sat studying, with a book open before him: Belasez was busied with embroidery.   Abraham was idle, so far as his hands were concerned; but any one who had studied him for a minute would have seen that his thoughts were very active, and by no means pleasant.

Ten calm days passed over, and nothing happened. They heard, through neighbours, that Genta was going through all the phases of a tedious illness, and that Licorice was a most attentive and valuable nurse.

At the end of those ten days, Delecresse came in with an order for some of the exquisite broidery which only Belasez could execute. It was wanted for the rich usurer's wife, Rosia: and she wished Belasez to come to her with specimens of various patterns, so that she might select the one she preferred.

A walk through the city was an agreeable and unusual break in the monotony of existence; and Rosia's house was quite at the other end of the Jews' quarter. Belasez prepared to go out with much alacrity. Her father escorted her himself, leaving Delecresse to mind the shop.

The embroidery was exhibited, the pattern chosen, and they were nearly half-way at home, when they were overtaken by a sudden hailstorm, and took refuge in the lych-gate of a church. It was growing dusk, and they had not perceived the presence of a third person,—like themselves, a refugee from the storm.

"This is heavy!" said Abraham, as the hailstones came pouring and dancing down.

"I am afraid we shall not get home till late," was the response of his daughter.

"No, not till late," said Abraham, absently.

"Belasez!" came softly from behind her.

She turned round quickly, her hands held out in greeting, her eyes sparkling, delight written on every feature of her face.

"Father Bruno! I never knew you were in Norwich."

"I have not been here long, my child. I wondered if we should ever meet."

Ah, little idea had Belasez how that meeting had been imagined, longed for, prayed for, through all those weary weeks. She glanced at her father, suddenly remembering that her warm welcome to the Christian priest was not likely to be much approved by him. Bruno's eyes followed hers.

"Abraham!" he said, in tones which sounded like a mixture of friendship and deprecation.

Abraham had bent down as though he were cowering from an expected blow. Now he lifted himself up, and held out his hand.

"Bruno de Malpas, thou art welcome, if God hath sent thee."

"God sends all events," answered the priest, accepting the offered hand.

"Aye, I am trying to learn that," replied Abraham, in a voice of great pain. "For at times He sends that which breaks the heart."

"That He may heal it, my father."

The title, from Bruno's lips, surprised and puzzled Belasez.

"It may be so," said Abraham in a rather hopeless tone. "'It is Adonai; let Him do what seemeth Him good.' So thou hast made friends with—my Belasez."

"I did not know she was thine when I made friends with her," said Bruno, with that quiet smile of his which had always seemed to Belasez at once so sweet and so sad.

"'Did not know'? No, I suppose not. Ah, yes, yes! 'Did not know'!"

"Does this child know my history?" was Bruno's next question.

"She knows," said Abraham in a troubled voice, "nearly as much as thou knowest."

"Then she knows all?"

"Nay, she knows nothing."

"You speak in riddles, my father."

"My son, I am about to do that which will break my heart. Nay,—God is about to do it. Let

me put it thus, or I shall not know how to bear
it."

"I have no wish nor intention to trouble you,
my father," said Bruno hastily. "If I might, now
and then, see this child,—to tell truth, it would be a
great pleasure and solace to me: for I have learned
to love her,—just the years of my Beatrice, just
what Beatrice might have grown to be. Yet—if I
speak I must speak honestly—give me leave to see
Belasez, only on the understanding that I may speak
to her of Christ. She is dear as any thing in this
dreary world, but He is dearer than the world and
all that is in it. If I may not do this, let me say
farewell, and see her no more."

"Thou hast spoken to her—of the Nazarene?"
asked Abraham in a low tone.

"I have," was Bruno's frank reply.

"Thou hast taught her the Christian faith?"

"So far as I could do it."

Belasez stood trembling. Yet Abraham did not
seem angry.

"Thou hast baptized her, perhaps?"

"No. That I have not."

"Not?—why not?"

"She was fit for it in my eyes; and—may I say

it, Belasez?—she was willing But my hands were not clean enough. I felt that I could not repress a sensation of triumphing over Licorice, if I baptized her daughter. May the Lord forgive me if I erred, but I did not dare to do it."

"O my son, my son!" broke from Abraham. "Thou hast been more righteous than I. Come home with me, and tell the story to Belasez thyself; and then—Adonai, Thou knowest. Help me to do Thy will!"

Bruno was evidently much astonished, and not a little perplexed at Abraham's speech; but he followed him quietly. The storm was over now, and they gained home and the chamber over the porch without coming in contact with Delecresse. Abraham left Bruno there, while he desired Belasez to take off her wet things and rejoin them. Meantime he changed his coat, and carried up wine and cake to his guest. But when Belasez reappeared, Abraham drew the bolt, and closed the inner baize door which shut out all sound.

"Now, Bruno de Malpas," he said, "tell thy story."

And sitting down at the table, he laid his arms on it, and hid his face upon it.

"But, my father, dost thou wish *her* to hear it?"

"The Blessed One does, I believe. She has heard as yet but a garbled version. I wish what He wishes."

"Amen!" ejaculated Bruno. And he turned to Belasez.

She, on her part, felt too much astonished for words. If any thing could surprise her more than that Bruno should be actually invited to tell the tapued story, it was the calm way in which Abraham received the intimation that she had all but professed Christianity. Mortal anger and scathing contempt she could have understood and expected; but this was utterly beyond her.

"Belasez," said Bruno, "years ago, before thou wert born, thy father had another daughter, and her name was Anegay."

"Father! you said Anegay was not my sister!" came in surprised accents from Belasez. But a choking sob was the only answer from Abraham.

"She was not the daughter of thy mother, Belasez; but of thy father's first wife, whose name was Floria. Perhaps he meant that. She was twenty years older than thou. And—I need not make my tale long— we met, Belasez, and we loved each other. I told her of Christ, and she became a Christian, and received holy baptism at my hands. By that time thy father had wedded thy mother. As thou knowest, she is a staunch Jewess; and though she did not by any means discover all, she did find that Anegay had Christian friends, and forbade her to see them again. Time went on, and we could scarcely ever meet, and Anegay was not very happy. At length, one night, a ring was brought to me which was her usual token, praying me to meet her quickly at the house of Isabel de Fulshaw, where we had usually met before. I went, and found her weeping as though her heart would break. She told me that Licorice had been—not very gentle with her, and had threatened to turn her out of the house the next morning unless she would trample on the cross, as a sign that she abjured all her Christian friends and Christ. That, she said, she could not do. 'I could tread on the piece of wood,' she said, 'and that would be nothing: but my mother means it for a sign of abjuring Christ.' And she earnestly implored me to get her into some nunnery, where she might be safe. Perhaps I ought to have done that. But I offered her another choice of safety. And the next morning, as soon as the canonical hours had dawned, Anegay was my wife."

Abraham spoke here, but without lifting his head. "I was on a journey, Belasez," he said. "I never persecuted my darling—never!"

"No, Belasez," echoed Bruno; "he never did. I believe he was bitterly grieved at her becoming a Christian, but he had no hand in her sufferings at that time. A year or more went on, and the Lord gave us a baby daughter. I baptized her by the name of Beatrice, which was also the name that her mother had received in baptism. She was nearly a month old, when a message came to me from the Bishop, requiring me to come to him, which involved a journey, there and back, of about a week. I went: and I returned—to find my home desolate. Wife, child—even the maid-servant,—all were gone. An old woman, who dwelt in my parish, was in the house, but she could tell me nothing save that a message had come to her from Frethesind the maid, begging her to come and take charge of the house until my return, but not giving a word of explanation. I could think of no place to which my wife would be likely to go, unless her mother had been there, and had either forced or overpersuaded her to return with her. I hurried to Norwich with as much speed as possible. To my surprise, Licorice received me with apparent kindliness, and inquired after Anegay as though no quarrel had ever existed."

Belasez thought, with momentary amusement, that Bruno was not so well acquainted with Licorice as herself.

" I asked in great distress if Anegay were not with her. Licorice assured me she knew nothing of her. ' Then you did not fetch her away?' said I. ' How could I?' she answered. 'I have a baby in the cradle only five weeks old.' Well, I could not tell what to think; her words and looks were those of truth. She was apparently as kind as possible. She showed me her baby—thyself, Belasez; and encouraged me to play with Delecresse, who was then a lively child of three years. I came away, baffled, yet unsatisfied. I should have been better pleased had I seen thy father. But he, I was told, was again absent on one of his business journeys."

" True," was the one word interpolated by Abraham.

" I went to the house of my friend, Walcheline de Fulshaw. He was an apothecary. I told my story to him and to Isabel his wife, desiring their counsel as to the means whereby I should get at the truth. Walcheline seemed perplexed; but Isabel said,

'Father, I think I see how to find out the truth. Dost thou not remember,' she said, turning to her husband, 'the maiden Rosia, daughter of Aaron, whom thou didst heal of her sickness a year past? Let me inquire of her. These Jews all know each other. The child is bright and shrewd, and I am sure she would do what she could out of gratitude to thee.' Walcheline gave consent at once, and a messenger was sent to the house of Aaron, requesting that his daughter would visit Isabel de Fulshaw, who had need of her. The girl came quickly, and very intelligent she proved. She was about twelve years of age, and was manifestly loving and desirous to oblige Isabel, who had, as I heard afterwards, shown her great kindness. She said she knew Abraham thy father well, and Licorice and Anegay. 'Had Anegay been there of late?' Isabel asked her. 'Certainly,' answered Rosia. 'Was she there now?' The child hesitated. But the truth came out when Isabel pressed her. Licorice had been absent from home, for several weeks, and when she returned, Anegay was with her, and four men were also in her company. Anegay had been very ill: very, very ill indeed, said the child. But—after long hesitation—she was better now. 'What about

the baby?' asked Isabel. Rosia looked surprised.
She had heard of none, except Licorice's own—thee,
Belasez. Had she spoken with Anegay? The girl
shook her head. Had she seen her? Yes. How
was it, that she had seen her, but not spoken with
her? The child replied, she was too ill to speak;
she knew no one."

"She did not know me, Belasez," said Abraham
sorrowfully, lifting his white, troubled face. "I
came home to find her there, to my great surprise.
But she did not know me. She took me for some
other man, I cannot tell whom. And she kept
begging me pitifully to tell Bruno—to let Bruno
know the moment he should come home: he would
never, never leave her in prison; he would be sure
to rescue her. I asked Licorice if Anegay had come
of her own will, for I was very much afraid lest
some force had been used to bring her. But she
assured me that my daughter had returned of her
own free will, only a little reluctantly, lest her husband should not approve it. There had been no
force whatever, only a little gentle persuasion. And
—fool that I was!—I believed it at the time. It
was not until all was over that I heard the real truth.
What good could come of telling Bruno then? It

would be simply to make him miserable to no purpose. And yet—Go on, my son."

And Abraham returned to his former position.

"Then," continued Bruno, "Isabel pressed the child Rosia harder. She told her that she felt certain she knew where Anegay was, and she must tell it to her. At last the child burst into tears. 'Oh, don't ask me!' she said, 'for I did love her so much! I cannot believe what Licorice says, that she is gone to Satan because she believed in the Nazarene. I am sure she went to God.' 'But is she dead, Rosia?' cried Isabel. And the child said, 'She is dead. She died yesterday morning.'"

Bruno paused, apparently to recover his composure.

"I went back at once to this house. I saw that Licorice instantly read in my face that I had heard the truth: and she tried to brazen it out no longer. Yes, it was true, she said in answer to my passionate charges: Anegay was dead. I should see her if I would, to convince me. So I passed into an inner chamber, and there I found her lying, my own fair darling, white and still, with the lips sealed for ever which could have told so much "——

Bruno nearly broke down, and he had to wait for a minute before he could proceed.

"I stood up from my dead, and I demanded of Licorice why she had done this cruel thing. And she said, 'Why! How little does a Christian know the heart of a Jew! Canst thou not guess that in our eyes it is a degradation for a daughter of Israel to be looked on by such as you Gentiles—that for one of you so much as to touch her hand is pollution that only blood can wipe away? Why! I wanted to revenge myself on thee, and if it were not too late, to save the child's soul. Thou canst hang me now, if thou wilt: I have had my revenge!' And I said, 'Licorice, my faith teaches me that revenge must be left to God, and that only forgiveness is for the lips of men. I, a sinner as thou art, must have nothing to do with vengeance. But, O Licorice, by all that thou deemest dear and holy, by the love that thou bearest to that babe of thine in the cradle, I conjure thee to tell me what has become of my child. Is she yet living?' She paused a while. Then she said in a low voice, 'No, Bruno. The journey was too much, in such a season, for so young an infant. She died the day after we arrived here. Perhaps,' said Licorice, 'thou wilt not believe me; but I am sorry that the child is dead. I meant to bring her up a strict

Jewess, and to wed her to some Jew. That would have been sweet to me. She and my Belasez would have grown together like twin sisters, for they were almost exactly of an age.' I could not refuse credence, for her look and tone were those of truth. It explained, too, if Beatrice had died so soon after arrival, why the child Rosia had not heard of her. So then I knew, Belasez, that the life to which my God called me thenceforward was to be a lonely walk with Him, sweetened by no human love any more, only by the dear hope that Heaven would hold us all, and that when we met in the Golden City we should part no more."

Tears were dimming Belasez's eyes. Bruno turned to Abraham.

"Now, my father, I have done thy will. But suffer me to say that it is no slight perplexity to me, why thou hast thought it meet that this sorrowful story should be told to the child of her that did the wrong."

Abraham made no answer but to rise from the position in which he had been sitting all the time, and to walk straight to the window. He seemed unwilling to speak, and his companions looked at him in doubtful surprise. They had to wait, however, till he turned from the window, and came and stood before Bruno.

"Son," he said, "what saith thy faith to this question?—When a man hath taken the wrong road, and hath wandered far away from right, from truth, and God, is it ever too late, while life lasts, for him to turn and come back?"

"Never," was Bruno's answer.

"And is it, under any circumstances, lawful for a man to lie unto his neighbour?"

Bruno, like many another, was better than his system; and at that time the Church herself had not reached those depths of legalised iniquity wherein she afterwards plunged. So that he had no hesitation in repeating, "Never."

"Then hear the truth, Bruno de Malpas; and if it well-nigh break an old man's heart to tell it, it is better that I should suffer and die for God's sake than that I should live for mine. On one point, Licorice deceived thee to the last. And until now, I, even I, have aided her in duping thee. Yet it is written, 'He that confesseth and forsaketh his sin shall find mercy.' May it not be too late for me!"

"Assuredly not, my father. But what canst thou mean?"

"Bruno, thy child did not die the day after she came hither."

"Father! Thou art not going to tell me "——

Bruno's voice had in it a strange mixture of agony and hope.

"Son, thy Beatrice lives."

Before either could speak further, Belasez had thrown herself on her knees, and flung her arms around Abraham.

"O Father, if it be so, speak quickly, and end his agony! For the sake of the righteous Lord, that loveth righteousness, do, do give Father Bruno back his child!"

Abraham disengaged himself from Belasez's clinging arms with what seemed almost a shudder. He took up his long robe, and tore it from the skirt to the neck. Then, with a voice almost choked with emotion, he laid both hands, as if in blessing, on the head of the kneeling Belasez.

"Beatrice de Malpas," he said, "THOU art that child."

A low cry from Bruno, a more passionate exclamation from Belasez, and the father and daughter were clasped heart to heart.

CHAPTER XI.

WHAT CAME OF IT.

> " Content to fill Religion's vacant place
> With hollow form, and gesture, and grimace."
>
> — *Cowper.*

"NAY, my son, it is of no use. I shall never forsake the faith of my fathers. For this child, if she can believe it,—well: she is more thine than mine,—*ay Dios!* And perhaps there is this much change in me, that I have come to think it just possible that it may not be idolatry to fancy the Nazarene was the Messiah. How can I tell? We know so little, and Adonai knows so much! But the cowslip is easily transplanted: the old oak will take no new rooting. Let the old oak alone. And there are other things in thy faith, my son,—a maiden whom I should deem it sin to worship, images of stone before which no Jew may bow down, a thing you call the Church, which we cannot understand, but which seems to bind you all, hand and foot, soul and body, as a slave is bound by his master. I cannot take up with those."

"Nor I," said Belasez in a low voice.

"Then do not," was the quiet answer of Bruno. "I shall never ask it of either of you."

"But thou believest all these?" said Abraham.

"I believe Jesus Christ my Lord. The rest is all to me a very little matter. I never pray with an image; I need it not. If another man think he does need it, to his own conscience I leave it before God. For Mary, Mother and Maid, I honour her, as you maybe honour your mother. *I* do not worship her: about other men I say nothing. And as to the Church,—why, what is the Church but a congregation of saved souls, to whom Christ is Lawgiver and Saviour? Her laws are His: or if not, then they have no right to be hers."

"Ah Bruno," said Abraham rather sadly, "thy religion is not that of other Christians."

"It is better," said Belasez softly.

"Father, my Christianity is Christ. I concern not myself with other men, except to save them, so far as it pleases God to work by me."

"Well, well! May Adonai forgive us all!—My

son, what dost thou mean to do with the child? It is for thee to decide now."

"My father, I shall endeavour to obtain absolution from my vows, and to become once more a parish priest, so that my Beatrice may dwell with me. Until then, choose thou whether she shall remain with thee, or go back to Bury Castle. I am sure the Lady would gladly receive her."

"Nay, Bruno, do not ask me to choose! If the child be here when Licorice returns, she will never dwell with thee. I believe she would well-nigh stab us both to the heart sooner than permit it. And I fear she may come any day."

"Then she had better come with me to Bury."

"'It is Adonai!' So be it."

"But I shall see thee, my father?" asked Belasez, addressing Abraham.

"Trust me for that, my Belasez! I can come to thee on my trade journeys, so long as it pleases the Holy One that I have strength to take them. And after that—He will provide. My son, wilt thou come for the child to-morrow? I will let thee out at the postern door; for thou hadst better not meet Delecresse."

And Abraham drew back the bolt, and opened the baize door.

R

"Father Jacob!" they heard him instantly ejaculate, in a very different tone from that of his last words.

"What hast thou been about now?" demanded the shrill voice of Licorice in the passage outside. "When folks are frightened at the sight of their lawful wives, it is a sure sign they have been after some mischief. Is there any one in yon chamber except thyself?—Ah, Belasez, I am glad to see thee; 'tis more than I expected. But, child, thou shouldst have set the porridge on half an hour ago; go down and look to it.—Any body else? Come, I had best see for myself."

And Licorice pushed past her husband, and walked into the room where Bruno was standing. He came forward to meet her, with far more apparent calmness than Abraham seemed to feel.

"Good even, my mother," he said courteously.

"If I were thy mother, I would hang myself from the first gable," hissed Licorice between her closed teeth. "I know thee, Bruno de Malpas, thou vile grandson of a locust! Nay, locust is too good for thee: they are clean beasts, and thou art an unclean. Thou hare, camel, coney, night-hawk, raven, lobster, earwig, hog! I spit on thee seven times"—and she did it—"I deliver thee over to Satan thy master"——

"That thou canst not," quietly said Bruno.

"I sweep thee out of my house!" And suiting the action to the word, Licorice caught up a broom which stood in the corner, and proceeded to apply it with good will. Bruno retreated, as was but natural he should.

"Licorice, my dear wife!"

"I'll sweep *thee* out next!" cried Licorice, brandishing her broom in the very face of her lord and master. "I'll have no Christians, nor Christian blood, nor Christian faith, in *my* house, as I am a living daughter of Abraham! Get you all out hence, ye loathsome creeping things, which whosoever toucheth shall be unclean! Get ye out, I say!—Belasez, bring me soap and water. I'll not sleep till I've washed the floor. I'd wash the air if I could."

"Your pardon, Mother, but if you will have no Christian blood in your house, you must sweep me out," answered Belasez, with a mixture of dignity and irrepressible amusement.

Licorice turned round to Abraham.

"Thou hast told her?"

"It was better she should know, wife."

"I'll chop thy head off, if I hear thee say that again!—And dost thou mean to be a Christian, thou wicked girl?"

"I do, Mother. And I mean to go with my father."

"Go, then—like to like!—and all the angels of Satan go with thee!"

And the broom came flying after Belasez.

"Nay, wife, give the child her raiment and jewels."

"I'll give her what belongs to her, and that's a hot iron, if she does not get out of that door this minute!"

"Wife!"

"I'll spoil her pretty face for her!" shrieked Licorice. "I never liked the vain chit overmuch, nor Anegay neither: but if she does not go, I'll give her something she won't forget in a hurry!"

"Come, my Beatrice,—quick!" said Bruno.

"Go, go, my Belasez, and God keep thee!" sobbed Abraham.

And so Belasez was driven away from her old home. She had hardly expected it. It had always been a trouble to her, and a cause of self-reproach, that she and Licorice did not love each other better: and she was not able to repress a sensation of satisfaction in making the discovery that Licorice was not her mother. Yet Belasez had not looked for this.

"What are we to do, Father?" she asked rather blankly.

"I must lodge thee with the Sisters of St. Clare, my child; there is nothing else to be done. I will come and fetch thee away so soon as my arrangements can be made."

Beatrice,—as we must henceforth call her,—did not fancy this arrangement at all. Bruno detected as much in her face.

"Thou dost not like it, my dove?"

"I do not like being with strangers," she said frankly. "And I am afraid the nuns will think me a variety of heathen, for I cannot do all they will want me."

"They will not, if I tell the Abbess that thou art a new convert," said Bruno. "They may very likely attempt to instruct thee."

"Father, why should there be any nuns?"

Beatrice did not know how she astonished Bruno. But he only smiled.

"Thine eyes are unaccustomed to the light," was all he answered.

"But, Father, among our people of old,—I mean," said Beatrice hesitatingly, "my mother's people"——

"Go on, my Beatrice. Let it be 'our people.' Speak as it is nature to thee to do."

"Thank you, my father. Among our people, there were no nuns. So far from it, that for a woman to remain unwed was considered a reproach."

"Why?—dost thou know?"

"I think, because every woman longed for the glory of being the mother of the Messiah."

"True. Therefore, Christ being come, that reproach is done away. Let each woman choose for herself. 'If a virgin marry, she hath not sinned.' Nevertheless, 'she that is unmarried thinks of the things of the Lord, that she may be holy, body and soul.'"

"Father, do you wish *me* to be a nun?"

"Never!" hastily answered Bruno. "Nay, my Beatrice; I should not have said that. Be thou what the Lord thinks best to make thee. But I do not want to be left alone again."

Beatrice's heart was set at rest. She had terribly feared for a moment lest Bruno, being himself a monk, might think her absolutely bound to be a nun.

They soon reached the Franciscan Convent. The Abbess, a rather stiffly-mannered, grey-haired woman, received her young guest with sedate kindliness, and committed her to the special charge of Sister Eularia. This was a young woman of about twenty-five, in whose mind curiosity was strongly developed. She took Beatrice up to the dormitory, showed her where she was to sleep, and gave her a seat on the form beside her at supper, which was almost immediately served. Beatrice noticed that whenever Eularia helped herself to any thing edible, she made the sign of the cross over it.

"Why dost thou do that?" asked the young Jewess.

"It is according to our rule," replied the nun. "Surely thou knowest how to cross thyself?"

"Indeed I do not. And I do not see why I should."

"Poor thing!—how sadly thou lackest teaching! Dost thou not know that our Lord Christ suffered on the cross?"

"Oh yes! But why must I cross myself on that account?"

"In respect to Him!" exclaimed Eularia.

"Pardon me. If one whom I loved were slain by the sword, I should not courtesy to every sword I saw, because I loved him. I should hate the very sight of one."

Eularia was scarcely less puzzled than Beatrice.

" It is the symbol of our salvation," she said.

" I should look on it rather as the symbol of His suffering."

" True : but He suffered for us."

" For which reason I should still less admire that which made Him suffer."

Eularia shrugged her shoulders.

" Thou art very ignorant."

The discussion slumbered until they rose from supper; when Eularia seated Beatrice beside her on the settle, and offered to instruct her in the use of the rosary.

" What a pretty necklace! I thought nuns did not wear ornaments ?"

" Ornaments ! Of course not."

" Then what do you do with that ?"

" We pray by it."

" Pray—by—it ! I do not understand."

" We keep count of our prayers."

" Count !—why ?"

" Why, how could we remember them else ?"

" But why should you remember ?"

"Poor ignorant child! When thou comest to make confession, thou wilt find that the priest will set thee for penance, so many Aves and so many Paternosters."

"What are those?"

"Dost thou never pray?" gasped Eularia.

"I never say so many of one thing, and so many of another," answered Beatrice, half laughing. "I never heard anything so absurd. The holy prophets did not pray in that way."

"Of course they did!" exclaimed Eularia. "How could they obtain help of our Lady, without repeating Ave and Salve?"

"How could they, indeed, before she was born?" was the retort.

"Oh dear, dear!" said Eularia. "Why, thou knowest nothing."

Beatrice privately thought that she would prefer not to know all that rubbish. Plenty of it was served up to her before she left the convent, by the holy Sisters of St. Clare.

It was nearly three weeks before Bruno came for her, and very weary of her hosts she was. They were no less astonished and dismayed by her. The ignorant heathen would not worship the holy images, would not use holy water, would not kneel before the holy Sacrament, would not do this, that, and the other: and, not content with this series of negations, she actually presumed to reason about them !

"What dost thou believe?" despairingly demanded Sister Eularia at last.

"I believe in God," said Beatrice gravely. "And I believe that Jesus of Nazareth was the Sent of God."

"And in the Holy Ghost?" asked Eularia.

"If I understand you, certainly. Is it not written, 'The Spirit of God hath made me'?"

"And in holy Church?"

"I do not know. What is it?"

"How shocking! And in the forgiveness of sins?"

"Assuredly."

"And in the resurrection and eternal life?"

"Undoubtedly."

"And in the invocation of the holy saints?"

"I believe that there have been holy men and women."

"And dost thou invoke them?"

"Do you mean, pray to them?"

"Dost thou beg of them to intercede for thee?"

"No, indeed, not I!"

"Did I ever see such ignorance! And thou wilt not learn."

"I will learn of my father, and no one else. I am sure he does not believe half the rubbish you do."

"*Sancta Hilaria, ora pro nobis!*"

"What language is that?" innocently asked Beatrice.

"The holy tongue, of course."

"It is not our holy tongue."

"Have Jews a holy tongue?" responded Eularia, in surprise.

"Yes, indeed,—Hebrew."

"I did not know they believed any thing to be holy. Have they any relics?"

"I do not know what those are."

Eularia led the way to the sacristy.

"Look here," she said, reverently opening a golden reliquary set with rubies. "Here is a small piece of the holy veil of our foundress, St. Clare. This is the finger-bone of the blessed Evangelist Matthew. Here is a piece of the hoof of the holy ass on which our Lord rode. Now thou knowest what relics are."

"But what can make you keep such things as those?" asked Beatrice, opening wide her lustrous eyes.

"And this," enthusiastically added Eularia, opening another reliquary set with emeralds and pearls, "is our most precious relic,—one of the small feathers from the wing of the holy angel, St. Gabriel."

To the intense horror of Eularia, a silver laugh of unmistakable amusement greeted this holy relic.

"Beatrice! hast thou no reverence?"

"Not for angels' feathers," answered Beatrice, still laughing. "Well, I did think you had more sense!"

"I can assure thee, thou wilt shock Father Bruno if thou allowest thyself to commit such improprieties."

"I shall shock him, then. How excessively absurd!"

Eularia took her unpromising pupil out of the sacristy more hastily than she had led her in. And perhaps it was as well for Beatrice that Father Bruno arrived the next day.

They reached Bury Castle in safety. The Countess had been very much interested in Father Bruno's story, and most readily acceded to his request to leave Beatrice as her visitor until he should have a home to which he could take her. And Beatrice de Malpas, the daughter of a baronial house in Cheshire, was a very different person in the estimation of a Christian noble from Belasez, daughter of the Jew pedlar.

Rather to her surprise, she found herself seated above the salt, that is, treated as a lady of rank: and the embargo being over which had confined her to Margaret's apartments, she took her place at the Earl's table in the banquet-hall. Earl Hubert's quick eyes soon found out the addition to his supper-party, and he condescended to remark that she was extremely pretty, and quite an ornament to the hall. Beatrice herself was much pleased to find her old friend Doucebelle seated next to her, and they soon began to converse on recent events.

It is a curious fact as concerns human nature, that however long friends may have been parted, their conversation nearly always turns on what has happened just before they met again. They do not speak of what delighted or agonised them ten years ago, though the effect may have extended to the whole of their subsequent lives. They talk of last week's journey, or of yesterday's snow-storm.

Beatrice fully expected Doucebelle's sympathy on the subject of relics, and she was disappointed to find it not forthcoming. Doucebelle was rather inclined to be shocked than amused. The angel's feather, in her eyes, was provocative of any thing rather than ridicule: and Beatrice, who had anticipated her taking the common-sense view of the matter, felt chilled by the result.

Life had fallen back into its old grooves at Bury Castle. Grief, with the Countess, was usually a passionate, but also a transitory feeling. Her extremely easy temper led her to get rid of a sorrow as soon as ever she could. Pain, whether mental or bodily, was in her eyes not a necessary discipline, but an unpleasant disturbance of the proper order of events. In fact, she was one of those persons who are always popular by reason of their gracious affability, but in whom, below the fair flow of sweet waters, there is a strong substratum of stony selfishness. She objected to people being in distress, not because it hurt them, but because it hurt her to see them. And the difference between the two, though it may scarcely show at times on the surface, lies in an entire and essential variety of the strata underneath.

It was only natural that, with this character, the Countess should expect others to be as little impressed by suffering as herself. She really had no conception of a disposition to which sorrow was not an easily-healed scratch, but a scar that would be carried to the grave. In her eyes, the calamity which had happened to her daughter was a disappointment, undoubtedly, but one which she would find no difficulty in surmounting at all. There were plenty of other men in the world, quite as handsome, as amiable, as rich, and as noble, as Richard de Clare. If such a grief had happened to herself, she would have wept incessantly for a week, been low-spirited for a month, and in a year would have been wreathed with smiles, and arranging her trousseau for a wedding with another bridegroom. The only thing which could really have distressed her long, would have been if the vacant place in her life had *not* been refilled.

But Margaret's character was of a deeper type. For her the world held no other man, and life's blossom once blighted, no second crop of happiness could grow, at least on the same tree. To such a character as this, the only possibility of throwing out fresh bloom is when the tree is grafted by the great Husbandman with amaranth from Heaven.

Yet it was not in Margaret's nature—it would have been in her mother's—to say much of what she felt. Outwardly, she showed no difference, except that her *cœur léger* was gone, never to return. She did not shut herself up and refuse to join in the employments or amusements of those around her. And the majority of those around never suspected that the work and the amusement alike had no interest for her, nor would ever have any: that she "could never think as she had thought, or be as she had been, again."

One person only perceived the truth, and that was because he was cast in a like mould. Bruno saw too plainly that the hope expressed by the Countess that "Magot was getting nicely over her disappointment" was not true,—never would be true. In his case the amaranth had been grafted in, and the plant was blossoming again. But there was no such hope for her, at least as yet.

Beatrice was unable to enter into Margaret's feelings, not so much through want of capacity as of experience. Eva was equally unable, being naturally at once of a more selfish and a less concentrated disposition : her mind would have been more easily drawn from her sorrow,—an important item of the healing process. Doucebelle came nearest ; but as she was the most selfless of all, her grief in like case would have been rather for the sufferings of Richard than for her own.

Beatrice soon carried the relic question to her father for decision, though with some trepidation as to what he would say. If he should not agree with her, she would be sorely disappointed. Bruno's smile half reassured her.

"So thou canst not believe in the genuineness of these relics?" said he. "Well, my child, so that thou hast full faith in Christ and His salvation, I cannot think it much matters whether thou believest a certain piece of stuff to be the veil of St. Clare or not. Neither St. Clare nor her veil is concerned in thine eternal safety."

"But Doucebelle seems almost shocked. She does believe in them."

"Perhaps it will not harm her—with the like proviso."

"But, Father !—the honour in which they hold these rags and bones seems to me like idolatry !"

"Then be careful thou commit it not."

"But *you* do not worship such things ?"

"Dear child, I find too much in Christ and in this perishing world, to have much time to think of them."

Beatrice was only half satisfied. She would have felt more contented had Bruno warmly disclaimed the charge. It was at the cost of some distress that she realised that what were serious essentials to her were comparatively trivial matters to him. The wafts of polluted air were only too patent to her, which were lost in the purer atmosphere, at the altitude where Bruno stood.

The girls were gathered together one afternoon in the ante-chamber of Margaret's apartments, and Bruno, who had come up to speak to his daughter, was with them. Except in special cases, no chamber of any house was sacred from a priest. Eva was busy spinning, but it would be more accurate to say that Marie, who was supposed to be spinning also, was engaged in breaking threads. Margaret was employed on tapestry-work; Doucebelle in plain sewing; and Beatrice with her delicate embroidery.

"Father," said Beatrice, looking up suddenly, "I was taught that it was sin to make images of created things, on account of the words of the second commandment. What do you say ?"

"'*Non facies tibi sculptile, neque omnem simili-tudinem,*'" murmured Bruno, reflectively. "I think, my child, that it depends very much on the meaning of '*tibi.*' Ah, I see in thy face thou hast learned no Latin. 'Thou shalt not make *to thee* any sculptured image.' Then a sculptured image may be made otherwise. The latter half of the commandment, I think, shows what is meant. '*Non adorabis ea, neque coles*'—'thou shalt not worship them.' At the same time, St. Paul saith, '*Omne autem, quod non est ex fide, peccatum est*'—'all that is not of faith is sin;' and '*nisi ei qui existimat quid commune esse, illi commune est*': namely, 'to him who esteemeth a thing unclean, to him it is unclean.' If thou really believest it sin, by no means allow thyself to do it."

"But, Father, suppose we cannot be sure?" said Doucebelle.

"Thou needst not fear that thou wilt ever walk *too* close to Christ, daughter," quietly answered Bruno.

"But, Father! are we bound to give up all that can possibly be sin, or even can become sin?" asked Eva, in a tone which decidedly indicated dissent.

"I should like to hear thy objection, daughter."

"Why, we should have to give up every thing nice!" said Eva, disconsolately. "There are all sorts of delightful things, which are not exactly sins, but "——

"Not quite virtues," interposed Beatrice, with an amused expression, as Eva paused.

"Well, no. Still they are not wrong—in themselves. But they make one waste one's time, or forget to say one's beads, or be cross to one's sister,—just because they are so delightful, and one does not want to give over. And being cross is sin, I suppose; and so it is when one forgets to say one's prayers: I don't know whether wasting time is exactly a sin."

"I see," said Bruno, in the same quiet tone. "Had our Lord sent thee to clear His Temple of the profane who desecrated it by traffic, thou wouldst have overthrown the tables of the money-changers, but not the seats of them that sold doves."

Beatrice and Doucebelle answered by a smile of intelligence; Eva looked rather dissatisfied.

"But it is not a sin to be happy, Father?" asked Margaret in a low voice.

"Not if God give thee the happiness."

"That is just it!" said Eva, discontentedly. "How is one to know?"

"My child," answered Bruno, ignoring the tone, "God never means His children to put any thing into the place of Himself. The moment thou dost that, that thing is sin to thee."

"But when do we do that, Father?" asked Doucebelle.

"When it makes thee forget to say thy prayers, I should think," drily observed Beatrice.

"When it comes in the way between Him and thee," said Bruno.

"And is it a sin to waste time, Father?" queried Eva.

"It is a sin to waste any thing," answered Bruno. "But if it be more a sin to waste one thing than another, surely it is to waste life itself."

He rose and went away. Eva shrugged her shoulders with a wry face.

"There never was any body so precise as Father Bruno! I would rather ask questions of Father Nicholas, ten times over."

"Well, I don't like asking questions of Father Nicholas," responded Doucebelle, "because he never answers them. He never goes down to the bottom of things."

"*Ha, chétife!*" cried Eva. "Dost thou want to

get to the bottom of things ? That is just why I like Father Nicholas, because he never bothers one with reasons and distinctions. It is only, ' Yes, thou mayest do so,' or ' No, do not do that,'—and then I am satisfied. Now, Father Bruno will persist in explaining why I am not to do it, and that sometimes makes me want to do it all the more. It seems to leave it in one's own hands."

Beatrice broke into a laugh. "Why, Eva, thou wouldst rather be a chair to be moved about, than a woman to be able to go at pleasure."

"I would rather have a distinct order," said Eva, a little scornfully. "' Do,' or ' Don't,' I can understand. But, ' St. Paul says this,' or ' St. John says that,' and to have to make up one's own mind,—I detest it."

"And I should detest the opposite."

"I am afraid, Beatrice, thou art greatly wanting in the virtue of holy obedience. But of course one can make allowances for thine unhappy education."

Eva had occasion to leave the room at the conclusion of this unflattering speech: and Beatrice indulged in a long laugh.

"Well, what I am afraid of," she said to Margaret and Doucebelle, "is that Eva is rather wanting in the virtue of common sense. But whether I am to lay that on her education, I do not know."

There was no answer: but the thoughts of the hearers were almost opposites. Margaret considered Beatrice rash and self-satisfied. Doucebelle thought heartily with her, and only wished that she had as much courage to say so.

CHAPTER XII.

WHAT IS LOVE ?

"She only said, 'My life is dreary,
    He cometh not,' she said :
She said, ' I am aweary, weary,
    I would that I were dead !'"
                                    —*Tennyson.*

IT was fortunate for Bruno de Malpas that he
had a friend in Bishop Grosteste, whose large
heart and clear brain were readily interested in his
wish to return from regular to secular orders. He
smoothed the path considerably, and promised him
a benefice in his diocese if the dispensation could be
obtained. But the last was a lengthy process, and
some months passed away before the answer could
be received from Rome.

It greatly scandalised Hawise and Eva—for different reasons—to see how very little progress was
made by Beatrice in that which in their eyes was

the Christian religion. It was a comfort to them to reflect that she had been baptized as an infant, and therefore in the event of sudden death had a chance of going to Heaven, instead of the dreadful certainty of being shut up in Limbo,—a place of vague locality and vaguer character, being neither pleasant nor painful, but inhabited by all the hapless innocents whose heathen or careless Christian parents suffered them to die unregenerated. But both of them were sorely shocked to discover, when she had been about two months at Bury, that poor Beatrice was still ignorant of the five commandments of the Church. Nor was this all: she irreverently persisted in her old inquiry of "What is the Church?" and sturdily demanded what right the Church had to give commandments.

Hawise was quite distressed. It was not *proper*,—a phrase which, with her, was the strongest denunciation that could be uttered. Nobody had ever asked such questions before: *ergo*, they ought never to be asked. Every sane person knew perfectly well what the Church was (though, when gently urged by Beatrice, Hawise backed out of any definition), and no good Catholic could possibly require telling. And as to so shocking a supposition as that the Church had no right to issue her own commands, —well, it was not proper!

Eva's objection was quite as strong, but of a different sort. She really could not understand what Beatrice wanted. If the priest—or the Church—they were very much the same thing—told her what to do, could she not rest and be thankful? It was a great deal less trouble than everlastingly thinking for one's self.

"No one of any note ever thinks for himself," chimed in Hawise.

"Then I am glad I am not of any note!" bluntly responded Beatrice.

"You a De Malpas! I am quite shocked!" said Hawise.

"God made me with a heart and a conscience," was the answer. "If He had not meant me to use them, He would not have given them to me."

At that point Beatrice left the room in answer to a call from the Countess; and Hawise, turning to her companions, remarked in a whisper that it must be that dreadful Jewish blood on the mother's side which had given her such very improper notions. They were *so* low! "For my part," she added, "if it were proper to say so, I should remark that I cannot imagine why Father Bruno does not see that she understands something of Christianity—but of course one must not criticise a priest."

" Speak truth, my daughter," said a voice from the

doorway which rather disconcerted Hawise. "Thou canst not understand my actions—in what respect?"

"I humbly crave your pardon, Father; but I am really distressed about Beatrice."

"Indeed !—how so ?"

"She understands nothing about Christian duties."

"I hope that is a little more than truth.   But if not, —let her understand Christ first, my child : Christian duties will come after."

"Forgive me, Father—without teaching?"

"Not without His teaching," said Bruno, gravely. "Without mine, it may be."

"But, Father, she does not know the five commandments of holy Church. Nay, she asks what 'the Church' means."

"If she be in the Church, she can wait to know it. Thy garments will not keep thee less warm because thou hast never learned how to weave them."

Hawise did not reply, but she looked unconvinced.

A few days after this, Eva was pleased to inform Beatrice that she had been so happy as to reach that point which in her eyes was the apex of feminine ambition.

"I am betrothed to Sir William de Cantilupe."

Margaret sighed.

"Dost thou like him?" asked Beatrice, in her straightforward way, which was sometimes a shade too blunt, and was apt to betray her into asking direct questions which it might have been kinder and more delicate to leave unasked.

Eva blushed and simpered.

"I'll tell thee, Beatrice," said little Marie, dancing up. "She's over head and ears in love—so much over head"—and Marie's hand went as high as it would go above her own: "but it's my belief she has tumbled in on the wrong side."

"'The wrong side'!" answered Beatrice, laughing. "The wrong side of love? or the wrong side of Eva?"

"The wrong side of Eva," responded Marie, with a positive little nod. "As to love, I'm not quite sure that she knows much about it: for I don't believe she cares half so much for Sir William as she cares for being married. That's the grand thing with her, so far as I can make out. And that's not my notion of love."

"Thou silly little child of twelve, what dost thou know about it?" contemptuously demanded Eva. "Thy time is not come."

"No, and I hope it won't," said Marie, "if I'm to make such a goose of myself over it as thou dost."

"Marie, Marie!"

"It's true, Margaret!—Now, Beatrice, dost thou not think so? She makes a regular misery of it. There is no living with her for a day or two before he comes to see her. She never gives him a minute's peace when he is here; and if he looks at somebody else, she goes as black as a thunder-cloud. If he's half an hour late, she's quite sure he is visiting some other gentlewoman, whom he loves better than he loves her. She's for ever making little bits of misery out of nothing. If he were to call her 'honey-sweet Eva' to-day, and only 'sweet Eva' to-morrow, she would be positive there was some shocking reason for it, instead of, like a sensible girl, never thinking about it in that way at all."

Beatrice and Doucebelle were both laughing, and even Margaret joined in a little.

"Of course," said Marie by way of postscript, "if Sir William had been badly hurt in a tournament, or anything of that sort, I could understand her worrying about it : or if he had told her that he did not love her, I could understand that : but she worries for nothing at all! If he does not tell her that he loves her every time he comes, she fancies he doesn't."

"Marie, don't be so silly !"

"Thanks, I'll try not," said Marie keenly. "And she calls that love! What dost thou think, Beatrice ?"

"Why, I think it does not sound much like it, Marie—in thy description."

"Why, what notion of love hast thou ?" said Eva

scornfully. "I have not forgotten how thou wert wont to talk of thy betrothed."

"But I never professed to love Leo," said Beatrice, looking up. "How could I, when I had not seen him ?"

"Dost thou want to see, in order to love?" sentimentally inquired Eva.

"No," answered Beatrice, thoughtfully. "But I want to know. I might easily love some one whom I had not seen with my eyes, if he were always sending me messages and doing kind actions for me : but I could not love somebody who was to me a mere name, and nothing more."

"It is plain thou hast no sensitiveness, Beatrice."

"I'd rather have sense,—wouldn't you?" said little Marie.

"As if one could not have both !" sneered Eva.

"Well, if one could, I should have thought thou wouldst," retorted Marie.

"Well! I don't understand you !" said Eva. "I cannot care to be loved with less than the whole heart. I should not thank you for just the love that you can spare from other people."

"But should not one have some to spare for other people ?" suggested Marie.

"That sounds as if one's heart were a box," said Beatrice, "that would hold so much and no more.

Is it not more like a fountain, that can give out perpetually and always have fresh supplies within?"

"Yes, for the beloved one," replied Eva, warmly.

"For all," answered Beatrice. "That is a narrow heart which will hold but one person."

"Well, I would rather be loved with the whole of a narrow heart than with a piece of a broad one."

"O Eva!"

"What dost thou mean, Doucebelle?" said Eva, sharply, turning on her new assailant. "Indeed I would! The man who loves me must love me supremely—must care for nothing but me: must find his sweetest reward for every thing in my smile, and his bitterest pain in my displeasure. That is what I call love."

"Well! I should call that something else—if Margaret wouldn't scold," murmured Marie in an undertone.

"What is that, Marie?" asked Margaret, with a smile.

"Self-conceit; and plenty of it," said the child.

"Ask Father Bruno what he thinks, Beatrice," suggested Margaret, after a gentle "Hush!" to the somewhat too plain-spoken Marie. "Thou canst do it, but it would not come so well from us."

"Dost thou mean to say I am conceited, little

piece of impertinence?" inquired Eva, in no dulcet tones.

"Well, I thought thou saidst it thyself," was the response, for which Marie got chased round the room with the wooden side of an embroidery frame, and, being lithe as a monkey, escaped by flying to the Countess's rooms, which communicated with those of her daughter by a private staircase.

Father Bruno came up, as he often did, the same evening: but before Beatrice had time to consult him, the small Countess of Eu appeared from nowhere in particular, and put the crucial question in its crudest form.

"Please, Father Bruno, what is love?"

"Dost thou want telling?" inquired Bruno with evident amusement.

"Please, we all want telling, because we can't agree."

Bruno very rarely laughed, but he did now.

"Then, if you cannot agree, you certainly do need it. I should rather like to hear the various opinions."

"Oh! Eva says—" began the child eagerly; but Bruno's hand, laid gently on her head, stopped her.

"Wait, my child. Let each speak for herself."

There was silence for a moment, for no one liked to begin—except Marie, whom decorum alone kept silent.

"What didst thou say, Eva?"

"I believe I said, good Father, that I cared not for the love of any that did not hold me first and best. Nor do I."

"'Love seeketh not her own,'" said Bruno. "That which seeks its own is not love."

"What is it, Father?" modestly asked Doucebelle.

"It is self-love, my daughter; the worst enemy that can be to the true love of God and man. Real love is unselfish, unexacting, and immortal."

"But love can die, surely!"

"St. Paul says the contrary, my daughter."

"It can kill, I suppose," said Margaret, in a low tone.

"Yes, the weak," replied Bruno.

"But, Father, was the holy Apostle not speaking of religious love?" suggested Eva, trying to find a loophole.

"What is the alternative,—irreligious love? I do not know of such a thing, my daughter."

"But there is a wicked sort of love."

"Certainly not. There are wicked passions. But love can never be wicked, because God is love."

"But people can love wickedly?" asked Eva, looking puzzled.

"I fail to see how any one can *love* wickedly. Self-love is always wicked."

T

"Then, Father, if it be wicked, you call it self-love?" said Eva, leaping (very cleverly, as she thought) to a conclusion.

"Scarcely," said Bruno, with a quiet smile. "Say rather, my daughter, that if it be self-love, I call it wicked."

The perplexed expression returned to Eva's face.

"My child, what is love?"

"Why, Father, that is just what we want to know," said Marie.

But Bruno waited for Eva's answer.

"I suppose," she said nervously, "it means liking a person, and wishing for his company, and wanting him to love one."

"And I suppose that it is caring for him so much that thou wouldst count nothing too great a sacrifice, to attain his highest good. That is how God loved us, my children."

Eva thought this extremely poor and tame, beside her own lovely ideal.

"Then," said Marie, "if I love Margaret, I shall want *her* to be happy. I shall not want her to make me happy, unless it would make her so."

"Right, my child," said Bruno, with a smile of approbation. "To do otherwise would be loving Marie, not Margaret."

"But, Father!" exclaimed Eva. "Do you mean

to say that if my betrothed prefers to go hawking rather than sit with me, if I love him I shall wish him to leave me?"

"Whom wouldst thou be loving, if not?"

"I could not wish him to go and leave me!"

"My child, there is a divine self-abnegation to which very few attain. But those few come nearest to the imitation of Him who 'pleased not Himself,' and I think—God knoweth—often they are the happiest. Let us all ask God for grace to reach it. 'This is My commandment, that ye have love one to another.'"

And, as was generally the case when he had said all he thought necessary at the moment, Bruno rose, and with a benediction quitted the room.

"Call that loving!" said Eva, contemptuously, when he was gone. "Poor tame stuff! I should not thank you for it."

"Well, I should," said Doucebelle, quietly.

"Oh, thou!" was Eva's answer, in the same tone. "Why, thou hast no heart to begin with."

Doucebelle silently doubted that statement.

"O Eva, for shame!" said Marie. "Doucebelle always does what every body wants her, unless she thinks it is wrong."

"Thou dost not call that love, I hope?"

"I think it is quite as like it as wishing people to

do what they don't want, to please you," said Marie, sturdily.

"I don't believe one of you knows any thing about it," loftily returned Eva. "If I had been Margaret, now, I could not have sat quietly to that broidery. I could not have borne it!"

Margaret looked up quickly, changed colour, and with a slight compression of her lower lip, went back to her work in silence.

"But what wouldst thou have done, Eva?" demanded the practical little Marie. "Wouldst thou have stared out of the window all day long?"

"No!" returned Eva with fervent emphasis. "I should have wept my life away. But Margaret is not like me. She can get interested in work and other things, and forget a hapless love, and outlive it. It would kill me in a month."

Margaret rose very quietly, put her frame by in the corner, and left the room. Beatrice, who had been silent for some time, looked up then with expressive eyes.

"It is killing her, Eva. My father told me so a week since. He says he is quite sure that the Countess is mistaken in fancying that she is getting over it."

"She! She is as strong as a horse. And I don't think she ever felt it much! Not as I should have done. I should have taken the veil that very day.

Earth would have been a dreary waste to me from that instant. I could not have borne to see a man again. However many years I might have lived, no sound but the *Miserere*"——

"But, Eva! I thought thou wert going to die in a month."

"It is very rude to interrupt, Marie. No sound but the *Miserere* would ever have broken the chill echoes of my lonely cell, nor should any raiment softer than sackcloth have come near my seared and blighted heart!"

"I should think it would get seared, with nothing but sackcloth," put in the irrepressible little Lady of Eu.

"But what good would all that do, Eva?"

"Good, Beatrice! What canst thou mean? I tell thee, I could not have borne any thing else."

"I don't believe much in thy sackcloth, Eva. Thou wert making ever such a fuss the other day because the serge of thy gown touched thy neck and rubbed it, and Levina ran a ribbon down to keep it off thee."

"Don't be impertinent, Marie. Of course, in such a case as that, I could not think of mere inconveniences."

"Well, if I could not think of inconveniences when I was miserable, I would try to make less fuss over them when I was happy."

"I am not happy, foolish child."

"Why, what's the matter? Did Sir William look at thee only twenty-nine times, instead of thirty, when he was here?"

"Thou art the silliest maiden of whom any one ever heard!"

"No, Eva; her match might be found, I think," said Beatrice.

Marie went off into convulsions of laughter, and flung herself on the rushes to enjoy it with more freedom.

"I wonder which of you two is the funnier!" said she.

"What on earth is there comical about *me?*" exclaimed Eva, the more put out because Beatrice and Doucebelle were both joining in Marie's amusement.

"It is of no use to tell thee, Eva," replied Beatrice; "thou wouldst not be able to see it."

"Can't I see any thing you can?" demanded Eva, irritably.

"Why, no!" said Marie, with a fresh burst: "canst thou see thine own face?"

"What a silly child, to make such a speech as that!"

"No, Eva," said Beatrice, trying to stifle her laughter, increased by Marie's witticism: "the child is any thing but silly."

"Well, I think you are all very silly, and I shall not talk to you any more," retorted Eva, endeavouring to cover her retreat ; but she was answered only by a third explosion from Marie.

Half an hour later, the Countess, entering her bedchamber, was startled to find a girl crouched down by the side of the bed, her face hidden in the coverlet, and her sunny cedar hair flowing over it in disorder.

"Why, what—Magot! my darling Magot! what aileth thee, my white dove?"

Margaret lifted her head when her mother spoke. She had not been shedding tears. Perhaps she might have looked less terribly wan and woful if she had done so.

"Pardon me, Lady! I came here to be alone."

The Countess sat down in the low curule chair beside her bed, and drew her daughter close. Margaret laid her head, with a weary sigh, on her mother's knee, and cowered down again at her feet.

"And what made thee wish to be alone, my rosebud?"

"Something that somebody said."

"Has any one been speaking unkindly to my little one?"

"No, no. They did not mean to be unkind. Oh

dear no! nothing of the sort. But—things sting—when people do not mean it."

The Countess softly stroked the cedar hair. She hardly understood the explanation. Things of that sort did not sting her. But this she understood and felt full sympathy with—that her one cherished darling was in trouble.

"Who was it, Magot?"

"Do not ask me, Lady. I did not mean to complain of any one. And nobody intended to hurt me."

"What did she say?"

"She said"—something like a sob came here—"that I was one who could settle to work, and get interested in other things, and forget a lost love. But, she said, it would kill her in a month."

"Well, darling? I began to hope that was true."

"No," came in a very low voice. It was not a quick, warm denial like that of Eva, yet one which sounded far more hopelessly conclusive. "No. O Mother, no!"

"And thou art still fretting in secret, my dove?"

"I do not know about fretting. I think that is too energetic a word. It would be better to say—dying."

"Magot, mine own, my sunbeam! Do not use such words!"

"It is better to see the truth, Lady. And that is true. But I do not think it will be over in a month."

The Countess could not trust herself to speak. She went on stroking the soft hair.

"Father Bruno says that love can kill weak people. I suppose I am weak. I feel as if I should be glad when it is all done with."

"When what is done with?" asked the Countess, in a husky tone.

"Living," said the girl. "This weary round of dressing, eating, working, talking, and sleeping. When it is all done, and one may lie down to sleep and not wake to-morrow,—I feel as if that were the only thing which would ever make me glad any more."

"My heart! Dost thou want to leave me?"

"I would have lived, Lady, for your sake, if I could have done. But I cannot. The rosebud that you loved is faded: it cannot give out scent any more. It is not me,—me, your Margaret—that works, and talks, and does all these things. It is only my body, which cannot die quite so fast as my soul. My heart is dead already."

"My treasure! I will have Master Aristoteles to see to thee. I really hoped thou wert getting over it."

"It is of no use trying to keep me," she answered quietly. "You had better let me go—Mother."

The Countess's reply was to clap her hands—at that time the usual method of summoning a servant. When Levina tapped at the door, instead of bidding her enter, her mistress spoke through it.

"Tell Master Aristoteles that I would speak with him in this chamber."

The mother and daughter were both very still until the shuffling of the physician's slippered feet was heard in the passage. Then the Countess roused herself and answered the appeal with "Come in."

"My Lady desired my attendance?"

"I did, Master. I would fain have you examine this child. She has a strange fancy, which I should like to have uprooted from her mind. She imagines that she is going to die."

"A strange fancy indeed, if it please my Lady. I see no sign of disease at all about the damsel. A little weakness, and low spirits,—no real complaint whatever. She might with some advantage wear the fleminum,[1]—the blood seems a little too much in the head : and warm fomentations would help to restore her strength. Almond blossoms, pounded with pearl,

---

[1] A garment which was supposed to draw the blood downwards from the brain.

might also do something.   But, if it please my Lady —let my Lady speak."

"I was only going to ask, Master, whether viper broth would be good for her?"

"A most excellent suggestion, my Lady.   But, I was about to remark, the physician of Saint Albans hath given me a most precious thing, which would infallibly restore the damsel, even if she were at the gates of death.   Three hairs of the beard of the blessed Dominic,[1] whom our holy Father hath but now canonised.   If the damsel were to take one of these, fasting, in holy water, no influence of the Devil could have any longer power over her."

"*Ha, jolife!*" cried the Countess, clasping her hands.   "Magot, my love, this is the very thing. Thou must take it."

"I will take what you command, Lady."

But there was no enthusiasm in Margaret's voice.

"Then to-morrow morning, Master, do, I beseech you, administer this precious cordial!"

"Lady, I will do so.   But it would increase the efficacy, if the damsel would devoutly repeat this evening the Rosary of the holy Virgin, with twelve Glorias and one hundred Aves."

---

1 "Hairs of a saint's beard, dipped in holy water, and taken inwardly," are given by Fosbroke (Encycl. Antiq., p. 479) in his list of medieval remedies.

"Get thee to it, quickly, Magot, my darling, and I will say them with thee, which will surely be of still more benefit. Master, I thank you inexpressibly!"

And hastily rising, the Countess repaired to her oratory, whither Margaret followed her. Father Warner was there already, and he joined in the prayers, which made them of infallible efficacy in the eyes of the Countess.

At five o'clock the next morning, in the oratory, the holy hair was duly administered to the patient. All the priests were present except Bruno. Master Aristoteles himself, after high mass, came forward with the blessed relic,—a long, thick, black hair, immersed in holy water, in a golden goblet set with pearls. This Margaret obediently swallowed (of course exclusive of the goblet); and it is not very surprising that a fit of coughing succeeded the process.

"Avaunt thee, Satanas!" said Father Warner, making the sign of the cross in the air above Margaret's head.

Father Nicholas kindly suggested that a little more of the holy water might be efficacious against the manifest enmity of the foul Fiend. Master Aristoteles readily assented; and the additional dose calmed the cough: but probably it did not occur to any one to think whether unholy water would not have done quite as well.

When they had come out into the bower, the Countess took her daughter in her arms, and kissed her brow.

"Now, my Magot," said she playfully—it was not much forced, for her faith was great in the blessed hair—"now, my Magot, thou wilt get well again. Thou must!"

Margaret looked up into the loving face above her, and a faint, sad smile flitted across her lips.

"Think so, dear Lady, if it comfort thee," she said. "It will not be for long !"

CHAPTER XIII.

FATHER BRUNO'S SERMON.

> " And speak'st thou thus,
> Despairing of the sun that sets to thee,
> And of the earthly love that wanes to thee,
> And of the Heaven that lieth far from thee?
> Peace, peace, fond fool !   One draweth near thy door,
> Whose footprints leave no print across the snow.
> Thy Sun has risen with comfort in His face,
> The smile of Heaven to warm thy frozen heart,
> And bless with saintly hand.   What ! is it long
> To wait and far to go ?   Thou shalt not go.
> Behold, across the snow to thee He comes,
> Thy Heaven descends, and is it long to wait ?
> Thou shalt not wait.   ' This night, this night,' He saith,
> ' I stand at the door and knock.' "
>
> *—Jean Ingelow.*

EARL HUBERT went very pale when his wife told him of the conversation which she had had with Margaret. She was his darling, the child of his old age, and he loved her more dearly than he was himself aware. But the blessed hair, and the holy water, were swallowed by him in a figurative sense, with far more implicit faith than they had been, physically, by Margaret. He was quite easy in his mind after that event.

The Countess was a little less so. The saintly relic did not weigh quite so much with her, and the white, still, unchanged face of the girl weighed more. With the restless anxiety of alarm only half awake, she tried to bolster up her own hopes by appeals to every other person.

"Father Nicholas, do you think my daughter looks really ill?"

Father Nicholas, lost at the moment in the Egean Sea, came slowly back from "the many-twinkling smile of ocean" to the consideration of the question referred to him.

"My Lady? Ah, yes! The damsel Margaret. To be sure. Well,—looking ill? I cannot say, Lady, that I have studied the noble damsel's looks. Perhaps—is she a little paler than she used to be? Ah, my Lady, a course of the grand old Greek dramatists,—that would be the thing to set her up. She could not fail to be interested and charmed."

The Countess next applied to Father Warner.

"The damsel does look pale, Lady. What wonder, when she has not confessed for over a fortnight? Get her well shriven, and you will see she will be another maiden."

"She sighs, indeed, my Lady; and I do not think she sleeps well," said Levina, who was the third authority. "It strikes me, under my Lady's pleasure, that she would be the better for a change."

This meant, that Levina was tired of Bury St. Edmund's.

"Oh, there's nothing the matter with her!" said Eva, testily. "She never takes things to heart as I do. She'll do well enough."

"Lady, I am very uneasy about dear Margaret," was Doucebelle's contribution. "I am sure she is ill, and unhappy too. I only wish I knew what to do for her."

Beatrice looked up with grave eyes. "Lady, I would so gladly say No! But I cannot do it."

The last person interrogated was Bruno; and by the time she came to him, the Countess was very low-spirited. His face went grave and sad.

"Lady, it never does good to shut one's eyes to the truth. It is worse pain in the end. Yes: the damsel Margaret is dying."

"Dying!" shrieked the unhappy mother. "Dying, Father Bruno! You said *dying!*"

"Too true, my Lady."

"But what can I do? How am I to stop it?"

"Ah!" said Bruno, softly, as if to himself.

" There is a ' Talitha Cumi ' from the other side too. The Healer is on that side now. Lady, He has called her. In her face, her voice, her very smile, it is only too plain that she has heard His voice. And there is no possibility of disobeying it, whether it call the living to death, or the dead to life."

"But how am I to help it?" repeated the poor Countess.

"You cannot help it. Suffer her to rise and go to Him. Let us only do our utmost to make sure that it is to Him she is going."

"Oh, if it be so, would it be possible to have her spared the pains of Purgatory? Father, I would think it indeed a light matter to give every penny and every jewel that I have!"

"Do so, if it will comfort you. But for her, leave her in His hands without whom not a sparrow falleth. Lady, He loves her better than you."

"Better? It is not possible! I would die for her!"

"He has died for her," answered Bruno, softly. "And He is the Amen, the Living One for ever: and He hath the keys of Hades and of death. She cannot die, Lady, until He bids it who counts every hair upon the head of every child of His."

"But where will she be?—what will she be?" moaned the poor mother.

U

"If she be His, she will be where He is, and like Him."

"But He does not need her, and I do!"

"Nay, if He did not, He would not take her. He loves her too well, Lady, to deal with this weak and weary lamb as He deals with the strong sheep of His flock. He leads them for forty years, it may be, through the wilderness: He teaches them by pain, sorrow, loneliness, unrest. But she is too weak for such discipline, and she is to be folded early. It is far better."

"For her,—well, perhaps—if she can be got past Purgatory. But for me!"

"For each of you, what she needs, Lady."

"O Father Bruno, she is mine only one!"

"Lady, can you not trust her in His hands who gave His Only One for her salvation?"

One evening about this time, Levina came up with the news that Abraham of Norwich wished to see the Damoiselle de Malpas. Her words were civil enough, but her tone never was when she spoke to Beatrice; and on this occasion she put an emphasis on the name, which was manifestly not intended to be flattering. Beatrice, however, took no notice of it. Indeed, she was too glad to see Abraham to feel an inclination to quarrel with the person who announced his arrival in any terms whatever. She threw aside her work in haste, and ran down into the hall.

"My Belasez, light of mine eyes!" said the old man fervently, as he folded her in his arms and blessed her. "Ah, there is not much light for the old pedlar's eyes now!"

"Dost thou miss me, my father?"

"Miss thee! Ah, my darling, how little thou knowest. The sun has gone down, and the heavens are covered with clouds."

"Was my mother very angry after I went away?"

It was not natural to speak of Licorice by any other name.

"Don't mention it, Belasez! She beat me with the broom, until Delecresse interfered and pulled her off. Then she spat at me, and cursed me in the name of Abraham, Isaac, and Jacob, and all the twelve tribes of Israel. She threw dirt at my beard, child."

The last expression, as Beatrice well knew, was an Oriental metaphor.

"Is she satisfied now?"

"Satisfied! What dost thou mean by satisfied? She gives me all the sitten[1] porridge. That is not

[1] Burnt to the pan : a variety of porridge which few would wish to taste twice.

very satisfying, for one can't eat much of it. I break
my fast with Moss, when I can."

Beatrice could not help laughing.

"My poor father! I wish I could just fly in every
morning, to make the porridge for thee."

"Blessed be the memory of the Twelve Patriarchs!
Child, thou wouldst scarcely escape with whole
bones. If Licorice hated Christians before, she
hates them tenfold now.—Dost thou think, Belasez,
that the Lady lacks anything to-day? I have one of
the sweetest pieces of pale blue Cyprus that ever
was woven, and some exquisite gold Damascene
stuffs as well."

"I am sure, Father, she will like to look at them,
and I have little doubt she will buy."

"How are matters going with thee, child? Has
thy father got leave to abandon his vows?"

"He hopes to receive it in a few days."

"Well, well! Matters were better managed in
Israel. Our vows were always terminable. And
Nazarites did not shut themselves up as if other men
were not to be touched, like unclean beasts. We
always washed ourselves, too. There is an old monk
at Norwich, that scents the street whenever he goes
up it : and not with otto of roses. I turn up a side
lane when I see him coming. Even the Saracens
are better than that. I never knew any but Chris-

tians who thought soap and water came from Satan." [1]

"Well, we all wash ourselves here," said Beatrice, laughing, "unless it be Father Warner; I will not answer for him."

"This world is a queer place, my Belasez, full of crooked lanes and crookeder men and women. Men are bad enough, I believe : but women !"——

Beatrice could guess of what woman Abraham was especially thinking.

"Is Cress come with thee, my father ?"

"No—not *here*," answered the old Jew, emphatically. "And he never can."

"Why ?"

"Belasez, I have a sad tale to tell thee."

"O my father ! Is there anything wrong with Cress ?"

It was impossible to recognise Delecresse as uncle instead of brother.

"Aye, child, wrong enough !" said Abraham sadly.

---

[1] "These monks imagined that holiness was often proportioned to a saint's filthiness . . . St. Francis discovered, by certain experience, that the devils . . were animated by clean clothing to tempt and seduce the wearers ; and one of their heroes declares that the purest souls are in the dirtiest bodies. . . Brother Juniper was a gentleman perfectly pious, on this principle ; indeed, so great was his merit in this species of mortification, that a brother declared he could always nose Brother Juniper when within a mile of the monastery, provided the wind were at the due point."—Disraeli's *Curiosities of Literature,* i. 92.

"Is he so ill, my father?"

"Ah, my Belasez, there is a leprosy of the soul, worse than that of the body. And there is no priest left in Israel who can purge that! Child, hast thou never wondered how Sir Piers de Rievaulx came to know of the damsel's marriage—she that is the Lady's daughter?"

"Margaret? I never could tell how it was."

"It was Delecresse who told him."

"Delecresse!"

"Ah, yes—may the God of Israel forgive him!"

"But how did Delecresse know?

"I fancy he guessed it, partly—and perhaps subtlely extracted some avowal from thee, in a way which thou didst not understand at the time."

"But, Father, I could not have told him, even unwittingly, for I did not know it myself. I remember his asking me who Sir Richard was, as we passed through the hall,—yes, and he said to old Hamon that he owed him a grudge. He asked me, too, after that, if Sir Richard were attached to Margaret."

"What didst thou say?"

"That I thought it might be so; but I did not know."

"Well! I am thankful thou couldst tell him no more. I suppose he pieced things together, and very likely jumped the last yard. Howbeit, he did it. My son, my only one! If there were an altar yet left in Israel, it should smoke with a hecatomb of lambs for him."

"All Israelites would not think it wicked, my father. They think all Gentiles fair prey."

"What, after they have eaten of their salt? Child, when the Lady had been kind to thee, I could not have touched a hair of any head she loved. Had the Messiah come that day, and all Gentiles been made our bond-slaves, I would have besought for her to fall to me, that I might free her without an instant's suspense."

"Yes, my father, *thou* wouldst," answered Beatrice, affectionately. "But I do not think thou ever didst hate Christians as some of our nation do."

"Child, Belasez! how could I, when the best love of my white dove's heart had been given to a Christian and a Gentile? I loved her, more than thou canst imagine. But would my love have been true, had I hated what she loved best? Where is thy father, my darling?"

Beatrice was just about to say that she could not tell, when she looked up and saw him. The greeting between Abraham and Bruno was very cordial now. Bruno smiled gravely when he heard of the further exploits of Licorice with the broom; but a very sad, almost stern, expression came into his eyes, when he was told the discovery concerning Delecresse.

"Keep it quiet, my father," he said. "The Lord will repay. May it be not in justice, but with His mercy!"

Then Abraham and his pack were had up to the bower, and large purchases made of Damascene and Cyprus stuffs. When he went away, Bruno walked with him across the yard, and as they clasped hands in farewell, suddenly asked him what he thought of the damsel Margaret.

"Can there be any question?" answered Abraham, pityingly. "Hath not Azrael[1] stamped her with his signet?"

"I fear so. Wilt thou pray for her, my father?"

Abraham looked up in amazement.

"A Christian ask the prayers of a Jew!" exclaimed he.

"Why not?" replied Bruno. "Were not Christ and all His apostles Jews? And thou art a good and true man, my father. The God of Israel heareth the prayers of the righteous."

"Canst thou account a Jew righteous?—one who believes not in thy Messiah?"

"I am not so sure of that," said Bruno, his eyes meeting those of Abraham in full. "I think thy

---

[1] The Angel of Death.

heart and conscience are convinced, but thou art afraid to declare it."

Abraham's colour rose a little.

"May Adonai lead us both to His truth!" he replied.

But Bruno noticed that he made no attempt to deny the charge.

Bruno's chief wish now was to get hold of Margaret, and find out the exact state of her mind. Without knowing his wish, she helped him by asking him to hear her confession. Bruno rose at once.

" Now ? " said Margaret, with a little surprise.

"There is no time but now," was the reply.

They went into the oratory, and closed the door on curious ears ; and Margaret poured out the secrets of her restless and weary heart.

"I longed to confess to you, Father, for I fancied that you would understand me better than the other priests. You know what love is ; I am not sure that they do : and Father Warner at least thinks it weakness, if not sin. And now tell me, have you any balm for such a sorrow as mine ? Of course it can never be undone ; that I know too well. And I do not think that any thing could make me live ; nor do I wish it. If I only knew where it is that I am going ! "

" Let the where alone," answered Bruno.

"Daughter, to whom art thou going? Is it to a Stranger, or to Him whom thy soul loveth?"

Not unnaturally, she misunderstood the allusion.

"No; he will not necessarily die, because I do."

She was only thinking of Richard.

"My child!" said Bruno, gently, "thou art going to the presence of the Lord Jesus Christ. Dost thou know any thing about Him?"

"I know, of course, what the Church teaches."

"Well; but dost thou know what He teaches? Is He as dear to thee as thine earthly love?"

"No." The reply was in a rather shamefaced tone; but there was no hesitation about it.

"Is He as dear to thee as the Earl thy father?"

"No."

"Is He as dear to thee as any person in this house, whomsoever it be,—such as thou hast been acquainted with, and accustomed to, all thy life?"

"Father," said the low, sad voice, "I am afraid you are right. I do not know Him."

"Wilt thou not ask Him, then, to reveal Himself to thee?"

"Will He do it, Father?"

"'Will He'! Has He not been waiting to do it, ever since thou wert brought to Him in baptism?"

"But He can never fill up this void in my heart!"

"He could, my daughter. But I am not sure that

He will, in this world. I rather think that He sees how weak thou art, and means to gather thee early into the warm shelter of His safe and happy fold."

"Father, I feel as if I could not be happy, even in Heaven, if *he* were not there. I can long for the grave, because it will be rest and silence. But for active happiness, such as I suppose they have in Heaven,—Father, I do not want that; I could not bear it. I would rather stay on earth—where Richard is."

"Poor child!" said Bruno half involuntarily. "My daughter, it is very natural. It must be so. 'Where is thy treasure, there is also thine heart.'"

"And," the low voice went on, "if I could know that he had given over loving me, I fancy it would be easier to go."

Bruno thought it best rather to raise her thoughts out of that channel than to encourage them to flow in it.

"My child, Christ has not given over loving thee."

"That does not seem real, like the other. And, O Father! He is not Richard!"

"Dear child, it is far more real: but thine heart is too sore to suffer thine eyes to see it. Dost thou not know that our Lord is saying to thee in this very sorrow, "Come unto Me, and I will give thee rest'?"

"It would be rest, if He would give me Richard," she said. "There is but that one thing for me in all the world."

Bruno perceived that this patient required not the plaster, as he had supposed, but the probe. Her heart was not merely sore; it was rebellious. She was hardening herself against God.

"No, my daughter; thou art not ready for rest. There can be no peace between the King and an unpardoned rebel. Thou art that, Margaret de Burgh. Lay down thine arms, and put thyself in the King's mercy."

"Father!" said the girl, in a voice which was a mixture of surprise and alarm.

"Child, He giveth not account of any of His matters. Unconditional submission is what He requires of His prisoners. Thou wouldst fain dictate terms to thy Sovereign: it cannot be. Thou must come into His terms, if there is to be any peace between Him and thee. Yet even for thee there is a message of love. He is grieved at the hardness of thine heart. Listen to His voice,—'It is hard *for thee* to kick against the pricks.' It is for thy sake that He would have thee come back to thine allegiance."

The answer was scarcely what he expected.

"Father, it is of no use to talk to me. I hear

what you say, of course; but it does me no good. My heart is numb."

"Thou art right," gently replied Bruno. "The south wind must blow upon the garden, ere the spices can flow out. Ask the Lord—I will ask Him also—to pour on thee the gift of the Holy Ghost."

"How many Paters?" said the girl in a weary tone.

"One will do, my daughter, if thou wilt put thy whole heart into it."

"I can put my heart into nothing."

"Then say to Him this only—'Lord, I bring Thee a dead heart, that Thou mayest give it life.'"

She said the words after him, mechanically, like a child repeating a lesson.

"How long will it take?"

"He knows—not I."

"But suppose I die first?"

"The Lord will not let thee die unsaved, if thou hast a sincere wish for salvation. He wants it more than thou."

"He wants it!" repeated Margaret wonderingly.

"He wants it. He wants thee. Did He die for thee, child, that He should let thee go lightly? Thou art as precious in His sight as if the world held none beside thee."

"I did not think I was that to any one—except my parents and—and Richard."

"Thou art that, incomparably more than to any of them, to the Lord Jesus."

The momentary exhibition of feeling was past.

"Well!" she said, with a dreary sigh. "It may be so. But I cannot care about it."

Bruno's answer was not addressed to Margaret.

"Lord, care about it for her! Breathe upon this dead, that she may live! Save her in spite of herself!"

There was a slight pause, and then Bruno quietly gave the absolution, and the confession was over.

The next Sunday, there was the unwonted occurrence of a sermon after vespers. Sermons were not fashionable at that time. When preached at all, they were usually extremely dry scholastic disquisitions. Father Warner had given two during his abode at the Castle: and both were concerning the duty of implicit obedience to the Church. Father Nicholas had preached about a dozen; some on the virtues—dreary classical essays; three concerning the angels; and one (on a Good Friday) which was a series of fervent declamations on the Passion.

But this time it was Bruno who preached; and on a very different topic from any mentioned above. His clear, ringing voice was in itself a much more interesting sound than Father Nicholas's drowsy monotone, or Father Warner's dry staccato. He at least was interested in his subject; no one could doubt that. As soon as the last note of the last chant had died away, Bruno came forward to the steps of the altar. He had given due notice of his intention beforehand, and every one (with Beatrice in particular) was prepared to listen to him.

The text itself—to hearers unfamiliar with the letter of Scripture—was rather a startling one.

"'O all ye that pass by the way, hearken and see if there be sorrow like unto my sorrow, wherewith the Lord hath trodden me as in the wine-press, in the day of the wrath of His anger.'"

Margaret looked up quickly. This seemed to her the very language of her own heart. She at least was likely to be attentive.

Perhaps no medieval preacher except Bruno de Malpas would even have thought of alluding to the literal and primary meaning of the words. From the first moment of their joint existence, Jerusalem and Rome have been enemies and rivals. Not content with, so far as in her lay, blotting out the very name of Israel from under heaven, Rome has calmly arrogated to herself—without even offering proof of it— that right to the promises made to the fathers, which, St. Paul tells us, belongs in a higher and richer sense to the invisible Church of Christ than to the literal and visible Israel. But Rome goes further than the

Apostle: for in her anxiety to claim the higher sense for herself, she denies the lower altogether. No Romanist will hear with patience of any national restoration of Israel. And whether the Anglo-Israelite theory be true or false, it is certainly, as a theory, exceedingly unpalatable to Rome.

With respect, moreover, to this particular passage, it had become so customary to refer it to the sufferings of Christ, that its original application to the destruction of Jerusalem had been almost forgotten.

But here, Bruno's Jewish proclivities stood him in good stead. He delighted Beatrice by fully stating the original reference of the passage. But then he went on to say that it was no longer applicable to the Babylonish captivity. Since that time, there had been another sorrow to which the sufferings of Israel were not to be compared—to which no affliction ever suffered by humanity could be comparable for a moment. He told them, in words that burned, of that three hours' darkness that might be felt—of that "Eli, Eli, lama sabachthani" into which was more than concentrated every cry of human anguish since the beginning of the world. And then he looked, as it were, straight into the heart's depths of every one of his hearers, and he said to each one of those hearts, "This was your doing!" He told them that for every sin of every one among them, that Sacrifice was a sufficient atonement: and that if for any one the atonement was not efficacious, that was not Christ's fault, but his own. There was room at the marriage-supper for every pauper straying on the high-way; and if one of them were not there, it would be because he had refused the invitation.

Then Bruno turned to the other half of his subject, and remarked that every man and woman was tempted to think that there was no sorrow like to his sorrow. Yet there was a balm for all sorrow: but it was only to be had at one place. The bridge which had been strong enough to bear the weight of Christ and His cross, carrying with Him all the sins and sorrows of all the world for ever, would be strong enough to bear any sorrow of theirs. But so long as man persisted in saying, "*My* will be done," he must not imagine that God would waste mercy in helping him. "Not my will, but Thine," must always precede the sending of the strengthening angel. And lastly, he reminded them that God sent grief to them for their own sakes. It was not for His sake. It gave Him no pleasure; nay, it grieved Him, when He had to afflict the children of men. It was the medicine without which they could not recover health: and He always gave the right remedy, in the right quantities, and at the right time.

"And now," said Bruno at last, "ye into whose

hands the Great Physician hath put this wholesome yet bitter cup,—how are ye going to treat it? Will ye dash it down, and say, 'I will have none of this remedy?' For the end of that is death, the death eternal. Will ye drink it, only because ye have no choice, with a wry face and a bitter tongue, blaspheming the hand that gives it? It will do you no good then; it will work for evil. Or will ye take it meekly, with thanksgiving on your lips, though there be tears in your eyes, knowing that His will is better than yours, and that He who bore for you the pangs that no man can know, is not likely to give you any bitterness that He can spare you? Trust me, the thanksgivings that God loves best, are those sobbed from lips that cannot keep still for sorrow.

"And, brethren, there is no sorrow in Heaven. 'Death there shall be no more, neither sorrow, nor crying, nor pain shall be any more.'[1] We who are Christ's shall be there before long."

He ended thus, almost abruptly.

The chapel was empty, and the congregation were critical. Earl Hubert thought that Father Bruno had a good flow of language, and could preach an excellent discourse. The Countess would have preferred a different subject: it was so melancholy!

---

[1] All quotations from Scripture in this story are of course taken from the Vulgate, except those made by Jews.

Sir John thought it a pity that man had been wasted on the Church. Hawise supposed that he had said just what was proper. Beatrice wished he would preach every day. Eva was astonished at her; did she really like to listen to such dolorous stuff as that? Doucebelle wondered that any one should think it dolorous; she had enjoyed it very much. Marie confessed to having dropped asleep, and dreamed that Father Bruno gave her a box of bonbons.

There was one of them who said nothing, because her heart was too full for speech. But the south wind had begun to blow upon the garden. On that lonely and weary heart God had looked in His mercy that day, and had said, " Live! "

Too late for earthly life. That was sapped at the root. God knew that His best kindness to Margaret de Burgh was that He should take her away from the evil to come.

CHAPTER XIV.

EVIL TIDINGS.

" Too tired for rapture, scarce I reach and cling
  To One that standeth by with outstretched hand ;
  Too tired to hold Him, if He hold not me :
  Too tired to long but for one heavenly thing,—
  Rest for the weary, in the Promised Land."

PERMISSION for Bruno to lay aside the habit of Saint Augustine reached Bury Castle very soon after his sermon. And with it came two other items of news, — the one, that Bishop Grosteste offered him a rich living in his diocese; the other, that the Bishop's life had been attempted by poison. It was not to be wondered at in the least, since Grosteste had coolly declared the reigning Pope Innocent to be an exact counterpart of Anti-Christ (for which the head of the Church rewarded him by terming him a wicked old dotard), and his attachment to monachism in general was never allowed to stand in the way of the sternest rebuke to disorderly monks in particular. He also presumed to object to his clergy having constant recourse to Jewish money-lenders, and especially interfered with their favourite amusement of amateur theatricals, which he was so unreasonable as to think unbecoming the clerical office.

Bruno hastened to the Countess with the news, accompanying it by warm thanks for the shelter afforded to himself and his daughter, and informing her that he would no longer burden her with either. But she looked very grave.

"Father Bruno," she said, "I have a boon to ask."

"Ask it freely, Lady. I am bound to you in all ways."

"Then I beg that you and Beatrice will continue here, so long—*ha, chétife !*—so long as my child lives."

Father Bruno gravely assented. He knew too well that would not be long. Yet it proved longer than either of them anticipated.

Stormy times were at hand. The Papal Legate had effected between Earl Hubert and the Bishop of Winchester a reconciliation which resembled a quiescent volcano ; but Hubert was put into a position of sore peril by his royal brother-in-law of Scotland, who coolly sent an embassy to King Henry, demanding as his right that the three northernmost counties of England should be peaceably resigned to him. After putting him off for a time by an evasive message, King Henry consented to meet Alexander at York, and discuss the questions on which they differed. His Britannic Majesty was still vexing his nobles by the favour he showed to foreigners. At this time he demanded a subsidy of one-thirtieth of all the property in the kingdom, which they were by no means inclined to give him. As a sop to Cerberus, the King promised thenceforth to abide by the advice of his native nobility, and the subsidy was voted. But his next step was to invite his father-in-law, the Count of Provence, and to shower upon him the gold so unwillingly granted. The nobles were more angry than ever, and the King's own brother, Richard Earl of Cornwall, was the first to remonstrate. Then Archbishop Edmund of Canterbury took a journey to Rome, and declined to return, even when recalled by the Legate. But the grand event of that year was the final disruption of Christendom. The Greek Church had many a time quarrelled with the Latin, chiefly on two heads,—the worship of images and the assumption of universal primacy. On the first count they differed with very little distinction, since the Greek Church allowed the full worship of pictures, but anathematised every body who paid reverence to statues,—a rather odd state of things to Protestant eyes. Once already, the Eastern Church had seceded, but the quarrel was patched up again. But after the secession of 1237, there was never to be peace between East and West again.

The new year came in with a royal marriage. There were curious circumstances attending it, for the parties married in spite of the King, who was obliged to give away the bride, his sister Alianora, "right sore against his will:" and though the bride had taken the vow of perpetual widowhood,[1] they did not trouble themselves about a Papal dispensation till they had been married for some weeks. The bridegroom was the young Frenchman, Sir Simon de Montfort, whom the King at last came to fear more than thunder and lightning. The English nobility were extremely displeased, for they considered that the Princess had been married beneath her dignity; but since from first to last she had had her own wilful way, it was rather unreasonable in the nobles to vent their wrath upon the King. They rose against him furiously, headed by his own brother, and by the husband of the Princess Marjory of Scotland, till at last the royal standard was deserted by all but one man,—that true and loyal patriot, Hubert, Earl of Kent,—the man whom no oppression could alienate

---

[1] She was the young widow of William, Earl of Pembroke, the eldest brother of the husband of Marjory of Scotland.

from the Throne, and whom no cruelty could silence when he thought England in danger. But now his prestige was on the wane. The nobles were not afraid of him, on account of his old age, his wisdom, and a vow which he had taken never to bear arms again. In vain King Henry appealed privately to every peer, asking if his fidelity might be relied on. From every side defiant messages came back. The citizens of London, as their wont was, were exceptionally disloyal. Then he sent the Legate to his brother, urging peace. Cornwall refused to listen. At last, driven into a corner, the King begged for time, and it was granted him, until the first Monday in Lent. When that day came, the nobles assembled in grand force at London, to come to a very lame and impotent conclusion. Earl Richard of Cornwall, the King's brother, suddenly announced that he and his new brother-in-law, Montfort, had effected a complete reconciliation. The other nobles were very angry at the desertion of their leader, and accused him, perhaps not untruly, of having been bribed into this conduct: for Cornwall was quite as extravagant, and nearly as acquisitive, as his royal brother. Just at this time died Joan, Queen of Scotland, the eldest sister of King Henry, of rapid decline, while on her way home from England ; and her death was quickly followed by that of Hubert's great enemy, the Bishop of Winchester. The filling up of the vacant see caused one of the frequent struggles between England and Rome. The Chapter of Winchester wished to have the Bishop of Chichester: the King was determined to appoint the Queen's uncle, Guglielmo of Savoy; and, as he often did to gain his ends, Henry sided with Rome against his own people.

The disruption between the Greek and Latin Churches being now an accomplished fact, the Archbishop of Antioch went the length of excommunicating the Pope and the whole Roman Church, asserting that if there were to be a supreme Pontiff, he had the better claim to the title. This event caused a disruption on a small scale in Margaret's bower, where Beatrice scandalised the fair community by wanting to know why the Pope should not be excommunicated if he deserved it.

"Excommunicate the head of the Church!" said Hawise, in a horrified tone.

"Well, but here are two Churches," persisted Beatrice. "If the Pope can excommunicate the Archbishop, what is to prevent the Archbishop from excommunicating the Pope?"

"Poor creature!" said Hawise pityingly.

"The Eastern schism is no Church!" added Eva.

"Oh, I do wish some of you would tell me what you mean by a Church!" exclaimed Beatrice, earnestly, laying down her work. "What makes one thing a Church, and another a schism?"

But that was just what nobody could tell her. Hawise leaped the chasm deftly by declaring it an improper question. Eva said, "*Si bête!*" and declined to say more.

"Well, I may be a fool," said Beatrice bluntly: "but I do not think you are much better if you cannot tell me."

"Of course I could tell thee, if I chose!" answered Eva, with lofty scorn.

"Then why dost thou not?" was the unanswerable reply.

Eva did not deign to respond. But when Bruno next appeared, Beatrice put her question.

"The Church is what Christ builds on Himself: a schism is bred in man's brain, contrary to holy Scripture."

In saying which, Bruno only quoted Bishop Grosteste.

"But, seeing men are fallible, how then can any human system claim to be at all times The Church?" asked Beatrice.

"The true Church is not a human system at all," said he.

"Father, Beatrice actually fancies that the Archbishop of Antioch could excommunicate the holy Father!" observed Hawise in tones of horror.

"I suppose any authority can excommunicate those below him, in the Church visible," said Bruno, calmly: "in the invisible Jerusalem above, which is the mother of us all, none excommunicates but God. 'Every branch in Me, not fruit-bearing, He taketh it away.' My daughters, it would do us more good to bear that in mind, than to blame either the Pope or the Archbishop."

And he walked away, as was his wont when he had delivered his sentence.

That afternoon, the Countess sent for Beatrice and Doucebelle to her own bower. They found her seated by the window, with unusually idle hands, and an expression of sore disturbance on her fair, serene face.

"There is bad news come, my damsels," she said, when the girls had made their courtesies. "And I do not know how to tell my Magot. Perhaps one of you might manage it better than I could. And she had better be told, for she is sure to hear it in some way, and I would fain spare the child all I can."

"About Sir Richard the Earl, Lady?" asked Beatrice.

"Yes, of course. He is married, Beatrice."

"To whom, Lady?" asked Beatrice, calmly: but Doucebelle uttered an ejaculation under her breath.

"To Maud, daughter of Sir John de Lacy, the Earl of Lincoln. It is no fault of his, poor boy! The Lord King would have it so. And the King has made a good thing of it, for I hear that the Earl of Lincoln has given him above three thousand gold pennies to have the marriage, and has remitted a debt of thirteen hundred more. A good thing for him!—and it may be quite as well for Richard. But my poor child! I cannot understand how it is that she does not rouse up and forget her disappointment. It is very strange."

It was very strange, to the mother who loved Margaret so dearly, and yet understood her so little. But Doucebelle silently thought that any thing else would have been yet stranger.

"And you would have us tell her, Lady?"

"It would be as well. Really, I cannot!"

The substratum was showing itself for a moment in the character of the Countess.

"Dulcie would *do* it better than I," said Beatrice. "I am a bad hand at beating about the bush. I might do it too bluntly."

"Then, Dulcie, do tell her!" pleaded the Countess.

"Very well, Lady." But all Doucebelle's unselfishness did not prevent her from feeling that she would almost rather have had any thing else to do.

She went back slowly to Margaret's bower, tenanted at that moment by no one but its owner. Margaret looked up as Doucebelle entered, and read her face as easily as possible.

"Evil tidings!" she said, quietly enough. "For thee, or for me, Dulcie?"

Doucebelle came and knelt beside her.

"For me, then!" Margaret's voice trembled a little. "Go on, Dulcie! Richard"——

She could imagine no evil tidings except as associated with him.

Doucebelle conquered her unwillingness to speak, by a strong effort.

"Yes, dear Margaret, it is about him. The"——

"Is he dead?" asked Margaret, hurriedly.

"No."

"I thought, if it had been that"—— she hesitated.

"Margaret, didst thou not expect something more to happen?"

"Something—what? I see!" and her tone changed. "It is marriage."

"Yes, Sir Richard is married to"——

"No! Don't tell me to whom. I am afraid I should hate her. And I do not want to do that."

Doucebelle was silent.

"Was it his doing," asked Margaret in a low voice, "or did the Lord King order it?"

"Oh, it was the Lord King's doing, entirely, the Lady says."

"O Dulcie! I ought to wish it were his, because there would be more likelihood of his being happy: but I cannot—I cannot!"

"My poor Margaret, I do not wonder!" answered Doucebelle tenderly.

"Is it very wicked," added Margaret, in a voice of deep pain, "not to be able to wish him to be happy, without me? It is so hard, Dulcie! To be shut out from the warmth and the sunlight, and to see some one else let in! I suppose that is a selfish feeling. But it is so hard!"

"My poor darling!" was all that Doucebelle could say.

"Father Bruno said, that so long as we kept saying, 'My will be done,' we must not expect God to comfort us. Yet how are we to give over? O Dulcie, I thought I was beginning to submit, and this has stirred all up again. My heart cries out and says, 'This shall not be! I will not have it so!' And if God will have it so!—How am I to learn to bend my will to His?"

Neither of the girls had heard any one enter,

and they were a little startled when a third voice replied—

"None but Himself can teach thee that, my daughter. If thou canst not yet give Him thy will, ask Him to take it in spite of thee."

"I have done that, already, Father Bruno."

"Then thou mayest rest assured that He will do all that is lacking."

That night, Bruno said to Beatrice,—"That poor, dear child! I am sure God is teaching her. But to-day's news has driven another nail into her coffin."

Would it have been easier, or harder, if the veil could have been lifted which hid from Margaret the interior of Gloucester Castle? To the eyes of the world outside, the young Earl behaved like any other bridegroom. He brought the Lady Maud to his home, placed her in sumptuous apartments, surrounded her with obsequious attendants, provided her with all the comforts and luxuries of life : but there his attentions ended. For four years his step never crossed the threshold of the tower where she resided, and they met only on ceremonial occasions. Wife she never was to him, until for twelve months the cold stones of Westminster Abbey had lain over the fair head of his Margaret, the one love of his tried and faithful heart.

Having now completed the wreck of these two young lives, His Majesty considerately intimated to Richard de Clare, that in return for the unusual favours which had been showered upon him, he only asked of him to feel supremely happy, and to be devoted to his royal service for the term of his natural life.

Only !

How often it is the case that we imagine our friends to be blessing us with every fibre of their hearts, when it is all that they can do to pray for grace to enable them to forgive us !

Not that Richard did any thing of the kind. So far from it, that he registered a vow in Heaven, that if ever the power to do it should fall into his hands, he would repay that debt an hundredfold.

The two chaplains of the Earl had shown no interest whatever in Margaret and her troubles. Father Warner despised all human affections of whatever kind, with the intensity of a nature at once cold and narrow. Father Nicholas was of a far kindlier disposition, but he was completely engrossed with another subject. Alchemy was reviving. The endless search for the philosopher's stone, the elixir of life, and other equally desirable and unattainable objects, had once more begun to engage the energies of scientific men. The real end which they were approaching was the invention of gunpowder, which can hardly be termed a blessing to the world at large. But Father Nicholas fell into the snare, and was soon absolutely convinced that only one ingredient was wanting to enable him to discover the elixir of life. That one ingredient, of priceless value, remains undiscovered in the nineteenth century.

Yet one thing must be said for these medieval philosophers,—that except in the way of spending money, they injured none but themselves. Their search for the secret of life did not involve the wanton torture of helpless creatures, nor did their boasted knowledge lead them to the idiotic conclusion that they were the descendants of a jelly-fish.

Oh, this much-extolled, wise, learned, supercilious Nineteenth Century! Is it so very much the superior of all its predecessors, as it complacently assumes to be?

King Alexander of Scotland married his second wife in the May of 1239, to the great satisfaction of his sisters. The Countess of Kent thought that such news as this really ought to make Margaret cheer up: and she was rather perplexed (which Doucebelle was not by any means) at the discovery that all the gossip on that subject seemed only to increase her sadness. An eclipse of the sun, which occurred on the third of June, alarmed the Countess considerably. Some dreadful news might reasonably be expected after that. But no worse occurrence (from her point of view) happened than the birth of a Prince—afterwards to be Edward the First, who has been termed "the greatest of all the Plantagenets."

The occasion of the royal christening was eagerly seized upon, as a delightful expedient for the replenishing of his exhausted treasury, by the King who might not inappropriately be termed the least of the Plantagenets. Messengers were sent with tidings of the auspicious event to all the peers, and if the gifts with which they returned laden were not of the costliest description, King Henry dismissed them in disgrace. "God gave us this child," exclaimed a blunt Norman noble, "but the King sells him to us!"

Four days after the Prince's birth came another event, which to one at least in Bury Castle, was enough to account for any portentous eclipse. The Countess found Beatrice drowned in tears.

"Beatrice!—my dear maiden, what aileth thee? I have scarcely ever seen thee shed tears before."

The girl answered by a passionate gesture.

"'Oh that mine head were waters, and mine eyes a fountain of tears, that I might weep day and night for the slain of the daughter of my people!'"

"*Ha, chétife !*—what is the matter ?"

"Lady, there has been an awful slaughter of my people." And she stood up and flung up her hands towards heaven, in a manner which seemed to the Countess worthy of some classic prophetess. "'Remember, O Adonai, what is come upon us; consider, and behold our reproach!' 'O God, why hast Thou cast us off for ever? why doth Thine anger smoke against the sheep of Thy pasture? We see not our signs: there is no more any prophet.' 'Arise, O Adonai, judge the earth! for Thou shalt inherit all nations.'"

The Countess stood mute before this unparalleled outburst. She could not comprehend it.

"My child, I do not understand," she said, kindly enough. "Has some relative of thine been murdered? How shocking!"

"Are not all my people kindred of mine?" exclaimed Beatrice, passionately.

"Dost thou mean the massacre of the Jews in London?" said the Countess, as the truth suddenly flashed upon her. "Oh yes, I did hear of some such dreadful affair. But, my dear, remember, thou art now a De Malpas. Thou shouldst try to forget thine unfortunate connection with that low race. They are not thy people any longer."

Beatrice looked up, with flashing eyes from which

some stronger feeling than sorrow had suddenly driven back the tears.

"'If I forget thee, O Jerusalem, let my right hand forget her cunning!' Lady, thou canst not fathom the heart of a Jew. No Christian can. We are brethren for ever. And you call my nationality unfortunate, and low! Know that I look upon that half of my blood as the King does upon his crown, —yea, as the Lord does upon His people! 'We are Thine; Thou never barest rule over them; they were not called by Thy name.' But you do not understand, Lady."

"No,—it is very strange," replied the Countess, in a dubious tone. "Jews do not seem to understand their position. It is odd. But dry thine eyes, my dear child; thou wilt make thyself ill. And really "——

The Countess was too kind to finish the sentence. But Beatrice could guess that she thought there was really nothing to weep over in the massacre of a few scores of Jews. She found little sympathy among the younger members of the family party. Margaret said she was sorry, but it was evidently for the fact that her friend was in trouble, not for the event over which she was sorrowing. Eva openly expressed profound scorn of both the Jews and the sorrow.

Marie wanted to know if some friend of Beatrice were among the slain: because, if not, why should she care any thing about it? Doucebelle alone seemed capable of a little sympathy.

But before the evening was over, Beatrice found there was one Christian who could enter into all her feelings. She was slowly crossing the ante-chamber in the twilight, when she found herself intercepted and drawn into Bruno's arms.

"My darling!" he said, tenderly. "I am sent to thee with heavy tidings."

Poor Beatrice laid her tired head on her father's breast, with the feeling that she had one friend left in the world.

"I know it, dear Father. But it is such a comfort that you feel it with me."

"There are not many who will, I can guess," answered Bruno. "But, my child, I am afraid thou dost not know all."

"Father!—what is it?" asked Beatrice, fearfully.

"One has fallen in that massacre, very dear to thee and me, my daughter."

"Delecresse?" She thought him the most likely to be in London of any of the family.

"No. Delecresse is safe, so far as I know."

"Is it Uncle Moss?—or Levi my cousin?"

"Beatrice, it is Abraham the son of Ursel, the father of us all."

The low cry of utter desolation which broke from the girl's lips was pitiful to hear.

"'My father, my father! the chariot of Israel, and the horsemen thereof!'"

Bruno let her weep passionately, until the first burst of grief was over. Then he said, gently,

"Be comforted, my Beatrice. I believe that he sleeps in Jesus, and that God shall bring him with Him."

"He was not baptized?" asked Beatrice, in some surprise that Bruno should think so.

"He was ready for it. He had spoken to a friend of mine—one Friar Saher de Kilvingholme—on the subject. And the Lord would not refuse to receive him because his brow had not been touched by water, when He had baptized him with the Holy Ghost and with fire."

Perhaps scarcely any priest then living, Bruno excepted, would have ventured so far as to say that.

"Oh, this *is* a weary world!" sighed Beatrice, drearily.

"It is not the only one," replied her father.

"It seems as if we were born only to die!"

"Nay, my child. We were born to live for ever. Those have death who choose it."

"A great many seem to choose it."

"A great many," said Bruno, sadly.

"Father," said Beatrice, after a short silence, "as a man grows older and wiser, do you think that he comes to understand any better the reason of the dark doings of Providence? Can you see any light upon them, which you did not of old?"

"No, my child, I think not," was Bruno's answer. "If any thing, I should say they grow darker. But we learn to trust, Beatrice. It is not less dark when the child puts his hand confidingly in that of his father; but his mind is the lighter for it. We come to know our Father better; we learn to trust and wait. 'What I do, thou knowest not now: but thou shalt know hereafter.' And He has told us that in that land where we are to know even as we are known, we shall be satisfied. Satisfied with His dealings, then: let us be satisfied with Him, here and now."

"It is dark!" said Beatrice, with a sob.

"'The morning cometh,' replied Bruno. "And 'in the morning is gladness.'"

Beatrice stood still and silent for some minutes, only a slight sob now and then showing the storm through which she had passed. At last, in a low, troubled voice, she said,—

"There is no one to call me Belasez now!"

Bruno clasped her closer.

"My darling!" he said, "so long as the Lord spares us to each other, thou wilt always be *belle assez* for me!"

CHAPTER XV.

" Joy for the freed one !   She might not stay
    When the crown had fallen from her life away :
    She might not linger, a weary thing,
    A dove with no home for its broken wing,
    Thrown on the harshness of alien skies,
    That know not its own land's melodies.
    From the long heart-withering early gone,
    She hath lived—she hath loved—her task is done !"
                                        —*Felicia Hemans.*

"NOW, Sir John de Averenches, what on earth dost *thou* want ?"

" Is there no room, Damsel ?"

" Room !   There is room enough for thee, I dare say," replied Eva, rather contemptuously. She looked down on Sir John supremely for four reasons, which in her own eyes at least were excellent ones. First, he was rather short; secondly, he was very silent;

thirdly, he was not particularly handsome; and lastly (and of most import), he had remained proof against all Eva's attractions.

"I thank thee," was all he said now; and he walked into Margaret's bower, where he took a seat on the extreme end of the settle, and never said a word to any body whilst he stayed.

"The absurd creature!" exclaimed Eva, when he was gone. "What an absolute ass he is! He has not an idea in his head."

"Oh, I beg thy pardon, Eva," interposed Marie, rather warmly. "He's plenty of ideas. He'll talk if one talks to him. Thou never dost."

"He is clever enough to please thee, very likely!" was the rather snappish answer.

From that evening, Sir John de Averenches took to frequenting the bower occasionally, much to the annoyance of Eva, until the happy thought struck her that she might have captivated him at last. Mentally binding him to her chariot wheels, she made no further objection, but on the contrary, became so amiable that the shrewd little Marie noticed the alteration.

"Well, Eva is queer!" said that acute young lady. "She goes into the sulks if Sir William de

Cantilupe so much as looks at any body; but she does not care how many people she looks at! I think she should be jealous on both sides!"

Eva's amenities, however, seemed to have no more effect on Sir John than her displeasure. Night after night, there he sat, never speaking to any one, and apparently not noticing one more than another.

"He's going out of his mind," suggested Marie.

"Not he!" said Eva. "He's none to go out of!"

The mystery was left unsolved, except by Bruno, who fancied that he guessed its meaning; but since the clue was one which he preferred not to pursue, he discreetly left matters to shape themselves, or rather, to be shaped by Providence, when the time should come.

That was a dreary winter altogether. The King had openly insulted his sister and Montfort, when they made their appearance at the ceremony of the Queen's "up-rising;"[1] and they had left England, pocketing the affront, but as concerned Montfort, by no means forgetting it.

The Pope made further encroachments on the liberties of the Church of England, by sending over a horde of Italians to fill vacant benefices. The

[1] Churching.

nobles blazed out into open wrath "that the Pope, through avarice, should deprive them of their ancient right to the patronage of livings!" They were headed, as usual, by the King's brother, Richard Earl of Cornwall, who seems to have been not a true, living Christian (as there is reason to believe his son was), but simply a political opponent of the aggressions of Rome. The citizens of London were about equally disgusted with the King, who at this time received a visit from the Queen's uncle, Tomaso of Savoy, and in his delight, His Majesty commanded his loyal and grumbling subjects to remove all dirt from the streets, and to meet the Count in gala clothing, and with horses handsomely accoutred.

The hint thrown out by Levina had not been lost on the Countess. She thought a complete change might do good to the fading flower which was only too patently withering on its stem: and at her instance the whole household removed to Westminster at the beginning of this winter. They had hardly settled down in their new abode when a fresh storm broke on the now aged head of Earl Hubert.

Once more, all the old, worn-out charges were trumped up, including even that by which the Princess Margaret's name had been so cruelly aspersed. A flash of the early fire of the old man blazed forth when the accusation was made.

"I was never a traitor to you, nor to your father!" said Hubert de Burgh, facing his ungrateful King and pupil of long ago: "If I had been, under God, you would never have been here!"

It was true, and Henry knew it, best of all men.

The King, in the fulness of his compassionate grace, was pleased to let the Earl off very lightly. The sentence passed was, that he should only resign the four most valuable castles that he had. This, of course, was not because Hubert was guilty, but because His Majesty was covetous. Château Blanc, Grosmond, Skenefrith, and Hatfield, were given up to the Crown. Hubert bore it, we are told, very quietly and patiently. His own time could not be long now, for he was at least seventy; and the Benjamin of his love was dying of a broken heart.

King Henry himself was not without sorrow, for about All Saints' Day, Guglielmo of Savoy, the beloved uncle who had moulded him like wax, died rather suddenly at Viterbo. So grieved was the King, that he tore his royal mantle from his shoulders, and flung it into the fire. With that sudden and passionate reaction to the other side, often seen in weak natures, he now threw himself into the arms of the Predicants and Minorites—until he set up a new favourite, who was not long in appearing.

Before the winter was over, a second sorrow fell upon Richard de Clare, in the death of his mother, Isabel, wife of the King's brother. Cornwall grieved bitterly both for the loss of his wife and for the miserable state into which England was sinking; and declaring that he loved his country so much, that he could not bear to stay and see it go to ruin, he prepared to head a fresh crusade. Perhaps it did not occur to him that love and patriotism would have been shown better by staying at home and trying to keep his country from going to ruin. That was reserved for another Richard—the young Earl of Gloucester.

Another comet, and a violent hurricane, in the spring, made the augurs shake their heads and prophesy worse calamities than ever. There was a fresh one on the way, in the shape of a Papal exaction of one-fifth of the property of foreign bene-ficed clerks in England, in order to support the war then waged by the Pope on the Emperor of Germany. The royal Council was stirred, and told its listless master that he "ought not to suffer England to become a spoil and a desolation to immigrants, like a vineyard without a wall, exposed to wild beasts." His Majesty, like a true son of holy Church, replied that he "neither wished nor dared to oppose the Pope in any thing." As if to make confusion worse confounded, the Archbishop of Canterbury (subsequently known as St. Edmund of Pontigny) aspired to become a second Becket, and appealed to the Pope to do away with state patronage, which he of course considered ought to be vested in the Primate. King Henry, supine as he was, was roused at last, and sent a message to Rome to the effect that the appeal of the Archbishop was contrary to his royal dignity. The Pope declined to entertain the appeal: and the King, we are told (by a monk) "became more tyrannical than ever," and appointed Bonifacio of Savoy to the See of Winchester. The defeated Archbishop submitted to the Pope's demand of a fifth of his income: but when the Pope, emboldened by success, came to an agreement with the Italian priests occupying English benefices, that on condition of their helping him against the Emperor, all benefices in his gift should be bestowed upon

Italians, the Archbishop could bear no longer, and he left England, never to return. He died at Pontigny, his birthplace, on the sixteenth of November following; and not long afterwards, King Henry reverently knelt to worship at the tomb of the saint[1] who had been a thorn in his side as long as he lived.

Then the English Abbots, cruelly mulcted by the Pope, appealed to their natural Sovereign, to be met by a scowl, and to hear the Legate told that he might choose the best of the royal castles wherein to imprison them. Twenty-four Roman priests came over to fill English benefices: and at last, when the Legate left England (for which "no one was sorry but the King"), it was calculated that with the exception of church plate, he carried out of England more wealth than he left in it.

But in the halls of Earl Hubert at Westminster, all interest in outside calamities was lost in the inside. As that spring drew on towards summer, the blindest eyes could no longer refuse to see that the white lily had faded at last, and the star was going out.

The trial of patience had been long for Margaret, but it was over now.

<hr>

[1] *Rot. Exit., Pasc.,* 41 H. III.

Master Aristoteles could not understand it. The maiden had no disease that he could discover: and to think that the blessed hair of St. Dominic should have failed to restore her! It was most unaccountable.

There was no word of complaint from the dying girl. She no longer thought it strange that God should have made her young life short and bitter. The lesson was learned, at last.

So gradually her life went out, that no one expected the end just when it came. Weaker and weaker she grew from day to day; more unable to sit up, to work, to talk: but the transition from life to death was so quiet that it was difficult for those around to realise how near it was.

Margaret had risen and dressed every day, but had lain outside her bed when dressed, for the greater part of April. It was May Day now, and in all the streets were May-poles and May dancers, singing and sunshine.

Eva went out early, with a staff of attendants, to join in the festivities.

"Why, what good can there be in my staying at home?" she said, answering Doucebelle's face. "Margaret will not be any better because I am here. And then, when I come in at night, I can tell her all about it. And it is no use talking, Doucebelle! I really cannot bear this sort of thing! I get so melancholy, you have no idea! I don't know what would become of me if I had not some diversion."

Beatrice and Doucebelle stayed with Margaret: Doucebelle from a sort of inward sensation, she hardly knew what or why; Beatrice from a remark made by Bruno the night before.

"It will not be long, now, at least," he had said.

The day wore slowly on, but it seemed just like twenty days which had preceded it. Bruno paid his daily visit towards evening.

"Are the streets very full of holiday-makers?" asked Margaret.

"Very full, my daughter. There is a great crowd round the May-pole."

"I hope Eva will enjoy herself."

"I have no doubt she will."

"It seems so far off, now," said Margaret, dreamily. "As if I were where I could hardly see it—somewhere above this world, and all the things that are in the world. Father, have you any idea what there will be in Heaven?"

"There will be Christ," answered Bruno. "And what may be implied in ' His glory, which God hath given Him,'—our finite minds are scarcely capable of guessing. Only, His will is that His people shall behold it and share it. It must be something that He thinks worth seeing—He, who has beheld the glory of God before the worlds were."

"Father," said Margaret, with deep feeling, "it seems too much that *we* should see it."

"True. But not too much that He should bestow it. He gives,—as He forgives—like a king."

Like what king?—was the thought in Doucebelle's mind. Not like the one of whom she knew any thing—who was responsible before God for that death which was coming on so quietly, yet so surely.

Beatrice had left the room a few minutes before, and she was now returning to it through the ante-chamber. The dusk was rapidly falling, and, not knowing of any presence but her own, she was extremely startled to find herself grasped by the shoulder, by a firm hand which evidently had no intention of standing any trifling. She looked up into the face of a stranger, and yet a face which was not altogether strange. It was that of a tall, handsome man, with fair hair, and a stern, pained compression of brow and lips.

"Is it true?" he said in a husky voice.

"Is what true?" Beatrice was too startled to think what he meant.

The grasp upon her shoulder tightened till a weaker woman would have screamed.

"Belasez, do not trifle with me! Is she dying?"

And then, all at once, Beatrice knew who it was that asked her.

"It is too true, Sir Richard," she said sadly, pityingly, with almost a reverential compassion for that faithful love which had brought him there that night.

"I must see her, Belasez."

"Is it wise, Sir Richard?"

"Wise!"

"Pardon me—is it right?"

"Right!—what is the wrong? She is my wife, in God's sight—she and none other. What do I care for Pope or King? Is not God above both? We plighted our vows to Him, and none but He could part us."

"Let me break it to her, then," said Beatrice, feeling scarcely so much convinced as overwhelmed. "It will startle her if she be not told beforehand."

Richard's only answer was to release Beatrice from his grasp. She passed into Margaret's bower, and, was surprised to see a strange gleam in the eyes of the dying girl.

"Beatrice, Richard is here. I know I heard his voice. Bring him to me."

"God has told her," said Bruno, in an undertone, as he left the room, with a sign to Beatrice and Doucebelle to follow.

They stood in the ante-chamber, minute after minute, but no sound came through the closed door. Half an hour passed in total silence. At last Bruno said—

"I think some one should go in."

But no one liked to do it, and the silence went on again.

Then Hawise came in, and wanted to know what they were all doing there. She was excessively shocked when Doucebelle told her. How extremely improper! She must go in and put a stop to it that minute.

Hawise tapped at the door, but no answer came. She opened it, and stood, silenced and frightened by what she saw. Richard de Clare bent over the bed, pouring passionate, unanswered kisses upon dead violet eyes, and tenderly smoothing the tresses of the cedar hair.

"The Lord has been here!" said Beatrice involuntarily.

"O Lord, be thanked that Thou hast given Thy child quiet rest at last!" was the response from Bruno.

Richard stood up and faced them.

"Is this God's doing, or is it man's?" he said, in a voice which sounded almost like an execration of some one. "God gave me this white dove, to nestle in my bosom and to be the glory of my life. Who took her from me? Does one of you dare to say it was God? It was man!—a man who shall pay for it, if he coin his heart's blood to do so. And if the payment cost my heart's blood, it will be little matter, seeing it has cost my heart already."

He drew his dagger, and bending down again, severed one of the long soft tresses of the cedar hair.

"Farewell, my dove!" he murmured, in a tone so altered that it was difficult to recognise the same voice. "Thou at least shalt suffer no more. Thy place is with the blessed saints and the holy angels, where nothing may ever enter that shall grieve or defile. But surely as thou art safe housed in Heaven, and I am left desolate on earth, thy death shall be avenged by fair means or by foul!"

"'Vengeance is Mine; I will repay, saith the Lord,'" softly quoted Bruno as Richard passed him in the doorway.

"He will,—by my hands!"

And Richard de Clare was seen no more.

It was hard to tell the poor mother, who came into her Margaret's bower with a bright smile, guessing so little of the terrible news in store. Tenderly as they tried to break it, she fainted away, and had to be nursed back to life and diligently cared for. But all was over for the night, and Doucebelle and Beatrice were beginning to think of bed, before Eva made her appearance. Of course the news had to be told again.

"Oh dear, how shocking!" said Eva, putting down her bouquet. "How very distressing! (I am afraid those flowers will never keep till morning.) Well, do you know, I am really thankful I was not here. What good could it have done poor dear Margaret, you know?—and I am so easily upset, and so very sensitive! I never can *bear* scenes of that sort. (Dear, I had no idea my shoes were so splashed!) As it is, I shall not sleep a wink. I sha'n't get over it for a week,—if I do then! Oh, how very shocking! Look, Doucebelle, aren't these cowslips sweet?"

"Eva, wilt thou let me have some of the white flowers—for Margaret?" said Doucebelle.

"For Margaret!—why, what dost thou mean? Oh! To put by her in her coffin? Horrid! Really, Dulcie, I think that is great waste. And the bouquet is so nicely made up,—it would be such a pity to pull it to pieces! I spent half an hour at least in putting it together, and Brimnatyn de Hertiland helped me. Of course thou canst have them if thou must,—but "——

Doucebelle quietly declined the gift so doubtfully offered.

"I wish, Doucebelle, thou wouldst have more consideration for people's feelings!" said Eva in a querulous tone, smoothing the petals of her flowers. "I am sure, whenever I look at a bouquet for the next twelvemonth, I shall think of this. I cannot help it—things do take such hold of me! And just think, how easily all that might be avoided!"

"I beg thy pardon, Eva. I am sorry I asked thee," was the soft answer.

It was not far to Margaret's grave, for they laid her in the quiet cloisters of Westminster Abbey, and the King who had been an accessory to her end followed her bier. Hers was not the only life that his act had shortened. Earl Hubert had virtually done with earth, when he saw lowered into the cold ground the coffin of his Benjamin. He survived her just two years, and laid down his weary burden of life on the fourth of May, 1243.

When Margaret was gone, there was no further tie to Bury Castle for Bruno and his daughter. Bishop Grosteste was again applied to, and responded as kindly as before, though circumstances did not allow him to do it equally to his satisfaction. The rich living originally offered to Bruno had of course been filled up, and there was nothing at that moment in the episcopal gift but some very small ones. The best of these he gave; and about two months after the death of Margaret, Bruno and Beatrice took leave of the Countess, and removed to their new home. It was a quiet little hamlet in the south of Lincolnshire, with a population of barely three hundred souls; and Beatrice's time was filled up by different duties from those which had occupied her at Bury Castle. The summer glided away in a peaceful round of most unexciting events. There had been so much excitement hitherto in their respective lives, that the priest and his daughter were only too thankful for a calm stretch of life, all to themselves.

One evening towards the close of summer, as Bruno came home to his little parsonage, where the dog-roses looked in at the windows, and the honey-suckles climbed round the porch, a sight met him which assured him that his period of peace and content was ended. On the stone bench in the porch, alone, intently examining a honeysuckle, sat Sir John de Averenches.

Bruno de Malpas was much too shrewd to suppose that his society was the magnet which had attracted the silent youth some fifty miles across the country. He sighed, but resigning himself to the inevitable, lifted his biretta as he came up to the door. Sir John rose and greeted him with evident cordiality, but he did not appear to have any thing particular to say beyond two self-evident statements—that it was a fine evening, and the honeysuckles were pretty.

"Is Beatrice within?" said the priest, feeling pretty sure that he knew.

Sir John demurely thought not.

It was another half-hour before Beatrice made her appearance; and Bruno noticed that the unexpected presence of a third person evoked no expression of surprise on her part. The preparations for supper were made by Beatrice and her attendant handmaiden Sabina; and after the meal was over, Bruno discreetly went off, with the interesting observation that he was about to visit a sick person at the furthest part of the parish. Sir John had taken his seat on the extreme end of a form, and Beatrice came and sat with her embroidery at the other end. Ten minutes of profound silence intervened.

" Beatrice ! "

" Yes."

Another minute of silence.

" Beatrice ! "

" Well ? "

" Beatrice, what dost thou think of me ? "

Beatrice coolly cut off an end of yellow silk, and threaded her needle with blue.

" Ask my father."

" How does he know what thou thinkest ? "

" Well, he always does," said Beatrice, calmly fastening the blue silk on the wrong side of the material.

" Wilt thou not tell me thyself ? "

" I should, if I wanted to be rid of thee.

The distance between the two occupants of the form was materially lessened.

"Then thou dost not want to be rid of me?"

"I can work while I am talking," replied Beatrice, in her very coolest manner.

"Why dost thou think I came, Beatrice?"

"Because it pleased thee, I should think."

The needle was drawn from the blue silk, and a needleful of scarlet went in instead, while the end of the blue thread was carefully secured in Beatrice's left hand for future use.

"One, two, three, four"—Beatrice was half audibly counting her stitches.

"It did please me, Beatrice."

"Five, six—all right, Sir John—seven, eight, nine"—

"Does it please thee?"

"Thirteen, fourteen—it is pleasant to have some one to talk to—fifteen, sixteen—when I am not counting—seventeen, eighteen, nineteen."

And in went the needle, and the scarlet silk began to flow in and out with rapidity.

"Do I interrupt thee, Beatrice?"

"Thanks, I have done counting for the present."

" Would it interrupt thee very much to be married ?"

" Well, I should think it would." Beatrice stopped the scarlet, and rethreaded the blue.

" More than thou wouldst like ? "

" That would depend on circumstances."

" What circumstances ? " inquired the bashful yet persistent suitor.

" Who was to marry me, principally."

" Suppose I was ? "

" Thou canst not, till thou hast asked my father."

There was a gleam in the dark eyes veiled with their long lashes. It might be either resentment or fun.

" May I ask him, Beatrice ? "

" Did I not tell thee so at first ? "

This curious conversation had taken so long, and had been interrupted by so many pauses, that Bruno appeared before it had progressed further. He glanced at the pair with some amusement in his eyes, not unmixed with sadness, for he had a decided foreboding that he was about to lose his Beatrice. But no more was said that night.

The next morning, Sir John de Averenches made the formal appeal which Bruno was fully expecting.

"I am not good at words, Father," he said, with honest manliness; "and I know the maiden is fair beyond many. You may easily look higher for her; but you will not easily find one that loves her better."

"Truly, my son, that is mine own belief," said Bruno. "But hast thou fully understood that she is of Jewish descent, which many Christian knights would count a blot on their escocheons?"

"Being a Christian, that makes no difference to me."

"Well! She shall decide for herself; but I fancy I know what she will say. It will be hard to part with her."

"Why should you, Father? Will she not still want a confessor?—and could she have a better than you?"

"Thank you, Father!" said Beatrice demurely, when Bruno told her that his consent was given, contingent upon hers. "Then I will begin my wedding-dress."

In this extremely cool manner the fair maiden intimated her intention of becoming a matron. But Bruno, who knew every change of her features and colour, was well aware that she felt a great deal more than she said. The mask was soon dropped.

The wedding-dress was a marvel of her own lovely embroidery. It was worn about the beginning of winter, and once more Bruno resigned his parish duties, and became, as his son-in-law had wisely suggested, a family confessor.

They heard from Bury that the marriage of Eva de Braose took place about the same time. And the general opinion in the Lincolnshire parsonage was rather, as respected Sir William de Cantilupe, one of condolence than of congratulation.

Eighteen years after that summer, a solitary traveller was approaching the city of Tewkesbury. He sat down on a low wall which skirted the road, and wiped his heated brow. He was a tall, fine-looking man, with a dark olive complexion, and clustering masses of black hair. There was no one in sight, and the traveller began to talk in an undertone to himself, as solitary men are sometimes wont to do.

"A good two hours before sunset, I suppose," he said, looking towards the sun, which was blazing fiercely. "Pugh! where does that horrid smell come from? Ah, that is the vesper bell, as they call it—

the unclean beasts that they are! Well, we at least are pure from every shadow of idolatry.

"Yet are we pure from sin? I do think, now, it was a pity—a mistake—that visit of mine to Sir Piers de Rievaulx. I might have let that girl live— the girl that Belasez loved. Well! she is one of the creeping things now. She—our Belasez! This is a cross-grained, crooked sort of world. Faugh! that smell again!

"I suppose this is the wall of Tewkesbury Castle. Is my Lord the Earl at home, I wonder? How I did hate that boy!

"What is coming yonder, with those jingling bells? A string of pilgrims to some accursed shrine, most likely. May these heathen idolaters be all con- founded, and the chosen people of Adonai be brought home in peace! I could see, I dare say, if I stood on the wall. They may have some vile idol with them, and if I do not get out of the way "——

He had sprung upon the parapet, and stood trying so to twist himself as to catch a glimpse of the reli- gious procession which he supposed to be approach- ing, when suddenly he slipped and fell backwards. A wild cry for "Help!" rang through the startled air. Where was he going? Down, down, plunging overhead into some soft, evil-odoured, horrible mass, from which, by grasping an iron bar that projected above, he just managed so far to raise himself as to get his head free. And then the dreadful truth broke upon him, and his cries for help became piercing.

Delecresse had fallen into the open cess-pool of Tewkesbury Castle.

Suddenly he ceased to shriek, and all was still. Not that he needed help any the less, nor that he was less conscious of it, but because he remembered what at first he had forgotten in his terror and disgust, that until sunset it was the rest of the holy Sabbath unto the Lord. Perhaps, by clinging to the iron bar, he could live till the sun dropped below the horizon. At any rate, Delecresse, sternest of Pharisees to his heart's core, would not profane the Sabbath, even for life.

But now there was a little stir outside, and a voice shouted—

"What ho!—who cried for help?"

"I."

"Who art thou, and where?"

"I have fallen into the cess-pool; I pray thee, friend, whoever thou art, to bring or send me something on which I can rest till sunset, and then help me forth."

"The saints be blessed! a jolly place to fall into. But why, in the name of all the Calendar, dost thou want to wait till sunset?"

"Because I am a Jew, and until then is the holy Sabbath."

A peal of laughter answered the explanation.

"Hope thou mayest enjoy it! Well, if ever I heard such nonsense! Is it worth while pulling a Jew out?—what sayest thou, Anselm?"

"He is a man, poor soul!" returned a second voice. "Nay, let us not leave him to such a death as that."

"Look here, old Jew! I will go and fetch a ladder and rope. I should pull my dog out of that hole, and perhaps thou mayest be as good."

"I will not be taken out till sunset," returned Delecresse stubbornly.

"The fellow's a mule! Hie thee, Anselm, and ask counsel of our gracious Lord what we shall do."

A strange feeling crept over Delecresse when he heard his fate, for life or death, thus placed in the hands of the man whose life he had wrecked. Anselm was heard to run off quickly, and in a few minutes he returned.

"Sir Richard the Earl laughed a jolly laugh when I told him," was his report. "He saith, Let the cur be, if he will not be plucked forth until Monday morning: for if Saturday be his Sabbath, Sunday is mine, and what will defile the one will defile the other.'"[1]

"Monday morning! He will be a dead man, hours before that!"

"So he will. It cannot be helped, except——Jew, wilt thou be pulled out now, or not? If not now, then not at all."

For one moment, the heart of Delecresse grew sick and faint within him as he contemplated the awful alternatives presented to his choice. Then, gathering all his strength, he shouted back his final decision.

"No! I will not break the Sabbath of my God."

The men outside laughed, uttered an expression of contemptuous pity, and he heard their footsteps grow faint in the distance, and knew that he was left to die as horrible a death as can befal humanity. Only one other cry arose, and that was not for the ears of men. It was the prayer of one in utter error, yet in terrible extremity: and it was honestly sincere.

"Adonai! I have sinned and done evil, all my life long. Specially I have sinned against this man,

_____

[1] This part of the story is historical.

who has left me to die here in this horrible place. Now therefore, O my God, I beseech Thee, let the sufferings of Thy servant be accepted before Thee as an atonement for his sin, and let this one good deed, that I have preferred death rather than break Thy law, rise before Thee as the incense with the evening sacrifice!"

Yes, it was utter error. Yet the Christians of his day, one here and there excepted, could have taught him no better. And what had they offered him instead? Idol-worship, woman-worship, offerings for the dead,—every thing which the law of God had forbidden. In the day when the blood of the martyrs is demanded at the hand of Babylon, will there be no reckoning for the souls of those thousand sons of Israel, whom she has persistently thrust away from Christ, by erecting a rood-screen of idols between Him and them?

When day dawned on the Monday, they pulled out of the cess-pool the body of a dead man.

One month later, in the chapter-house at Canterbury, King Henry III. stood, an humble and helpless suppliant, before his assembled Barons. There he was forced, utterly against his will and wish, to sign an additional charter granting liberties to England, and binding his own hands. It was Simon de Montfort who had brought matters to this pass. But Simon de Montfort was not the tall, fair, stately man who forced the pen into the unwilling fingers of the cowering King, and who held out the Evangelisterium for the swearing of his hated oath. King Henry looked up into the cold steel-like glitter of those stern blue eyes, and the firm set expression of the compressed lips, and realised in an instant that in this man he would find neither misgiving nor mercy. It was a great perplexity to him that the man on whom he had showered such favours should thus take part against him. He had forgotten all about that April morning, twenty-three years before; and had no conception that between himself and the eyes of Richard de Clare, floated

"A shadow like an angel's, with bright hair,"

nor that when that scene in the chapter-house was over, and Richard returned his good Damascus blade to its scabbard, he murmured within his heart to ears that heard not,—

"I have avenged thee at last!"

But Richard never knew that his heaviest vengeance had been exacted one month sooner, when, with that bitter mirth which Anselm had misnamed, he left an unknown Jew to perish in misery.

The sun was setting that evening over Lincoln. Just on the rise of Steephill stood a handsome Norman house, with a garden stretching behind. In the garden, on a stone settle, sat an old priest and a very handsome middle-aged lady. Two young sisters were wandering about the garden with their arms round each other's waists; a young man stood at the ornamental fountain, talking playfully to the hawk upon his wrist; while on the grass at the lady's feet sat two pretty children, their laps full of flowers. A conversation which had been running was evidently coming to a conclusion.

"Then you think, Father, that it is never lawful, under any circumstances, to do evil that good may come?"

"God can bring good out of evil, my Beatrice. But it is one of His prerogatives."

HISTORICAL APPENDIX.

FAMILY OF DE BURGH.

HUBERT DE BURGH, whose ancestry is unknown with certainty (though some genealogists attempt to derive him from Herlouin de Conteville, and his wife Arlette, mother of William the Conqueror), was probably *born* about 1168–70, and created Justiciary of England, June 15, 1214. He was also Lord Chancellor and Lord Chamberlain, with abundance of smaller offices. He was created Earl of Kent, Feb. 11, 1227. After all the strange viscissitudes through which he had passed, it seems almost surprising that he was allowed to die in his bed, at Banstead, May [4 ?], 1243, aged about 74, and surviving his daughter just two years. [Character historical.] He married—

A. Margaret, daughter and heir of Robert de Arsic or Arsike: dates unknown. (Hubert had previously been contracted, Apr. 28, 1200, to Joan, daughter of William de Vernon, Earl of Devon; but the marriage did not take place.)

B. Beatrice, daughter and sole heir of William de

Warenne of Wirmgay, and widow of Dodo Bardolf: apparently *married* after 1209, and *died* in or about 1214.

C. Isabel, youngest daughter and coheir of William Earl of Gloucéster, made Countess of Gloucester by King John, to the prejudice of her two elder sisters: affianced by her father to John, Count of Mortaigne [afterwards King John], at Windsor, Sept. 28, 1176; married to him at Salisbury, Aug. 29, 1189: divorced on her husband's accession, 1200, on pretext of being within the prohibited degrees.   She married (2) Geoffrey de Mandeville, Earl of Essex, to whom she was sold by the husband who had repudiated her, for the sum of twenty thousand marks, in 1213.   In the wars of the Barons, she threw all her influence into the scale against the King; but she showed that her enmity was personal, not political, by at once returning to her allegiance on the accession of Henry III. She was then given in *marriage* (3) to Hubert de Burgh, into whose hands the manor of Walden was delivered, as part of her dower, Aug. 13, 1217; the marriage probably took place shortly before that date, and certainly before the 17th of September.   Isabel was Hubert's wife for so short a time, that some writers have doubted the fact of the marriage altogether; but it is amply authenticated.   She was dead on the 18th of November following, as the Close Rolls bear witness; and the Obituary of Canterbury Cathedral and the Chronicle of Rochester agree in stating that she died Oct. 14, 1217.   She was *buried* in Canterbury Cathedral.

D. MARGARET, eldest daughter of William I., King of Scotland, surnamed The Lion; affianced, 1196, to Otho of Brunswick; committed to the care of King John of England in 1209; *married* at York, June 25, 1221; *died* 1259, leaving no surviving issue. [Character inferentially historical.]

Issue of Earl Hubert.—A. *By Margaret Arsic :—*

1. JOHN, knighted Whit Sunday, 1229; *died* 1274–75, leaving issue. *Married—*
    HAWISE, daughter and heir of Sir William de Lanvalay: *married* before Nov. 21, 1234; *died* 1249; *buried* at Colchester. [Character imaginary.]
2. *Hubert*, living 1281–82; ancestor of the Marquis of Clanricarde. Whom he married is not known.

D. *By Margaret of Scotland :—*

3. MARGARET, OR MARGERY—she bears both names on the Rolls—*born* probably 1222; *married* at Bury St. Edmund's "when the Earl was at Merton"— probably Jan. 11–26, 1236,—clandestinely, but with connivance of mother, to Richard de Clare, Earl of Gloucester; divorced 1237; livery of her estates granted to brother John, May 5, 1241; therefore *died* shortly before that date. Most writers attribute to Earl Hubert another daughter, whom they call Magotta : but the Rolls show no evidence of any daughter but Margaret. Magotta, or Magot, is manifestly a Latinism of Margot, the French diminutive for Margaret; the Earl's gifts to monas-

teries for the souls of himself and relatives, include "M. his daughter," but make no mention of two; and the grants made by the King to Earl Hubert and Margaret his wife, and Margaret their daughter, certainly imply that Margaret was the sole heir of her mother. [Character inferentially historical, except as regards religion, for which no evidence is forthcoming.]

RICHARD DE CLARE.

He was the eldest son of Gilbert, Earl of Gloucester and his wife Isabel Marshal (who married, secondly, the King's brother, Richard Earl of Cornwall): *born* 1222, the same year as that which probably saw the birth of Margaret de Burgh. King Henry obliged him to *marry*, in or about January, 1239, Maud de Lacy, daughter of John, Earl of Lincoln, by whom (after the death of Margaret) he had a family of three sons and three daughters. His eldest daughter he named after his lost love; but she proved a far less amiable character. Earl Richard was one of several noblemen who *died*, we are told, from poison, in consequence of dining with Queen Eléonore's cousin, Count Pietro of Savoy, June 14, 1262. He was *buried* in Tewkesbury Abbey. Richard stood foremost of the English nobles in the wars of the Barons against Henry III., and with his own hand forced the King to swear to the terms they dictated, in 1259, as is stated in the story. [Character historical.]

Fictitious Characters

These are, the priests at Bury Castle; the various Jews introduced; Levina; Doucebelle de Vaux.

Eva de Braose, Marie de Lusignan, Sir John de Burgh and his wife Hawise, are historical so far as their existence is concerned, but the characters ascribed to them are imaginary.

The dreadful end of Delecresse is thus far true,—that a Jew was thus treated by Richard de Clare. But who it really was who revealed to King Henry the clandestine marriage of Richard and Margaret, is one of the inscrutable mysteries of which no evidence remains.

Stories of English Life.

By EMILY S. HOLT.

A.D. 597
I. **Imogen:**
A TALE OF THE EARLY BRITISH CHURCH.

A.D. 1066
II. **Behind the Veil:**
A STORY OF THE NORMAN CONQUEST.

A.D. 1159
III. **One Snowy Night;**
OR, LONG AGO AT OXFORD.

A.D. 1189
IV. **Lady Sybil's Choice:**
A TALE OF THE CRUSADES.

A.D. 1214
V. **Earl Hubert's Daughter;**
OR, THE POLISHING OF THE PEARL.

A.D. 1325
VI. **In all Time of our Tribulation:**
THE STORY OF PIERS GAVESTONE.

A.D. 1350
VII. **The White Lady of Hazelwood:**
THE WARRIOR COUNTESS OF MONTFORT.

A.D. 1352
VIII. **Countess Maud;**
OR, THE CHANGES OF THE WORLD.

A.D. 1360
IX. **In Convent Walls:**
THE STORY OF THE DESPENSERS.

A.D. 1377
X. **John De Wycliffe,**
AND WHAT HE DID FOR ENGLAND.

A.D. 1384
XI. **The Lord Mayor:**
A TALE OF LONDON IN 1384.

A.D. 1390
XII. **Under One Sceptre:**
THE STORY OF THE LORD OF THE MARCHES.

A.D. 1400
XIII. **The White Rose of Langley;**
OR, THE STORY OF CONSTANCE LE DESPENSER.

A.D. 1400
XIV. **Mistress Margery:**
A TALE OF THE LOLLARDS.

A.D. 1400
XV. **Margery's Son;**
OR, UNTIL HE FIND IT.

A.D. 1470
XVI. **Red and White;**
OR, THE WARS OF THE ROSES.

A.D. 1480
XVII. **The Tangled Web:**
A TALE OF THE FIFTEENTH CENTURY.

A.D. 1515
XVIII. **The Harvest of Yesterday:**
A TALE OF THE SIXTEENTH CENTURY.

A.D. 1530
XIX. **Lettice Eden;**
OR, THE LAMPS OF EARTH AND THE LIGHTS OF HEAVEN.

A.D. 1535
XX. **Isoult Barry of Wynscote:**
A TALE OF TUDOR TIMES.

A.D. 1544
XXI. **Through the Storm;**
OR, THE LORD'S PRISONERS.

A.D. 1555
XXII. **Robin Tremayne:**
A TALE OF THE MARIAN PERSECUTION.

Extracts from Press Notices of Miss Holt's Tales

The English Churchman

"There can be no question that Miss Holt stands in the front rank of Protestant tale-writers for young and old. Everything she writes may be fully trusted as sound in the faith, and uncompromising in its attitude towards Romish error. The extensive circulation of her books will prove one of the most effectual means of educating the people in Reformation principles."

The Morning Post

"'All's Well' is a charmingly-told tale of the persecuting times of three and a half centuries ago. We wonder how many of us in these easy-going days would prove as faithful to God and to conscience, should the need arise, as Mistress Benden, the heroine of the tale, who not only endured sore imprisonment but sealed her testimony at the stake at Canterbury. Miss Holt's portrayal of men and manners and the quaint speech of our forefathers is as fascinating as ever, while her industry is phenomenal. A story like this is worth a cart-load of the novels that are mostly in vogue at our circulating libraries."

The Record

"Miss Holt's Tales of English Life in the Olden Time form a very valuable course of reading. We do not know one of her stories which does not deserve high commendation on account of its own intrinsic interest, and also because of the sound Protestant principles by which it is animated. . . . There are few materials for a good work of light literature so fascinating as a well-selected portion of our 'fair Island story,' nor any better calculated to imbue young and receptive minds with right views as to the unspeakable blessings which have accrued to this country through the free circulation of the Word of God, and our national emancipation from 'the hateful yoke of Rome.'"

The Christian

"To read one of Miss Holt's old-time tales is like taking a trip to 'the Delectable Mountains'; only the visitor looks back instead of looking forward. . . . We have learned to look upon her as an historian *par excellence*, and the reading of one of her delightful tales is an experience that we would fain repeat more frequently than we do. The purity, dignity, and grace of her literary style, the fidelity and finish of her portraits, and the amount of essential Christian teaching which she so skilfully and lovingly conveys, combined with the historic value of her writings, lend to them a charm possessed by very few of the productions of living authors."

Stories of English Life—continued.

A.D. 1556
XXIII. **All's Well;**
OR, ALICE'S VICTORY.

A.D. 1556
XXIV. **The King's Daughters.**
HOW TWO GIRLS KEPT THE FAITH.

A.D. 1569
XXV. **Sister Rose;**
OR, THE EVE OF ST. BARTHOLOMEW.

A.D. 1579
XXVI. **Joyce Morrell's Harvest:**
A STORY OF THE REIGN OF ELIZABETH.

A.D. 1588
XXVII. **Clare Avery:**
A STORY OF THE SPANISH ARMADA.

A.D. 1605
XXVIII. **It Might Have Been:**
THE STORY OF GUNPOWDER PLOT.

A.D. 1635
XXIX. **Minster Lovel:**
A STORY OF THE DAYS OF LAUD.

A.D. 1662
XXX. **Wearyholme;**
A STORY OF THE RESTORATION.

A.D. 1712
XXXI. **The Maiden's Lodge;**
OR, THE DAYS OF QUEEN ANNE.

A.D. 1745
XXXII. **Out in the Forty-five;**
OR, DUNCAN KEITH'S VOW.

A.D. 1750
XXXIII. **Ashcliffe Hall:**
A TALE OF THE LAST CENTURY.

XXXIV.
A.D. 1556
For the Master's Sake;
OR, THE DAYS OF QUEEN MARY.

A.D. 1345
The Well in the Desert.
AN OLD LEGEND.

XXXV.
A.D. 1559
All for the Best;
OR, BERNARD GILPIN'S MOTTO

A.D. 1560
At the Grene Griffin:
A TALE OF THE SIXTEENTH CENTURY.

XXXVI.
A.D. 1270
Our Little Lady;
OR, SIX HUNDRED YEARS AGO.

A.D. 1652
Gold that Glitters;
OR, THE MISTAKES OF JENNY LAVENDER.

XXXVII.
A.D. 1290
A Forgotten Hero:
THE STORY OF ROGER DE MORTIMER.

A.D. 1266
Princess Adelaide:
A STORY OF THE SIEGE OF KENILWORTH.

XXXVIII.
IST CENTURY.
The Slave Girl of Pompeii.

2ND CENTURY.
The Way of the Cross.
TALES OF THE EARLY CHURCH.

A.D. 870 to 1580
XXXIX. **Lights in the Darkness:**
BIOGRAPHICAL SKETCHES.

A.D. 1873
XL. **Verena.**
SAFE PATHS AND SLIPPERY BYE-WAYS.
A Story of To-day.

LONDON: JOHN F. SHAW AND CO.,
48 PATERNOSTER ROW.

TALES BY EMILY S. HOLT

Extracts from Press Notices—continued

The Spectator

" Miss Holt, besides possessing much literary skill, is a careful student of history. Her books are not only highly readable, but historical studies of much value."

The Sword and Trowel

" The historical accuracy of Miss Holt's charming stories of old English life is a distinctive feature by which they may easily be recognised ; and her clear presentation of pure gospel truth, her tender persistence in pointing her readers to the only way of salvation by faith in the Lord Jesus Christ, will always insure them a warm welcome in Christian households."

Protestant Observer

" Miss Holt's life was devoted to promoting the cause of Protestantism by her literary work, and her tales rank in the highest class."

Evening Hours

" We wish these volumes could be placed in every Sunday School Library and every Protestant home. It would be a good thing for the sons and daughters of England to become acquainted with such reading as we find in the writings of this gifted authoress."

The Christian World

" Miss Holt's stories not only depict very vividly the life of the times to which they carry us back, but they contain so much that is soundly sensible, that it is impossible to read them without an unusual amount of pleasure and benefit."

The Leeds Mercury

" In 'The King's Daughters' Miss Holt recounts how two girls kept the faith in the dark and cruel years of Mary's reign. The refusal of these intrepid confessors to admit the doctrine of Transubstantiation brings them to the stake, where they die triumphantly. In these days when Ritualism is so prevalent, a story which brings the reader face to face with the simple teaching of the New Testament is doubly welcome."

LONDON : JOHN F. SHAW AND CO.

48 PATERNOSTER ROW